PRAISE FOR MELANIE SUMMERS

"A fun, often humorous, escapist tale that will have readers blushing, laughing and rooting for its characters."
~ Kirkus Reviews

A gorgeously funny, romantic and seductive modern fairy tale...
I have never laughed out loud so much in my life. I don't think that I've ever said that about a book before, and yet that doesn't even seem accurate as to just how incredibly funny, witty, romantic, swoony...and other wonderfully charming and deliriously dreamy *The Royal Treatment* was. I was so gutted when this book finished, I still haven't even processed my sadness at having to temporarily say goodbye to my latest favourite Royal couple. ~ MammieBabbie Book Club
I have to HIGHLY HIGHLY HIGHLY RECOMMEND *The Royal Treatment* to EVERYONE!
~ Jennifer, The Power of Three Readers

I was totally gripped to this story. For the first time ever the Kindle came into the bath with me. This book is unputdownable. I absolutely loved it.
~ Philomena (Two Friends, Read Along with Us)

Very rarely does a book make me literally hold my breath or has me feeling that actual ache in my heart for a character, but I did both." **~ Three Chicks Review for Netgalley**

ALSO AVAILABLE
ROMANTIC COMEDIES by Melanie Summers
The Crown Jewels Series
The Royal Treatment
The Royal Wedding
The Royal Delivery

Paradise Bay Series
The Honeymooner
Whisked Away
The Suite Life

Crazy Royal Love Series (Coming in 2020)
Royally Crushed
Royally Wild

WOMEN'S FICTION by Melanie Summers
The After Wife – coming January 2020

STEAMY OFFERINGS by MJ Summers
The Full Hearts Series
Break in Two
Don't Let Go – Prequel to Breaking Love - E-book only
Breaking Love
Letting Go - Prequel to Breaking Clear & The Break-up
Breaking Clear
Breaking Hearts
The Break-up

ISBN-978-0-9950301-6-9

The Royal Wedding
~ a crown jewels romantic comedy ~

By Melanie Summers

DEDICATION

For Mrs. Shank,
An amazing woman who was taken from this Earth far too
soon. You inspired those around you to be more patient, to
learn to let go of the little stuff, and to find the humour in life.
The sound of your gentle laugh will forever make me smile.
Melanie

AUTHOR'S NOTE

Dear Reader,

A quick note of warning: if you haven't read *The Royal Treatment*, you really won't enjoy this story in the way in which it is intended. This truly is a continuation of Tessa and Arthur's journey, so **please** go back and start at the beginning.

Otherwise, you may end up feeling like you're not in on the joke—like when you go for drinks with your best friend's workmates and they're all talking about the pervy guy who sits at the corner desk, or they're using acronyms you don't understand and they're killing themselves laughing and you start laughing, too, even though you don't have the first clue what's so funny. Then pretty soon one of them realizes you can't possibly know why you're laughing, and they give you that slightly disgusted-yet-filled-with-pity look, so you excuse yourself to the ladies room and sit on the toilet, scrolling through Pinterest for far too long, feeling terribly alone and wishing the night would just end. Then you realize it's been so long, they're all going to think you have some embarrassing digestive disorder. So, now the thought of going back to the table is *so* much more awkward than it was to sit and pretend laugh in the first place because you're certain you're going to be known as 'that weird friend of Christie's, you know, the one with irritable bowel syndrome.'

Yeah...I don't want you to feel like that.

Because, the whole point of this series is to let you escape, laugh (about jokes you get), swoon, and sigh happily.

Oh, you've read the first one? Well, then...enjoy!

XOXO,

Melanie

ONE

Adventures in Babysitting

Tessa

I have a secret. It's not a big secret, really. Nothing twisted or dark. It's a goofy thing I do that I don't want anyone to know about because, if the newspapers got a hold of it—or worse, if a video were taken of me doing it—it would be world news within a few hours.

The fact that *anything* I do is newsworthy has nothing whatsoever to do with me and everything to do with the man to whom I've recently become engaged. I'm an exceedingly ordinary woman. Well, apart from the fact that I tend to make a spectacular arse of myself on a regular basis. But that all has to change because, as of one week ago, I've started toward a whole new life—one I never imagined for myself, even as a little girl...okay, well maybe as a little girl. And a teenager. And possibly after too much wine on occasion.

I am now the fiancée of Arthur Langdon, Crown Prince of Avonia. The second he slid this gorgeous, enormous diamond ring on my finger, I knew I could no longer be Tessa Sharpe, clumsy blogger/struggling reporter. Instead, I must transform into an elegant, fabulous princess such as Grace Kelly (whose very *name* was even graceful).

Oh, this ring is really very shiny.

Anyway, as soon as I said, "Yes," I vowed to myself to no longer do things that will cause me to humiliate myself. From now on, I shall conduct myself with the utmost sophistication and decorum at all times.

Except for right now.

At the moment, I'm in my brother Finn's old room at my parents' house (where I now live after a series of publicly humiliating events caused me to lose most of my money, my flat, as well as the lion's share of my income). Living with your parents at the age of twenty-eight is no treat, let me tell you. Especially not *my* parents, Evi and Ruben Sharpe, who not only have a very active and adventurous sex life (which causes me to shudder randomly while trying not to gag), but who also believe me to be incapable of almost any worthwhile accomplishment.

I've been living here for close to five months now, and if I had my way, I would move out this evening. But that's not going to happen, not with the tiny salary I earn each month for my part-time job at *The Weekly Observer*, Avonia's leading independent weekly newspaper, with a whopping circulation of ten thousand units.

My main source of income comes from my two remaining blogs. (I used to run a fairly popular blog called *The Royal Watchdog* until I fell madly in love with the prince I had spent years criticizing. Whoops!). Anyway, I shut it down for obvious reasons, but still have my photography website and Smart Runner blog, on which I review clothing, shoes, and devices used by jogging enthusiasts. This is not without its dangers, of course, and if you caught the video of me testing out the Shock Jogger earlier this spring, you're already well aware of the perils involved in demonstrating running equipment.

Oh, crap! Look at the time. I only have forty-five minutes to get ready for my big date, and I *definitely* have more than an hour's worth of preening. Arthur and I haven't seen each other for six excruciatingly lonely days. He's had to go to Genovia for the annual EU currency conference—and I'm finding it hard to believe it's possible to miss someone this much. We've gotten into some very naughty texting to see us through this torturous week apart. *Hmm...what was that thing he wrote last night about the first thing we're going to do when we're alone?*

Oh, right! Back to my secret. Before each date with Arthur, I like to put on the song 'Then He Kissed Me' by The Crystals and dance around singing into my hairbrush like Elizabeth Shue in *Adventures in Babysitting*—which is what I'm doing right now when I really should be getting into the shower. But I *am* multitasking by laying out my dress and tights on my bed while I sing.

"Auntie Tessa? What are you doing?"

I turn to see my six-year-old nephew, Knox, standing in the doorway of my room, watching me as I dance around and sing like a lunatic. "Nothing. Goofing around, but I'm done."

"Grandmum says you and Prince Arthur are going on a big date. Are you guys going to smooch all night?" He wrinkles up his nose and starts to giggle.

I gasp, pretending to be scandalized by the notion. "Of course not. We're not married yet. We'll probably just have some dinner and polite conversation. Anyway, out you go." I clap my hands in the manner of a school teacher herding a class in from recess, but my clap must be broken because it has no effect on him. He remains rooted in the doorway, grinning up at me.

So instead, I shimmy past him and hurry down the hall to the bathroom.

Twenty minutes later, I've buffed, shaved, shampooed, and covered myself in a very luxurious lotion Arthur gave me for my birthday. Nuts! I forgot my bathrobe. I wrap a towel around myself, pick up my dirty clothes off the floor, and scurry down the hall as quietly as possible—hoping none of my other nephews or nieces will see me. When I arrive back in the dank cave I call home, I find two of my nieces, Tabitha and Poppy, sitting on the bed, giggling hysterically. *Grr.* They're sitting on top of my dress, no doubt wrinkling it beyond my limited capabilities with an iron. In Tabitha's hand is my mobile phone. *Oh, this can't be good.*

Poppy looks up at me, her sweet little seven-year-old eyes dancing with excitement. "Who's Excalibur? And why is he dying to get you naked?"

I grip the towel with one hand and cross the room in two steps, then swipe my phone out of Tabitha's hand. "Nope. Not For you. Those are *private* messages, and they are not for little eyes. Now, if you'll excuse me, I need to get dressed."

Tabitha stares up at me from under her eyelashes, clearly trying to act both innocent and hurt. "We only came in to see if you had some Jelly Babies for us, and maybe to see if you needed any help getting ready for your date."

"Nope. No Jelly Babies today, remember? Now that I'm living here and you come every single day after school to be babysat, I really can't afford to buy thirty-five packages of candies every week." I turn my back to them and slide my ratty old bathrobe over my shoulders and tie it up, not bothering to remove my towel.

"Dad says that's bollocks," says Poppy. "He said Prince Arthur will be giving you a large clothing allowance now that you're engaged."

"Oh, does he now? Well, tell your dad he's dead wrong. It's only been a week, and fiancés don't give you money anyway. Husbands don't, either, so make sure you study hard so you can get a good job and support yourself when you grow up."

"Like *you*?" Tabitha asks, her eyes hardening. Oh, she's developed quite the attitude since she turned eleven. It's like she went from my little darling to nasty preteen witch the moment she blew out the candles. "Maybe I'll be like you and live with my parents until I'm really old, then find a prince to marry me."

I take a deep, calming breath. *She's only a child. She's only a child.* "I have a job. It just doesn't pay very well. You know what? I don't have time for this. I really need to dress now."

I shoo them with my hands, but they just stare. Sighing loudly, I try to regain my patience. "Listen, girls. There really are very few handsome princes left in the world. In fact, there's a very good chance I may have snagged the last one, but even so, I'm never going to live off his money. I'm going to have my own career, and you should, too."

"Really?" Poppy asks. "I thought your job would be to be a princess."

"Well, there's no reason a princess can't be a hard-hitting reporter at the same time, is there?" *Is there?* Now that I say it, I'm not completely certain I'm right about that one.

"If the 'I Hate Tessa' people have their way, you won't ever be a princess," Tabitha says.

"The what?"

"You haven't heard of them? It's all over Twitter. Their hashtag is #Brookeisbetter. They're starting a movement to convince Arthur to marry her instead of you."

My stomach does an awful, flippy, twisty thing, and my knees go weak. "Brooke is better? As in, Lady Dr. Brooke Beddingfield?" I tap on my mobile, opening my Twitter app, only to see that Tabitha's more up on the news than me, apparently. Quite embarrassing, really, since she's eleven and I'm a reporter. I search the hashtag and scroll through, seeing hundreds of *I Hate Tessa* tweets, several with photos of me being shocked and my face wrinkled up in pain. "Oh, fuck," I mutter.

"You said, 'fuck!' I'm so telling Grandmum!" Tabitha screeches.

"Shh! Please don't." I glance at her, then continue scrolling, each tweet making my stomach twist a little more.

"What will you give me if I don't tell?" Tabitha asks.

My shoulders drop. "You can't just keep it our little secret because I'm your auntie who loves you very much?"

"Afraid not."

"Fine. Just tell her, then. I don't—" I glance down at the floor and see something black moving under the bed. "Are those my..."

Crouching, I see Mr. Whiskers, my parents' cat, clawing the sheer fabric of my tights furiously. "Oh, bugger." I yank them away from the scrawny tabby, which only results in more tearing since his claws are firmly affixed to them. He displays his unwillingness to relinquish the tights by hissing at my face.

"No, Mr. Whiskers!" I give one final tug, determined not to let him win, and land on my butt with my prize, which will now be deposited into the trash bin. Mr. Whiskers jumps from under the bed, hitting me square in the face with his belly, his front paws landing on top of my head and his back legs wrapped around my neck.

"Ack! Shit!" I shriek just as he flings himself off me and darts out the door.

Tabitha and Poppy collapse in fits of laughter, forming a heap of squirming, giggly girls on my bed. "You said, 'shit'!"

"Mr. Whiskers jumped on your face!"

"Out. Now!" I point furiously at the door until they both slide off the bed and move in the desired direction, laughing hysterically.

I usher them out the door and shut it, wishing my dad hadn't taken the lock off back when Finn was sixteen and developed a liking for weed and girly magazines.

My heart sinks when the whole 'Brooke is better' thing comes popping back into my head. *No, don't think about that now, Tessa. You've only got ten minutes to dry and style your hair, put on some make-up, and figure out what to wear.*

****

All of two minutes later, my phone dings to inform me of a text message. When I swipe the screen, I see it's from my mum, who, as of three weeks ago, has her own smart phone and is thoroughly enjoying the new world of texting.

Tessa, It's me, Mum. Xavier wanted me to let you know that the prince will be here in T minus five minutes. Xoxo, Mum

The problem is that she doesn't quite trust the texts will actually make it up to space and back, so in about thirty seconds, she'll be knocking on the door to ask me if I got her message.

Knock, knock. "It's me, Twinkle." My mum pokes her head in the door. "Just wanted to see if you got my text."

"Got it, thanks." I wink at her confidently.

"Good. Can you imagine that my message could make it all the way up to space and back like that? So quickly?"

"Hard to believe." I open my mouth extra wide so I can apply my mascara.

"Will That Handsome Xavier be joining you or staying here this evening?"

"Probably coming along, I guess."

She's taken to calling my new bodyguard 'That Handsome Xavier' for obvious reasons. I'm still trying to get used to the fact that I have a bodyguard assigned to me at all, but having one that looks like Gaston from *Beauty and the Beast* (on steroids) is a whole different level of craziness.

The first thing my future father-in-law, King Winston, did when he found out about our impending marriage was assign Xavier to me. I take this as his version of throwing down the gauntlet. He wants to go toe-to-toe with me to see if he can get rid of me before I make it down the aisle to his son. But I have news for him—it's not going to work. He could hire the entire cast of The Thunder from Down Under to guard me, it won't make a bit of difference. I'm completely and utterly in love with Arthur, and nothing is going to change that.

The ladies in my neighbourhood, however, have spent a significant amount of time ogling Xavier under the pretense of pulling those last few weeds before winter starts. Abbott Lane has never seen such tidy front gardens. And it's the first time in history that not one set of hair rollers has seen the sun on our street for a full week.

My mum crosses the tiny room and peers out the window so she can get a better view of Xavier, who is probably doing another set of one-armed push-ups on the sidewalk. "I just love how he says, 'T minus five minutes.' So clever, that one." She turns, then looks me up and down and wrinkles up her nose. "You're not wearing that, are you?"

"What's wrong with this? I think it looks nice." I stare at myself in the mirror, suddenly unsure of the wraparound knit dress paired with the tall black boots. Do princesses wear tall black boots? What would Brooke-who-is-so-much-better-than-me wear for an evening out in the autumn?

"Well, if you're going to wear that, at least put on some chunky jewelry. Grace next door told me she saw Veronica

Platt on that morning talk show saying chunky jewelry is back in this fall."

I turn and rummage through the shoebox that holds my costume jewelry, searching for a silver chunky necklace I bought a few years ago. As much as I don't love taking advice from Grace next door, she does manage to keep up on the latest fashion trends a lot better than I do. My mum appears next to me and starts digging through the box to help me out.

"What's-his-name is here!" my father hollers up the stairs. Arthur has gone from being called Artie and being quite a favourite of my dad's to being called 'what's-his-name' since he proposed without checking with my father first. I had no idea my dad would take it so hard but, as my mum explained to me, I'm his only daughter, and this would have been his one chance to thoroughly intimidate a young man.

My mum rushes off to greet Arthur while I finish applying my mascara. As soon as I'm alone again, that sick feeling comes back over me. I stare at myself for a second in the mirror and say, "Forget them, Tessa. They don't matter. Only Arthur matters."

Hurrying out of my room, I resolve not to tell Arthur about the 'I Hate Tessa' movement. No need to have him know about it. Who knows? Maybe they'll manage to convince him I'm not the woman for him...

TWO

What Not to Say About a Newborn...

Arthur

"O h, Christ, is that him?" I ask my bodyguard, Ollie, who's sitting in the passenger seat of the limo. I'm tucked safely in the back behind bulletproof tinted windows, which allow me to observe the ridiculous specimen my father hired to look after Tessa.

Ollie turns his head to face me and nods while rolling his eyes. "Apparently, Your Highness, but I can find a way to get rid of him if you like."

The vehicle rolls to a stop in front of the Sharpe home. "So long as his head isn't filled with muscle rather than brain matter, he can stay."

I open the back door before my driver, Ben, has a chance to get out and do it for me. My time with Tessa has certainly changed me in a lot of little—and not so little—ways.

New bodyguard steps toward me and nods. "Good evening, Your Highness; all ready for the big date, are we?"

He gives me a large grin, and I can almost imagine a glint of sparkling light coming from those shockingly white teeth of his.

"The important thing is if Ms. Sharpe is ready." I give him a smile and a nod.

"Yes, sir, she should be. I gave her the T minus five minutes almost six minutes ago." He taps his watch with one finger and smiles confidently.

"Well, thank you for that," I say as I jog up the steps and to the front door, then give it a sound knock.

Thunderous footsteps are heard behind the door, and it swings open, revealing the faces of several of Tessa's adorable nephews and nieces, all grinning up at me, no doubt hoping for presents or treats. "Hello, children, is your aunt ready?"

I am immediately bombarded by hugs from the sticky-fingered brood. They all start talking at once, their words jumbling together. Oddly enough, I do make out the words "Excalibur" and "naked" coming from one of them. Just when I'm starting to feel very concerned, Evi's voice comes from the top of the stairs, "Oh, now, children, go have some lemon tarts and let the prince get himself settled."

"I think they may have already helped themselves," I say, wiping pastry bits and yellow custard off the front of my trousers as the kids run off to the kitchen.

Ruben pokes his head out from the television room and glares at me. "Big plans tonight?"

The way he asks the question is meant to tell me that if I have big plans with his daughter, I need to inform him first, unlike what happened last weekend when I surprised her by proposing on what was meant to be a very romantic hot air balloon ride. I give him a conciliatory smile. "Just a quiet dinner for two at Chez Lawrence."

Evi comes to my rescue once again. "That sounds just lovely, Arthur. We're going to have a nice, quiet night to ourselves as soon as the children all get picked up." She glances at the door. "Isa's on her way to get her brood, but Lars should have been here by now, and I haven't had a word from him."

The phone rings, and she disappears down the hall toward the kitchen. "Excuse me, Arthur—that's probably him now."

Ruben disappears back into the TV room, leaving me standing alone on the mat at the front door for a moment.

Then I hear her voice, and it's the sweetest sound I think I've ever known.

"Hello, handsome." She descends the stairs quickly, rushing into my arms before I have a chance to get a good look at her. But I'll forgive her for not letting me really see her, since now she's doing that wonderful thing she does when she presses her body up against mine and kisses me hard on the mouth. Mmm, she tastes good.

"God, I missed you," I murmur in her ear. "I can't wait to get you alone so I can do very naughty things to you."

She pulls back a bit and grins. "Like what?"

The moment is interrupted by a shriek from the kitchen. "Quick! Everybody in the car! The baby's coming!"

Ruben is the first to make it down the hall to the front door to get his shoes. He's soon followed by his grandchildren and his flushed wife, whose hands and mouth work at a furious pace. She passes out coats to each of the children while she issues orders to us all. "Hurry now, it's her fifth baby, so it won't take long and I'm not going to miss it this time! Knox, put your shoes on. Stephen, come here! You've got custard all over your cheeks, love."

I watch in horror as she licks her fingers and wipes his grimacing face.

"We'll need a ride, Arthur—we can't fit all the kids in the car. Outside with you!" She taps Knox on the shoulder and points to the door.

"Ruben, you follow in our car and stop by Lars and Nina's for the overnight bag. It's sitting at the back door. They forgot it."

In under a minute, coats are zipped, shoes are tied, and we're all seated in the back of the limo while she barks at Ben to get to Valcourt Memorial Hospital as fast as he can.

Tessa, who is at the far end of the limo, sandwiched between the ruffian twins, Geoffry and Josh, mouths, 'I'm sorry' to me.

I give her a wink. No problem, it's her fifth baby. Like Evi said, how long could it take to push this one out of a well-paved path?

****

A long, long time, apparently. We've now been seated in the hallway of the maternity ward for three hours with four anxious, bored boys. Tessa's sister-in-law, Isa, zipped by and picked up her children, so we're left with Lars and Nina's kids, who are waiting to find out if their mum finally gets the girl she's been trying for.

The lights are so bright, I wouldn't mind wearing sunglasses if it wouldn't make me seem like a total douchebag trying to disguise himself. I've had to cancel our dinner. Shame, really. I had a lovely private room picked out for us there and had to call ahead to pre-order the chocolate soufflés. Well, Vincent, my assistant, called ahead, and then I texted him to have him cancel. But it was my idea, so I should at least get some of the credit.

Evi is in with Nina and Lars, leaving Tessa and me with a very surly and worried Ruben, Ollie, and Mr. Missing Neck, who's been doing squats against the wall for the last twenty minutes. The twins have decided to join him and are making farting sounds every time they squat down, then laughing hysterically on the way back up.

Ollie has had word from Ben that a small crowd of journalists is waiting outside for us to come out, apparently needing to hear it from me first-hand that we're really here to welcome a new member to Tessa's family, and not for some other, more scandalous reason. I could pop down and say a few words so they could all go home, but I prefer to reward the persistence of those who stick it out to find out there is literally no story to report.

The ironic thing is that one of Tessa's workmates is among the crowd and has even sent her a text to try to get the scoop straight from the horse's mouth. She's not answering it, under the pretense of having her mobile shut off due to hospital policy. Poor Tessa. The day after our engagement, her boss sat her down to let her know she was sorry, but they'd have to report on her just like everyone else in the Royal Family. She did promise not to take photos or report on her while at work, though, so I suppose her boss isn't completely evil. But still, what an awkward position to be in. I'm not sure if that whole business is what's on Tessa's mind, but I can tell something is bothering her by the way she keeps staring off into space with her eyebrows furrowed.

"You're awfully quiet," I say.

"Oh, it's nothing. I'm just a little anxious for the baby to arrive."

"You sure there's nothing else?"

"I'm fine, really." She sighs. "Well, I was just thinking how strange it is that the guy who I picked up a latte for this morning is currently waiting outside to get photos of us."

Yup. Knew it. "Yes, it would seem I've complicated your life as far as your career goes."

"I should've read the fine print." Tessa gives me a wry smile.

I chuckle and bump her shoulder with mine. "Buyer beware, but you can't take it back now. A promise is a promise."

Her smile fades after a few seconds. "I mean, on some level I knew this would happen, but...I don't know. I guess I didn't think it would happen so fast or in such an all-encompassing way. I know that makes me ridiculously naïve."

"You're being too hard on yourself. You need to allow more than a week to adjust to life in the public eye. In my case, the paparazzi have always been there in the background from the moment I was conceived. They're a part of life, like...morning breath or prostate exams after forty."

Laughing, Tessa says, "Is that the category my colleagues fall under?"

"Not everyone in your profession, but most."

She stares off into space again, then mutters, "I'm going to have to quit, aren't I?"

Nodding, I say, "I didn't want to suggest it—modern relationship and all that—but yes."

The look on her face is one of muted shock, and it squeezes my heart a bit. I give her a kiss on the forehead. "I'm sorry, but I just don't see how it can work for you to be both the *author* and *subject* of the news."

"No, I suppose not."

"If I had my way, you'd never have to give up anything you love."

She stares at her hands for a long moment, then puts on a brave face and looks up at me. "I'm not giving anything up. I'm trading one dream for a much better one."

Not caring who sees, I plant a big kiss on her mouth. "Christ, I love you."

She gets that twinkle in her eye, then says, "You better. I'm giving up my career for you."

Leaning into her ear, I whisper, "Yes, but I've been told the perks are *huge*."

****

An hour later, we get our hopes up when Evi comes out of the birthing room, but it turns out she's only going on another ice chip run. What do they do with all these ice chips? I'd Google it, but I'm afraid of the images that might pop up.

Tessa rests her head on my shoulder and says, "I'm glad you're here, even though I'm sure you're not."

I lace my fingers through hers and give them a squeeze. "There's nowhere I'd rather be." And the odd thing is that it's true. "I'd rather spend an eternity with you in this horrid hallway than be apart from you for another week."

Tessa lifts her head and smiles at me, looking a little teary-eyed. "You know what's crazy? That's exactly how I feel."

"We're a pair of lunatics."

Mr. Missing Neck, who clearly has been eavesdropping while he does arm raises with a twin hanging from each forearm, says, "That's because you two are madly in love. That's where the phrase comes from. *Madly* in love. Get it? Because you're mad for each other."

Tessa smiles at me but speaks to him. "You're exactly right, Xavier."

Oh, so that's his name. "Listen, Xavier, you certainly have a way with the children. Would you mind helping watch them for a moment so Tessa and I can pop down to the cafeteria for a tea?"

Ruben raises one eyebrow. "Is that what you're calling it these days? A tea?"

"Dad! He meant a tea, for goodness' sake." She shoots him a warning look.

Ruben withers, but just a bit, then nods. "I can watch my own grandkids."

"I'm happy to stay, sir. I love children!" Xavier, who now has all four boys hanging off his arms, adds.

I stand quickly and pull Tessa to her feet. "Excellent. Thanks, mate. We'll be back in a flash."

We hurry down the hall together, then turn the corner and run into a woman pushing a middle-aged man in a wheelchair. Both their faces light up with recognition. She smiles broadly at me and squeals out, "Your Highness!", then looks at Tessa and her face falls, while the man notices Tessa first and says, "The Royal Watchdog!" He then glances at me, and his face falls.

"You're still with *him*, then?" he says, sounding thoroughly disgusted.

The woman pipes up, sounding equally nonplussed. "He proposed to *her* last week on a hot air balloon. Did you not see it on the news? They accidentally ended up in the Netherlands?"

"No, I've been in ICU, remember, Phyllis?" He turns and glares up at her.

"How could I forget, Daniel? I was sitting in a sodding chair in the hall the entire time, so now, each time I move, my back reminds me of how I spent the week."

"Yes, that whole hot air balloon ride didn't quite turn out the way I'd planned," I say, smiling at the woman. "Did you know you can't determine the direction of a balloon? Only up or down."

Daniel shakes his head. "Of course we knew that. Even a small child could work that out."

"No need to be rude to the prince! Just because you're a little under the weather."

Daniel looks at Tessa and points behind him with one thumb. "A little under the weather, she says. I've had both me lungs replaced."

"Yes, well, if you hadn't been smoking like a bloody chimney since you were a teenager, maybe you'd still be on your first set." Phyllis looks at me. "You might want to rethink the whole marriage thing."

"Yes, you might," Daniel tells Tessa.

"Well, at least you both agree on that," I say, then I give them a bow. "Wonderful to meet you both. I wish you a speedy recovery, Daniel."

Tugging Tessa by the hand, I head straight for the stairwell. Ollie is following at a respectful distance. I turn to him. "I've got it from here."

He gives me a knowing look. "I'll wait here, sir."

The second we're alone, I turn her to me, ready to crush her lips with mine. She looks up at me, clearly worried.

"Don't worry about them. They obviously hated each other from day one."

"So did we."

"Yes, but we got over that, and now we like each other very much." I kiss her wildly on the mouth, pressing her up against the cement wall. Tessa's mind seems to be put at ease based on that little moaning sound that just escaped her throat. We snog each other senseless for several minutes, coming dangerously close to doing things a prince definitely cannot do in public, before we finally pull away from each other, panting and straightening our clothes. I grin down at Tessa, whose cheeks are flushed and whose hair looks like she's been doing exactly what we were just doing.

I press my forehead to hers. "I can't bear the thought of you going back home to your parents' tonight."

"Me neither. I miss you so much," she says, wrapping her arms around my waist.

"Maybe you could stay over?"

"My parents'll need my help with the boys."

"Right. Damn. Tomorrow night, then?"

"Don't you have that dinner with the Australian Prime Minister?"

"Shit. Yes. Sunday?"

"I can't stay over. I have an early work meeting on Monday morning."

"This is ridiculous. We've gone from living together to barely seeing each other." I sigh. "What would you say to getting married as soon as possible?"

"I'd say, is there a judge who'd do it right now?"

"Oh, I chose the right girl." She couldn't care less about the huge televised event and the designer gown. She just wants to be with me. "If there was no one else to consider, I'd be whisking you off to Vegas so we could have Elvis marry us."

"The King marrying a future king." Tessa laughs, then she says, "But you owe it to the people to let them share in the festivities."

"True." I nod. "Plus, imagine how pissed at me your dad would be if we had the wedding without him. If he had his way, he'd have been in the balloon with us for the proposal."

"Good point," she says. "How long can it possibly take to plan a royal wedding?"

"How long can it take for a woman to have her fifth baby?"

"*That* long?"

"Almost. For a lesser man, eighteen months, but I bet I can get it done in six."

"Six?" Her eyes grow wide.

"Excited or terrified?"

"Both." She lifts herself on her tiptoes and gives me a light kiss on the lips. "Excited to be marrying you, terrified of the wedding."

"Don't be. All you have to do is make it down the aisle, and I'll be right beside you the rest of the way." I give her a lingering kiss on the lips and feel the moment when her entire being relaxes into me. It's the most powerful feeling, to be able to affect a woman like this. Rather intoxicating.

Just when I'm getting extremely...umm...cocky, she pulls back. "Can we really do it in six months?"

"If I have anything to say about it, we will."

She leans in, and we're back to kissing, and I'm pretty sure we're about to break at least two of the public decency laws until we're interrupted by a knock at the door.

"Ms. Sharpe, you're needed elsewhere." Ollie's muffled voice makes its way through the steel door.

We scramble to get ourselves looking halfway presentable, then I swing the door open, expecting to see Ollie standing alone. "Thank..."

Ruben, who's standing next to Ollie, folds his arms across his chest. "Tea, eh?"

I break out in a cold sweat, feeling like I did when I was eight and got caught drawing a mustache on the painting of the late Queen Liliana. There is literally nothing I can say to fix this, is there?

He shakes his head and turns. "The baby's here."

****

Eugenia Rosemund Sharpe. That's the name with which they've saddled the poor little doll. She's adorable, by the way. Chubby and pink, with enormous bright blue eyes and the tiniest little fingernails I've ever seen.

Evi hands her to me almost as soon as we get into the room. "Have you ever held a baby this new before?" she asks quietly.

"No." My heart explodes with some sort of strangely amazing happiness as I stare down at her little face. I'm terrified of dropping her but absolutely mesmerized at the same time. Yes, I think I'd like having one of these very much. "Have you ever seen such tiny fingernails? Sorry, I just can't get over them. They're so...tiny."

I glance at Tessa for the briefest of seconds, which is about as long as I can tear my gaze from this baby. "Let's do this. Right away."

Tessa gasps in shock. "We only just got engaged."

"So what? We're not teenagers."

Eugenia opens her eyes and stares at me. I coo at her, "Your Auntie Tessa and I are going to get married in six months. Yes, we are. Yes, we are."

Evi makes a very quiet squealing sound and touches her new granddaughter's cheek. "You've just come into the world, and already you've inspired new love, little Eugenia Rosemund."

I smile. "That's because she's just so perfect."

Tessa stands next to me and runs her fingers gently over Eugenie's head. "She certainly is."

Except, now that I really look, her head isn't so much round as it is oblong in a rather alarming sort of way. Dear God, that is really pointy—like one of those Coneheads from *Saturday Night Live* back when I was a kid. "Is her...head okay? It's rather pointy..."

"What?" Nina barks. "What's wrong with her?"

"Nothing, it's just..." Shit. Why the fuck did I say that out loud?

Lars comes over and scoops the baby out of my arms, glaring at me. "It's perfectly normal for the head to get a little squished on the way out. Nothing to be alarmed about."

Evi deftly covers Eugenia's conehead with a little wool hat.

Good job, Grandmum—hide the deformity before anyone else notices.

THREE

Stale Coffee and Wobbly Chairs

Tessa

I t's eight a.m. on Monday, and I'm crammed into the tiny boardroom along with six other bleary-eyed staff members, all of whom want desperately to get an exclusive from me—a photo, a quote, anything—so that's not awkward in any way. Just kidding—it's every bit as bizarre as you'd imagine. None of them will actually come out and ask, because Hazel Nettlebottom, our editor-in-chief, told them not to, but they all look at me like they're about to go on the Paleo diet and I'm the last cupcake in the shop window.

Tyler, the new intern, is the hungriest of the bunch because he's desperate to get on the payroll. He's the one who was at the hospital on Friday night and was waiting outside the building this morning to catch a photo of me on my way into the office. Luckily, Xavier managed to block his view of me while I made my way from the car to the lobby door because I woke up late today, so I'm not exactly 'camera-ready.' The nation's biggest news channel, ABNC, has hired famous fashion critic Nigel Wood, and based on his first two appearances on the morning news, his sole purpose is to make fun of me. So far, he's had an absolute field day with what I wore on our hot air balloon date, calling me the dullest dresser in the kingdom and posing the question of my potential colour-blindness to the world.

Hazel sweeps into the room, her floor-length sweater vest fanning out behind her. She stands at the far end in front of a white board and goes over last week's circulation and advertising numbers in excruciatingly careful detail. It doesn't take me long before my mind starts to wander, as it always does during this bit. The numbers are always pretty much the same—terrible. We're barely making enough to get by, and none of the reporters on staff has managed to do what Hazel asks of us every week, which is to find Holy Grail of journalism: 'the big scoop.'

I've got a big scoop for them. I'm leaving. I just have to figure out when. Too soon, and I'm going to be labeled a gold-digger. Too late, and I'm going to look like a dullard who's too stupid to see the writing on the wall. I spent the better part of the weekend wrestling with the decision of *when* to quit my job, and if I'm to be really honest, I'm also troubled by the fact that I have to at all, no matter what I told Arthur at the hospital.

I know, I know, you're probably thinking, 'Tessa, you're going to be a queen one day. What the hell do you have to feel sorry for yourself about?', and you're not wrong. I'm one of the luckiest bitches on the planet, and I do know it, I promise.

But (there's always a but, isn't there?), since I was fourteen years old, the only thing I've only ever wanted was to be a successful journalist. I worked my tail off for four years of uni, followed by seven years of struggling to make it, suffering some serious setbacks—namely Barrett Richfield, my cheating, lying, firing boss/boyfriend—but did I give up? No. I pivoted, adjusted, and kept going in my pursuit of the truth because, if nothing else, I am dedicated to my craft.

Oh, but I should probably be paying attention. Hazel just said the words 'vital' and 'imperative' in one sentence. But it's just so distracting to know I have to quit. Whoops, I don't mean quit; I mean *trade* it for something better. And it will be better, right? Even though I have my very own 'hate' club and fashion critic on the national news?

Hmm...I wonder if Arthur can arrange some face time with Camilla for me. She's had decades to figure out how to handle being wildly unpopular.

"Tessa. Tessa...hello," Hazel says in that Canadian accent of hers.

I look up to see her smiling at me from behind her turquoise-rimmed glasses. Oh, shit. The rest of the staff are filing out, and I haven't the faintest clue as to what I'm meant to be doing this week.

"Can you stop by my office after break time?"

"Yes, absolutely."

****

Break time passes by at record speed, and I find myself sitting on the slightly wobbly metal chair across from Hazel's desk while she finishes up a phone call. As soon as she hangs up, she tucks her pencil behind her ear and sighs. "So, Tessa, I think we need to talk about your future here."

Oh, Christ, am I about to get fired? I mean, I know I need to leave, but please not *this* way.

My face must say exactly what I'm thinking, because Hazel shakes her head and smiles. "No, no. I'm not letting you go, but I do think we need to *repurpose* you for obvious reasons."

Repurpose me? Like an old dresser? "Righto. I was thinking the same thing. I mean, I know I won't exactly be able to blend in with the crowd at public events."

"Well, not with that big hunk of manliness following you everywhere you go." She glances out the glass wall at Xavier, who is sitting in the hall reading *More Muscles* magazine. Blushing, she looks back at me and says, "I was thinking perhaps you could move to the announcements, obits, and edits desk."

"Brilliant, yes." Shit. That's a *giant* step down in the reporting world. It also means I'll be here until after midnight every Friday, when we go to press. I chew on my thumbnail for a second while I think about what this will mean for my personal life.

Hazel jots something down in her day planner. "Good. That's settled, then."

I nod, knowing I should bring up the fact that I need to quit soon, but somehow, I just can't force the words to come out of my mouth. I'm just not ready to 'trade' this part of my life.

FOUR

The Unintended Consequences of True Love

Arthur

Text from me to Tessa: *How's your day going?*
Her: *Up to my eyeballs in proofreading. Other than that, fine.*
Me: *Come by tonight. I want to help rid you of your stress.*
Her: *Mmm. Sounds intriguing. Eight, okay?*
Me: *Follow the trail of Jelly Babies leading from the front door.*

I put my phone down on my desk and stare out the window, thinking about Tessa across the river in some stuffy office. I didn't get to wake up with her in my arms this morning or steal a kiss from her at breakfast. All we manage most days is just a few flirty texts until late evening, at which time we might see each other. But most of the time, we just increase the frequency of flirty texts followed by speaking on the phone until late into the night, ending the call with a disgustingly sweet, 'you hang up first,' 'no, you hang up first.'

I need to get the ball rolling on our nuptials so I'll never have to wake up without her again. I glance at the next item on my itinerary. I've got twenty-five minutes until I'm due to leave for a luncheon for the Muscular Dystrophy Society. Should be just enough time to plan a wedding...

"Vincent, can you pop in here for a moment?" I say into the intercom.

"Be right there, Your Highness."

I take one last gulp of fresh air as the door opens, and in walks my assistant, Vincent, whose smell rating today is at an all-time high of five on the 'reeks of blue cheese' ranking system I've devised (but not to worry—I haven't told anyone else about it. I would never want to embarrass him). "Tessa and I had a chat over the weekend, and we'd like to have a May wedding."

Vincent opens his iPad case and nods. "Excellent, Your Highness, a most lovely time of year for such an occasion. The tulips will still be in full bloom, the weather will be warm. We can schedule a meeting...two weeks from tomorrow with the advisory members, as well as the head of programming at ABNC to get started." He taps on his screen for a moment.

"I'm thinking we just choose a date now and then let everyone else catch up."

"But Prince Arthur, that's not how this is done. There are literally hundreds of stakeholders involved. The two of us can't simply *book* the wedding."

"Why not? We set dates for important events all the time. Nobody complains."

"We can try, Your Highness, but we may need to be somewhat flexible once everyone's been consulted."

"Fine, but only by a few days either way. The sooner, the better."

"Certainly. May 2019 or May 2020?"

"May 2018."

He looks up, his eyebrows creasing together. "As in *six months* from now?"

"Precisely."

"Can't be done."

"Of course it can. We regularly book catering with fewer than three months' notice for the largest of receptions. This is really no different when you think about it."

"No different? Sir, we need to invite the heads of state and royal families for over two-hundred nations, not to mention clearing the schedules of your own family two weeks prior to the auspicious occasion. There are the television networks to consider, and we certainly don't want it to conflict with any major world sporting events. Then there's the matter of Ms. Sharpe's dress, as well as that of the bridal party and outfitting her entire family with appropriate attire, which should be...interesting. The top designers will require, at minimum, one year. Can't be done, Your Highness." Suddenly, a look of understanding crosses his face. His eyes grow wide and his mouth hangs open for a second before he catches himself. "Oh, dear, are we required to hurry for a *certain reason,* sir? Because if that's the case, I think we'll find six months too long. She'll be showing by then."

"Showing? God, no. We're not expecting an heir." I stand and walk to the window, then open it to allow some cool, autumn air into the room, unable to stand the smell of blue cheese any longer.

"Then, if I may, why the rush?"

I sigh heavily. "You must not ever tell anyone what I'm about to say, Vincent."

"Do you really need to preface anything you tell me with the request to keep it confidential?"

"No, I suppose not." I pause, wishing I didn't have to admit it out loud. "It's just that we miss each other very much now that we're not under the same roof." Gluing my eyes to the view of the front lawn, I try not to imagine the incredulous look on the face of my right-hand man.

"Even so, there are still *all* the other factors to consider. No one can pull off a royal wedding in such a short time."

"Surely, there must be someone who's capable."

He sighs and taps his finger on his chin for a moment. "Well, there's the team that oversaw William and Kate's wedding. They're considered the best, although they did screw up royally by missing the chance to pre-approve Pippa's dress."

"Good Lord, so people could see her rather nicely-shaped bottom. You'd think she was wearing a set of pasties and a pair of Daisy Dukes. I was there, and I have to say, most of the guests rather enjoyed it. The male ones, anyway."

A slight smile escapes his lips, giving away that *he* rather enjoyed that dress, too. "Yes, well, I doubt they'll be available given your somewhat unrealistic time frame."

"Let's try anyway, shall we? What's the use of being a crown prince if you can't even have your own wedding when you want?"

Vincent nods and stands, closing his iPad case before he walks out the door without another word. This is a sign that he's very displeased, but he'll do what I've asked anyway. I'm not going to lie—it's good to be almost king.

****

"Good morning and welcome to The Morning Show, Friday Edition. Our top news today comes from Valcourt Palace, where a date has been set for the upcoming nuptials of Prince Arthur to the former Royal Watchdog and so-called Shock Jogger blogger, Tessa Sharpe. Giles Bigley joins us from in front of the palace with more on this story."

"Veronica, good morning."

"Good morning, Giles. What can you tell us about the announcement from the palace?"

"I can tell you it's not what anyone was expecting. It seems as though his Royal Highness Prince Arthur and Ms. Sharpe may be in rather a hurry to make it down the aisle. They've set the date for May seventh of *next year*. Only six months from now."

"Giles, royal weddings normally take at least two years to plan, so why the rush?"

"That's what we're all wondering. The only possible explanation is that, by Avonian law, a baby born out of wedlock cannot be considered an heir to the throne."

Blanching visibly, Veronica starts, "Certainly, you're not suggesting..."

"It's really the only possibility that makes sense. Why else would they want to rush this event?"

****

"Sir, I can get Sebastian Yates-Davenport, but we have to book him now." Vincent is standing at the door to my office, his headset in place.

"William and Kate's?"

"Couldn't get them. They're holding out in case Harry and Megan set a date. Mr. Yates-Davenport did Prince Quinton and Princess Charlotte's wedding, which is quite the miracle given the fact that she..."

"Tried to run away three times?"

"Allegedly."

"Hire him.

"He's charging double because of the time frame."

"Negotiate him down. Tell him I don't have any secret baby paternity tests pending."

"I'll see what I can do."

FIVE

W.W.G.D.?

Tessa

I stand inside the front hall of my parents' house, panting after my morning run with Xavier. Well, we don't run together so much as I run and he strolls next to me, calling out encouraging phrases like, "That's it, Ms. Sharpe. Pick up that pace. Think of all the calories you're burning! You'll be fit, yet!"

So, what used to be my escape from the world has now become a somewhat irritating and humbling daily experience. I wait at the door while he gives the house a once-over, which is ridiculous since my parents have been home since we left. I take out my earbuds and see my mum rushing toward me from the kitchen with tears in her eyes. "Twinkle, why didn't you tell me?"

She pulls me in for a big hug. Suddenly, my dad appears and he's hugging me, too. "No wonder you've been so moody lately. You shouldn't be running. Not in your condition."

I try to speak, but my mum's voice drowns out mine. "You should have told us. We're not going to be upset with you. It's not like you're a teenager or something."

"Exactly, you're at the age where you *should* be getting on this before there are...complications that can come with being a mature parent."

"What are you talking about?" I pulled back from them.

"The baby, of course." My mum plants both hands on her hips.

"What baby?"

"Yours and Arthur's," my mum says. "We saw it on the news this morning. The phone's been ringing off the hook since you left."

Dad shakes his head at me. "Do you know how embarrassing it is for your mum to find out about our next grandchild on the news?"

Mum jumps right in. "Really, Tessa, you should have come to us first. I've had to pretend I knew the whole time. I've managed to be very coy with people about the due date, but I'm pretty sure Grace next door knows I had no idea."

Dad makes a *tsk*ing sound. "If she suspects that, it'll be all over the street by lunchtime."

"What I can't understand is, if you're planning for a May wedding, will you even fit into your dress? You'll be as big as a house by then."

"Stop." I raise both hands as well as my voice. "There's no baby."

My mum's face crumples as she reaches for me again. "Oh, darling, come here. It can happen to anyone. Don't think one miscarriage means you're infertile."

"Lots of people go through this. You might just need the help of a doctor." My dad pats me on the shoulder. "We can call Dr. Fredericks straight away. She'll know what to do."

My mum pulls away from me and glares at my father. "Ruben, I'm sure the royal family has access to much better doctors than we do. There's that clinic in Sweden that has the most advanced techniques in the world. They'll probably send her *there*. You know the one. They managed to help a man bring a baby to full term." She turns to me. "If they can help *a man,* they can certainly help you."

Oh, for... "I'm not pregnant, and I've never been pregnant. I don't need to go to some clinic in Sweden, and I don't have the first freaking clue what you're talking about."

My mother looks at me for a moment, then straightens her spine. "There's no need to get snippy about it," at the same time my father says, "You don't have to pretend with us. We're your parents."

I sigh, and my shoulders drop. "I'm not lying. I don't have the first idea why the news is reporting I'm pregnant, because I'm not."

Dad's face relaxes. "Oh, so you don't have fertility issues, then?"

"No!" I say, my tone filled with irritation. "Well, I don't know. I may have. I've never tried, so I suppose it's a possibility."

"Cheese and rice!" my mum says, throwing her hands up in the air and turning from me. "Now I've gone and told all the neighbours *and* my cousins you *are* pregnant, and I'm going to look like a complete idiot!"

She disappears into the kitchen, her words trailing behind her. "What am I supposed to tell them now? If you weren't pregnant, you really should have told us!"

****

Text from Lars to Me: *Are you seriously pregnant? Have you not ever heard of birth control? Seriously, Tessa. Total embarrassment.*

Text from Bram: *So, you were knocking boots and now you're knocked up, hey? Dumb arse.*

Text from Nikki: *OMG! I can't believe you're having a baby! You probably should have at least waited until you were almost all the way down the aisle, but who cares? I'm so excited! I'm going to be an auntie! Well, sort of. Anyway, Yay!*

Email from Hazel:
RE: If You Need a Friend, My Door is Always Open
Dear Tessa,

I wanted to check with you to see if we're okay, since you didn't feel comfortable sharing the news of your pregnancy with me. Don't worry, I'm not mad that you let ABNC scoop us on your pregnancy story. Just concerned that, somehow, I've damaged our relationship.

I was also hoping that maybe you and Arthur would agree to an interview to give the due date and your true feelings about becoming a mother so quickly. Or perhaps even reveal the baby's sex on our website? But only if and when you'd be ready to talk about it. No pressure, sweetie. But it would be SUCH the big scoop for the team, wouldn't it?

All the very best,

Hazel

P.S. Let me know if you need anything. I've started looking into Avonia's maternity leave policy and see that it's horribly lacking. Only six months of paid leave? We may need to do a story about that. Back home, it's a full year.

****

It's exactly eight p.m. when we cross the bridge that leads to the tiny island on which Valcourt Palace sits. I have to admit, I was a bit on edge this afternoon because I made the mistake of looking at the #BrookeIsBetter Twitter feed during my lunch break. Those people really hate me with a vengeance. Wow. The crappy thing is that one of them has managed to dig up a photo of Brooke and Arthur standing together at a polo match from a few years back, and the picture is just so cozy. She's looking perfectly lovely in a fitted, light yellow dress and Arthur's in his polo uniform. They're laughing about something; her hand is on his chest in that 'Oh, Arthur, you are just too funny, please ask me to marry you' sort of way.

It shouldn't bother me. It was a long time ago, and as far as I know, they have never been more than friends. And even if they *were* more than friends at one point, that's over and he's with me. So, I will not now or ever lower myself by asking him about her. Grace Kelly would *never* have asked about an old girlfriend. She wouldn't have been bothered with silly, insignificant details like exes or stupid people posting nasty things on social media. A true princess rises above it all, never letting pettiness or insecurity cloud her sunny outlook on the world.

I may have slipped up and called Finn earlier this afternoon to ask his opinion of the whole 'can a man and a woman truly be platonic' debate. But now I'm over What's-Her-Name and her sickeningly gorgeous self with her hands all over my fiancé's chest. It was a million years ago. Well, technically three years ago. But it might as well be a million because it's done. *Finito.*

Even though Finn's words are still bashing around in my brain...

"Let me guess, Arthur has a close female friend and you're trying to determine how threatened to be?"

"I wouldn't say close."

"Don't go down this road, Tess. It's a dead end."

"Just, please, answer the question, Finn."

"Fine. Your funeral. How hot is she?"

"Pretty hot. Like a solid nine."

"Yeah, in that case, Arthur has definitely thought about shagging her."

I sighed. *"Really? What about if her personality isn't so great? Like maybe she's boring or something?"*

"Doesn't matter. Every guy does a quick sex inventory of every non-related women he meets. It's an automatic reflex, like breathing out after you breathe in. It just happens without you thinking about it. If she's hot, all her guy friends will want to nail her."

"Awesome. Glad I asked."

"My advice? Don't worry about whoever she is. Arthur proposed to you, not her. But, at the same time, keep your eyes open. It's not like you know him all that well, so who knows? He could be a cheating fuck."

Xavier stops the car at the front entrance to the palace and says what he always does when he parks. "Another safe landing, courtesy of yours truly." Then he chuckles as he gets out of the car and hurries around to try to beat me to the door, which he never does. I can open my own doors, thank you very much.

I look up and see Arthur sitting on the third step, grinning at me. He runs one hand through his dark blond hair, and God, he's so manly and gorgeous in jeans and that grey hoodie. How is he *so* good-looking? And that look on his face says he is not a cheating fuck, but a man very much in love. What was I worried about a minute ago?

We hurry to each other like a couple of cheesy fools in a Hallmark Christmas movie. He wraps his arms around me and picks me up as he plants a lingering kiss on my mouth. Oh, that was nice. There's a reason those movies are so popular. When he puts me down, he smiles at Xavier. "I've got her from here."

"Excellent. I'll be right here waiting. You two kids have fun, now." *You kids.* Xavier's only thirty-five.

Arthur takes my hand, and we walk along the path that leads to the back of the palace.

"Been looking forward to this for days. Quite the luxury to have you all to myself for an entire evening."

"Well, we're not really alone, are we?" I look up at him and smile. "There are, what, one hundred people on staff this evening?"

"Not where we're going." He lifts my hand and kisses my knuckles. "I know how badly you need time away from the world since you don't have your own place anymore."

"Oh, God, yes. It's a bit of a zoo. Kids and cats and parents in and out of my bedroom every few minutes."

"Well, tonight it's just you and me. I'm going to feed you chocolate and make sure that, by the time you leave here, you will be the most relaxed, most satisfied woman on the planet."

We stroll along in the cool evening air until we reach the solarium. Arthur opens the door and glances down at me excitedly. When we step inside, I gasp. There are tiny twinkling white lights and lit candles everywhere among the plants. The effect is magical, and I feel myself transported away from the real world as soon as the door closes behind us.

"This is amazing." I turn to Arthur and wrap my arms around his neck, then give him a long kiss on the mouth. "You're amazing," I say, smiling up at him.

"I know. Now come with me, my lady. I may have managed to rustle up that chocolate soufflé I promised you the other night."

He leads me to a table set for two with silver domes covering plates. When I sit, Arthur takes a cloth napkin and fans it out on my lap. He then lifts the dome to unveil a perfectly baked dark chocolate soufflé with a scoop of vanilla bean ice cream on the side, garnished with a few carefully placed raspberries and some mint leaves.

"I was thinking we should forget the rest of the world exists and spend the rest of the evening thoroughly enjoying each other."

"Sounds perfect." I watch as he fills two flutes with Champagne, then sits down. Handing me a glass, he then holds his up to mine. "Oh, wait. Should you be having Champagne? According to the media, I knocked you up already."

"Turns out it was fake news," I say.

"Then drink up." He smiles. "To us. To being alone. To being alone together."

Our glasses make a most satisfying clinking sound when they touch, and as the first burst of cool bubbles washes over my tongue, I all but forget about What's-Her-Name in the yellow dress and the I Hate Tessa people. See? I am definitely going to rise above it all.

The first bite of soufflé is mouth-wateringly amazing. Like, literally, my mouth is watering and begging me for more. Oh yes, mouth, I think I will. Besides, I don't have to fit into a wedding dress until spring. There'll be loads of time to get in shape after tonight. Well, not that much time, actually. Hmm...maybe I should decide now how much to leave on the plate.

"Eat up, Sharpe. You're already in perfect shape," he says, staring at me with one raised eyebrow. "Besides, I'll help you work it off. I promise."

I laugh as I pick up my Champagne and gesture with it. "How is it you can already read my thoughts?"

"Careful observation combined with a decent base knowledge of the fairer sex."

Oh dear, I hope he doesn't mean She-Who-Shall-Not-Be-Named. "Oh, and with whom have you acquired this base knowledge?"

"Not like that. I have a sister, remember? And a grandmother, of whom I'm very fond."

"Right. I almost forgot. Where are they this evening?"

"Gran is probably watching telly by now, and Arabella is chasing the sun. I think she's gone to Portugal, if I'm not mistaken." He has a bite of dessert and gives me a thoughtful look while he chews. "Where would you like to go on our honeymoon?"

Honeymoon. I haven't even thought of that yet, but oh my God, it's going to be amazing, isn't it? I fight the impulse to jump up and down and squeal like a fifteen-year-old girl at a Justin Bieber concert. "I haven't given it any thought, actually."

"Where have you always wanted to go but never got to? First place that pops into your mind."

"The Maldives. No, Mauritius. No, wait, Maui."

Arthur chuckles. "Let's do them all."

"Them all? We couldn't possibly...that would be far too expensive, and...and how much time could you actually take for a honeymoon?"

"I'm pretty sure I could take a month, but I imagine it really depends on whether you'll still have your job at that point."

I put down my fork. "Urgh. I still haven't worked out when to leave."

"I was thinking about that," Arthur says, topping off my Champagne. "Why don't we sit down and sort out which charities you'd like to be involved with so we can set that up ahead of time? That way, when you do leave the paper, it can be because of your charitable commitments, and not because you're a gold-digging hussy."

"Arse." I chuckle, feeling a hint of relief at having a possible solution. "You really do want to take care of me, don't you?"

"Of course I do. It's my main focus in life now, which is not necessarily a good thing, what with running the kingdom and all." Arthur picks up my hand and brushes his lips against my knuckles. "I say, as far as your job goes, we take it one step at a time. Set up the charities, talk to your boss about what will work well for her, then quietly make your exit when the moment is right."

"You're good at this."

"Good at what?" he asks, taking another bite of soufflé.

"All of it—sorting out problems, making me feel better, taking a bad day and turning it into something wonderful..."

He grins at me over the candle. "There is literally nothing I'd rather do than make you feel better. Now, back to the honeymoon. I want to take you to every magical place on the planet. Anywhere and everywhere you've ever wanted to see."

"What about you?" I ask. "Where have you always wanted to go but haven't had the chance?"

"Nowhere, really. I've pretty much been everywhere, but whatever I did before I met you is completely irrelevant. Traveling with you will be completely new and wonderful."

"So, I can decide?"

"Yes. You decide, and I'll happily take you." He places his napkin on top of his plate and stands, then walks over to a small sound system and turns it on. Almost immediately, John Legend's voice surrounds us. Arthur turns to me and holds out his hand. "Dance with me."

I stand and cross the candlelit room to him; we hold each other, and our bodies start moving together to the slow beat as I rest my head on his broad shoulder. "You'd better be careful, Arthur. I've heard it's a mistake to be too romantic at the beginning of a relationship because if you can't keep it up, your wife will forever long for the younger, better version of you."

"Oh, I'll be able to keep it up, all right." He spins and dips me, then lowers his face to my neck. Nibbling on my earlobe, he makes me giggle, then picks me back up and spins me again and pulls me back into his arms. "Things won't ever be dull between us, Tessa. I promise."

"Somehow, I believe that. I can just tell by looking at you. You mean every word, don't you?" I run a finger over his cheek and down to his lips.

"When it comes to you, I do." He gazes into my eyes, and the look is so intense, so full of emotion, I can't think of a witty response. Or any response at all, really.

Arthur kisses me on the neck, then says, "When it comes to you, I find myself saying far too much. It's rather stupid of me because, if I'm not careful, you're going to get the upper hand."

"I got the upper hand the first time we met. I'm surprised you've forgotten."

Arthur grins at the memory. "You only got the upper hand because I gave it to you."

"Ha! That's the biggest load of horseshit I've ever heard. I took it, and you bloody well know it."

"I let you take it because of your hotness." He twirls us with the grace of a ballroom dancer, and I know he's doing it to distract me. "I was desperate to get you into bed."

"*That*, I believe."

"Good, because it's true." And then he kisses me, and kissing turns into so much more. Before I know it, our clothes are in a pile on the old stone floor and we're on top of them, our bodies moving together in an entirely more satisfying and delicious type of dance. His eyes lock on mine, and he looks at me as though it's the first time he's ever seen my face. I'm suddenly overcome by how beautiful he can make me feel just by the way he stares at me. I want to be looked at this way for the rest of my life, and I know with every fiber of my being this is exactly the way it will always be between us. No matter how many people want us to break up.

An hour or so later, we're in his bed, having come back to his private apartment in the palace for round two. Our bodies are a tangled mass of sweaty human as we stare up at the ceiling, smiling and panting while we try to recover. The Champagne is wearing off, and as it does, that yucky little feeling settles back into my gut.

"That was mind-blowingly wonderful." Arthur turns his face and gives me a kiss on the forehead. "Seriously amazing." Kiss. "Award-winning level of sex. And don't pretend it wasn't that good for you just so you can get another round out of me. I'm up for it anyway. Well, in a few minutes I will be."

I laugh because that's exactly what I was about to do. "You can hardly blame me, can you? I mean, if you got to see yourself naked, you'd be doing whatever you could to get you into bed and keep you there."

"I *have* seen myself naked. We have mirrors all over the place here, and I can say, with one hundred percent certainty, I'd much rather look at you."

"Well, then, this should work out just fine."

"Yes, it should." He gives me a quick kiss on the lips, then says, "You look thirsty. I'll be right back."

He stands and pulls on a pair of boxer briefs, then strides across the bedroom, giving me a most spectacular view of his incredible backside. As soon as he leaves the room, I flop back on the pillow and think about how lucky I am. I don't know why I let those stupid I Hate Tessa people get to me. They don't know Arthur the way I do. We're perfect for each other, no matter what anyone else thinks.

Damn. That stupid photo just popped into my head, and now I'm thinking about the fact that, at some point, Arthur must have wanted to shag Brooke. Maybe I should come right out and ask him if he and Brooke have ever been an item. It would be the smart thing to do. Just get it out in the open.

He returns, carrying two tumblers and a large bottle of water, along with a bag of crisps under his arm. Dexter, Arthur's pot-bellied pig, who has been sleeping soundly on the couch, trots in behind him. Arthur hands me a glass, then fills both before he settles himself next to me.

I prop myself up on one elbow and look at him. I'm just going to leave it alone. But surely, even Grace Kelly would have asked Prince Rainer in a very roundabout, general sort of way. It's no good to let these things fester. And if I can just reassure myself, then I can let this whole thing go and forget it forever. Yes, best to ask. "Have you ever felt this way about anyone before?"

"Nope, never."

Good answer. *Stop now while you're ahead, Tessa.* "Promise?"

Arthur narrows his eyebrows. "What's this about?"

"I don't know. I'm just wondering."

"Why?"

"Why aren't you answering the question?" I sit up and tuck the sheet under my armpits.

"I did answer, which only led to you asking again. My Spidey senses are tingling right now, which means you've likely got a hell of a whammy queued up, and I'd rather get out ahead of it, if you don't mind."

"I don't have a *whammy* coming your way. I was just curious." I have a sip of water, and when I look at him, the expression on his face calls me on my evasiveness. Sighing, I say, "I saw an old photo of you and Brooke today online. It kind of bothered me."

He shrugs. "She's just a friend. You know that."

"Yes, but has she always been in the friend zone?"

"Of course she has, but even if she had been more to me at one point, would it really matter now? You have exes, so do I."

"I know it shouldn't bother me, but—"

"It does anyway?" He grins at me. "Ms. Sharpe, are you a little bit jealous?"

Rolling my eyes, I say, "Not jealous. More like needing to have some assurance."

Arthur purses his lips for a second, then says, "Explain, please."

"We've only known each other for seven months. I guess I found myself curious about whether you'll be..." *Oh, shit. How do I say this without saying it?*

He raises one eyebrow. "A cheating bastard?"

"I was going to say faithful."

"I'm really surprised you feel the need to ask that. It's a little insulting, actually."

"I'm not trying to insult you..." *What am I trying to do?*

"No, of course not. You're merely insinuating that you're not sure if I'll cheat on you or not." His smile is gone now.

"Well, it's not like we've ever discussed the matter of fidelity."

"Is it negotiable?"

My head snaps back. "What? No, of course not."

"Why discuss it if it's not negotiable?"

My muscles tense up. "People do discuss things that aren't negotiable. It's part of getting to know someone. And I'm pretty sure we should really know each other if we're going to get married. However, the fact that you have found a way to avoid answering the question is honestly a bit alarming."

"Avoided the question? I'm simply pointing out the fact that the question itself is unnecessary in hopes of putting to rest any other ridiculous accusations disguised as questions." He sets his water down on the night table and opens the bag of crisps.

"I'm not stupid, you know. You can't use your Jedi mind trickery to make me forget that you still haven't answered the question."

His eyes hardened. "Fine. I won't cheat on you. Next topic: are you going to murder me in my sleep one day?"

"What? That's a horrible thing to ask me!"

"Oh, you're avoiding the question. Must mean that you're thinking of doing it..." He pops a chip into his mouth and maintains eye contact while he chews.

"Don't do that."

"Do what?"

"The smug chewing. Don't do that. I don't like it."

"Smug chewing?" he asks, looking far too amused for my liking.

"You knew exactly what you were doing with that crisp." I narrow my eyes at him. "You know what? I'm not going to sit here being smugly chewed at." I stand and cross the room, picking up my knickers and sliding them on. I pluck my bra off the lamp shade and stick my arms through the straps furiously.

"What are you doing?"

"What does it look like?" I jam my sweater over my head, and I'm now standing in my socks and cardigan, having forgotten my T-shirt and jeans in my desire to flee.

"It looks to me like you're getting dressed and quite possibly preparing to leave, which would seem like a very bad idea given the fact that we're in the middle of an argument and we won't see each other for three days."

"I think it's a brilliant idea. It's exactly what you do when you don't want to be around a complete arse." I hunt around until I find my T-shirt, then tug my cardigan up over my head, managing to get my arms tangled in the sleeves. I struggle for a minute, my entire body heating up with irritation and embarrassment. *Very elegant, Tessa. Come on, arms, really? Don't do this right now when I'm trying to make a point.*

Just when I'm starting to feel that panic that sets in when you really have to pee and you can't get your wet swimsuit off, I feel the sweater being gently lifted off me.

"I've got it, thanks," I snap.

"Calm down. I'm just trying to help."

"You did *not* just say that." I cover myself with the cardigan and glare.

Arthur rolls his eyes. "Christ. What is it with women and being asked to calm down?"

"First of all, you didn't ask. You ordered." I waggle my finger in front of his nose. "And I'm surprised you don't know this about me yet, but here's a news flash for you: I don't exactly take well to being ordered around."

"And I don't like being accused of something I have not and would never do. So, perhaps you'd do well to apologize rather than getting all high and mighty. This really is not the way to get what you want."

"Thanks for the advice! Is that what you read in *The Art of War*?" I spit out. "Or did you learn that bit of wisdom watching *The Godfather*?"

"Wow. Tessa, I'm doing my best to stay calm and be logical about this. I would appreciate it if you could do the same."

"Sure, it's easy for you to stay all *calm* and *logical*. You're not the one having to look at photos of women everyone considers to be much more suitable for your fiancée!" I sigh and look down at Dexter, who is now sniffing along the bed in search of the bag of crisps. He looks up at me with his big black eyes, and I swear the look on his face is suggesting that I calm down. "You know what? I'm just gonna go. I'm sorry I brought it up."

I hop up and down until I finally have my jeans pulled up, then exit the bedroom to find my suede boots. By the time I'm fully dressed, my anger has drained away, and in its place regret fills my body. I turn to see Arthur in just his jeans, leaning against the door jamb, watching me. The look on his face melts me completely. I sigh and let my shoulders drop. "I don't want to go."

"I don't want you to."

"I don't know what I'm doing...I'm just really scared. There's about five million people who don't want us to be together, and only two people I know for sure who do. And now there's the *I Hate Tessa* Club..."

His eyes narrow. "What are you talking about?"

"On Twitter. It started the night we got engaged. #BrookeIsBetter."

"What? How the fuck did I not hear about this?"

I shrug. "I don't know. I've been pretending it's not happening, which includes not telling you about it."

"Oh, Christ. Come here, you." He holds out his arms to me.

"Are you sure you want me to?"

"Very much. I need to hold you until you forget all about those ugly people."

I walk to him, and he wraps his arms around me and holds me close to his chest.

Pressing his lips to my forehead, he holds them there for a long time before saying, "I had no idea you were under this kind of pressure. Is that really the hashtag? Brooke Is Better?"

"Yes," I groan.

Arthur sighs. "I'm sorry you've had to deal with that. People can be fucking awful."

"I suppose I deserve it. I spent years being one of those awful people."

"No, you—"

I look up at him with pursed lips. "It's okay, Arthur. You can admit it."

"Okay, so you were pretty much the most awful of the bunch," he says with a hint of a smile. "But you more than made up for all of that. Is it too much to ask for the rest of the nation to forgive and forget it?"

"I think it may be," I say. "We're going to have to accept the fact that a lot of people—in fact, most people—won't approve of our relationship or understand it. Quite possibly for a very long time."

"Which means it's even more imperative that *we* believe in us."

We hold each other for a deliciously long time. He rubs my back with one hand, and the feeling is so hypnotic, I find myself melting in his arms. "I believe in us, Arthur. I do. I guess I just let them get to me today."

"Promise me one thing," he says.

"Anything."

"That you'll come to me straightaway if you read, see, or hear *anything* in the news about us that upsets you."

"I promise."

Planting a kiss on my head, he says, "Good. It's the only way we're going to get through this together."

"Okay. Deal. I also promise I'll never murder you in your sleep."

"Aww. Thank you, baby. Same here."

SIX

Twitter Battles are the New Duels

Arthur

"Welcome to ABNC's Royal Wedding Watch. I'm Veronica Platt, reporting live. There's more news from Valcourt Palace today. Giles Bigly joins us live from just outside the palace gates."

"Good morning, Veronica."

"It looks chilly out there today, Giles." Veronica smiles.

"Yes. Quite." A bitter expression crosses his face. "I think I'll just get the reporting done so I can get back inside."

"Excellent."

"We've got a big report today on the upcoming wedding. Prince Arthur has broken his silence on Twitter today about speculation that he and his fiancée, Tessa Sharpe, are expecting. The tweet says, 'No need to send baby gifts just yet. Absolutely no reason for Tessa and me to marry quickly other than being madly in love.'"

Veronica nods and gives a thoughtful look into the camera. "Interesting. What do you make of that, Giles?"

Giles freezes for a moment, then says, "She's not pregnant."

****

I hate to admit it, but I've done something rather foolish. I've let my sense of protectiveness overrule my sense of intelligence and have started my own secret Twitter account with the handle @WeLoveTessa and #TessaIsTops. I know it's not terribly creative, but I think it should get the point across. The problem is, one can't just start a Twitter account aimed at demolishing the #BrookeIsBetter movement and then leave it unattended.

No, once you engage in this form of online fighting, you must be constantly vigilant, ever at the ready with a clever retort and irrefutable evidence to oppose one's enemy. Unfortunately, in this particular case, my enemy seems to have nothing better to do with his—or, most likely, *her*—time. Oh, I know you'll say, 'That's a little sexist, Arthur,' but let's be really honest. I'm Avonia's most eligible bachelor, which means there are more than a few ladies in the kingdom whose wishful thinking may have gotten away from them. One of them was bound to overreact and believe she can 'be the difference' between me tying the knot or remaining single long enough to find her standing alone in the spring rain and rushing to her to pledge my instant and undying love.

'But Arthur, why would she want to point out that Brooke Beddingfield is better?'

Because she knows I don't have any interest in Brooke, so she can use Brooke as a pawn in her little game to get Tessa out of the way. Well, I have news for you, @IHateTessa. It's not going to work. I'm not going to change my mind even if you tweet every hour, which you seem to do.

So, now I'm stuck in a ridiculous battle of wits that takes up time I don't have. And given the fact that I obviously must keep this endeavor a secret from absolutely everyone—so please keep it between us—I cannot enlist the help of Vincent or any of the other staff in this regard. So, I find myself sneaking off with my phone whenever I get a notification that the @IHateTessa person has tweeted something new. Most of the time, I end up using the excuse that I need to use the restroom, which has set off certain alarm amongst my staff, who have more than once in the past three days suggested we call the doctor to examine me. This morning, I found a pamphlet on my desk about prostate issues, which I can assure you I do not have. So, my idiotic plan is not only taking up massive quantities of time I don't have, it is also quite likely to lead to me bending over and coughing if I'm not careful.

At the moment, I'm meant to be reading over the fourth draft of a rather contentious trade agreement between Avonia and Spain. However, instead I'm in a three-way Twitter fight with some douche who calls himself @KingSlayer99 and @IHateTessa. I don't know who will emerge victorious in this little battle, but I can say without hesitation we're all the losers here.

A knock at the door interrupts me while I'm thinking up the perfect retort. I quickly set my phone down and pick up my pen, pretending I've been working on the agreement this entire time. "Come in."

When I look up, I see my father standing in front of me, a bored look on his face. He's just returned from two weeks in Singapore, so he's sporting a tan.

"When did you get back?" I ask.

"This morning. Heard you got engaged while I was gone."

"Yes, I did." I turn my attention back to the paper—a little power play I learned from him.

He crosses the room to the drink cart under the window and pours himself a scotch. "You didn't think you should clear that with me first?"

"If I had thought that, I would have done it."

"I suppose there's no way to talk you out of this, is there?"

"No more than I can talk you out of that glass of *Oban* in your hand."

Tipping back the drink, my father has a big swig. "It's a mistake, you know."

"You mean like threatening to cut all ties with Spain and calling their Prime Minister a mealy-mouthed worm?" My phone starts vibrating, and I know it's one of those #IHateTessa twats. My fingers itch to respond.

"He's a bell-end, and you know it."

"They're one of our biggest trading partners, and you've really screwed the wool exporters on this one." I consider bringing up his choice of bodyguard for Tessa, just to let him know I'm onto him, but that would be like admitting I'm threatened by Xavier—which I am not in any way, shape, or form.

"You're not smart enough to change the subject on me. We were talking about your completely unsuitable bride-to-be."

"She's in no way unsuitable, and she is not a topic I'm willing to discuss with you, so if there's nothing else, I'll get back to trying to sort out your latest *faux pas*."

"She'll never make it, Arthur. She's not cut from the right cloth, and you know it. You're setting yourselves up to fail miserably."

"You are not qualified to make that claim. You've spent all of one minute with her, and you know nothing about her."

"I know everything I need to—she's cheap, common, and clumsy. Now, it's time to stop thinking with your pecker and call this off already."

I stand, my fists balled up, the blood coursing through my veins so hard, it pounds in my ears. I cross the room in three steps and stand, towering over him, realizing for the first time how much smaller he is. "I have never wanted to punch someone the way I do you right now."

"That's because you know I'm right," my father scoffs. "She's not the one you marry. She's the side action."

A knock at the door saves me from what I was about to do. Vincent walks into my office, staring down at a folder he's holding. "Your Highness, I've got those forms for you to sign."

He looks up, sees my father with me, and stops. "Sorry, Your Majesty. I had no idea you were in here."

"That's fine. I was just leaving." Father glares at me for a second, then says, "I trust you'll do as I've asked."

I lower my voice and say, "Then you are mistaken. I think you'd do well to remember I take on the lion's share of the actual work of running this kingdom. If I stop, you won't be able to spend most of the year globe-hopping and doing...whatever it is you do while you're away."

My father sneers. "Is that a threat?"

"Call it a reality check."

Shrugging, my father puts the glass down on the cart. "It'll never work. The sooner you realize it, the less you'll humiliate yourself."

I turn on my heel and walk to my desk. "The draft of the trade agreement is one hundred- and-twelve pages long. It's taken me all morning to get to page seven." I pick it up and offer it to him. "I'm sure Vincent will be happy to brief you on what you need to know in order to make the necessary changes."

My father glances at the large bundle of pages but makes no move to take it from me.

Vincent chimes in just at the right moment. "I'd be more than happy to help, Your Majesty. You'll need to clear your schedule for approximately ninety-two minutes in order for me to walk you through it."

"Thank you, no," he says to Vincent, his eyes staying trained on me. "I shall leave this in the prince's capable hands."

We stare each other down for a moment, then he breaks eye contact first and I know I've won. He gives me a slight nod, then walks out of the office, leaving Vincent and me alone. I grin at my assistant. "How did you know?"

"I'd be no good at my job if I wasn't able to anticipate likely events."

"Have I told you lately I'd be in serious trouble without you?"

"You don't have to, Your Highness. It's enough that you know it."

SEVEN

The Tiny Nasty Man

Tessa

I never thought I'd say this, but having a bodyguard is kind of a pain in the arse. Especially when said bodyguard likes to think he's also being paid to provide morality instructions. Today, for example, he knows I'm blowing off work so I can attend the first of what I'm sure will be many wedding planning sessions at the palace. He happened to be not only driving, but also eavesdropping from the front seat when I phoned Hazel, pretending to be sick. I couldn't very well ask for permission to take the day off when she's still 'not at all upset with me, so don't worry' about the fake pregnancy scare.

So, I temporarily reverted to my old ways and made an excuse as to why I couldn't be at the weekly meeting today. When I hung up, Xavier, who was executing a left turn at a very busy intersection, also managed to exhibit his disappointment in my behaviour with a very loud *tsk*ing sound. I busied myself on my phone, answering texts and pretending I couldn't hear him until he finally cleared his throat and said, "Do you really think lying is the best way to go about this?"

"In this case, it's the *only* way to go about it."

"Well, I guess it just depends what your integrity is worth to you...oh, look at that, the line is still huge at Krispy

Kreme. Those people are going to kill themselves with all that artery-clogging fat and sugar."

Now I'm wishing I hadn't refused the limousine they'd originally offered me in favour of a Tesla with tinted windows. This would be one of the moments in which I wouldn't feel at all bad holding the button as the privacy screen went up. I always thought it looked so rude in movies when the main character would shut out the limo driver, but now that I have a two-hundred-eighty-pound shadow not only following, but commenting on my every move, I suddenly understand the need for a few minutes alone.

Oh, I'm sounding rather whiny today. Maybe I *am* pregnant. Hmm, let me see, today's the twenty-third, which would mean that...nope. Not pregnant. I don't even have PMS. I'm just plain bitchy. Maybe it's because it's been raining for three days straight. Or it could be because I'm extremely nervous about today's meeting. Or possibly because my parents are following in their car so they can meet the wedding planner Arthur hired and put their two cents in about the wedding itself.

Oh, God. The thought of that makes my stomach churn. You see, the Sharpe family has some...how to put this nicely...tacky as fuck traditions. Even though I've made it more than clear to them that there will be no 'money dance' at the reception, I'm pretty sure they're going to try to slide that one in, along with a few other gems from my father's side.

They didn't want to get a lift with Xavier and me because any time they come 'into the city,' which is literally a twelve-minute drive from their house, Mum needs to stop at her favourite cheese shop, then 'that little place with that lovely Indian woman who wears those colourful clothes and has such a lovely smile' so she can buy some turmeric for her arthritis.

If I were smart, I'd be using this time to meditate on all the things for which I'm grateful, and to convince myself that this meeting will go smoothly and that I am the captain of my fate's ship and a whole lot of other inspirational and calming thoughts. But the truth is, I'm very, very nervous. I'm about to come face-to-face with one of the world's top wedding planning teams, as well as several of the royal family's aides, most of whom I've never met but I know dislike me very much from my Royal Watchdog days.

Even the fact that we're having a wedding planning meeting at all tells me I'm out of my league. In my world, we normally host a backyard wedding on a hot summer's day and round up the ladies in the neighbourhood to bring potluck for the meal. A posh wedding on Abbott Lane would include a large white tent set up in the garden of the bride's parents', as well as a local acoustic band hired based on their availability and willingness to work for pints of lager. But the wedding I'm to have is a completely different beast, all together.

My gut churns when I think about being dressed up in front of the world's richest, most powerful people, not to mention all the folks parked in front of their tellies all day for the big event. Literally millions of eyes will be watching me as I make my way down the aisle towards Arthur. Millions of ears will be listening for me to mix up the order of his several middle names so they can have a good laugh. But I've got news for them—I've been working on it every night before bed, and I'm going to get it right. Arthur Winston Phillip George Charles Edward. Or is it Arthur Winston George Phillip Charles Edward? Shit.

Anyway, more money will be spent on this event than my entire extended family has collectively *earned*. And the thought of it makes me feel sick, even though I know the funds have already been set aside from landholding investments the Langdon family has made over the last several hundred years. So at least it's not tax dollars that will be wasted, but somehow it still feels—if not wrong—definitely strange. I take a few deep breaths and quietly mutter to myself, "Don't fuck up. Don't fuck up. Don't fuck up."

"You know, Ms. Sharpe, you'll want to be finding some replacement words for all that swearing you do. Once you're the princess, that type of language will be quite frowned upon." Xavier watches me in the rear-view mirror for a moment, and I can see from the expression in his eyes that he's smiling, believing he's being helpful at the moment.

"Thank you, Xavier," I say between my teeth. "I'll keep that in mind."

Hmm, what's this button? Maybe there's a privacy screen after all. Nope. That's just the window. Fuckity fuck fuck. Ha! It's my wedding and I'll swear if I want to.

"Oh, are you too hot? I can turn on the air conditioning."

"No, just hit it by accident."

"Sure. Just let me know if you're ever in need of a temperature change," he says. "You know, there are lots of good alternatives to curse words, even some amusing ones such as 'fudge-doodles,' 'forget about it,' or 'that's fine and dandy.' The trick to staying positive is to frame things in a funny way for yourself. You know, get yourself smiling, and pretty soon whatever is bothering you isn't going to seem so bad."

Oh Christ, he's about to break into *Hakuna Matata*, isn't he? "Okay, thank you, Xavier, but I'm a little nervous at the moment and just need to collect myself."

"Absolutely, but maybe this time try saying, 'Don't fudge-doodle it up.' See? Fun, right?"

I glance out the water-streaked window, only to see that the car is just passing over the Langdon River, named for my future husband's family. His family has an *entire river* named after them, and not a small one either. A wide, deep, fast-running river that empties into the North Sea.

What the fuck am I doing marrying a prince? I'm no princess. I keep my jewelry in an Adidas box and swear like a biker, for God's sake.

****

Xavier parks the car in front of the palace. Several young pages dressed in raincoats stand at the bottom of the steps, holding umbrellas, ready to greet guests. As soon as the car stops, the nearest one hurries over and opens my door. As I get out, I see my parents parking directly behind Xavier, their Volkswagen Golf sticking out like a sore thumb next to a Bentley, the Range Rover, and Arthur's limo.

I wait at the top of the steps while another page hurries to help my parents. The massive wooden doors swing open, welcoming us into the warmth of the Grande Hall.

My mother gasps audibly and clutches my arm with both hands. "Oh, my heavens! Have you ever seen something so amazing before?"

"Well, yes, Mum, I did live here for two months, so —"

"Let me get a picture. Grace next door is *never* going to believe this." My mum starts digging around in her purse and pulls out her new cell phone.

Oh, good lord. I look to my right in time to see a young woman dressed in a cream-coloured suit walking quickly towards us. She gazes at us, looking my parents and me up and down, only to immediately decide we are not her type of people.

I feel my face heat up with embarrassment. "Mum, put your phone away; we're here for the meeting."

"Oh, yes, I suppose you're right. I'll be able to get photos of this any time after the wedding," my mum says loudly.

The woman stops in front of us. "I'm Rory, Sebastian's senior assistant."

"And who might Sebastian be?" my father asks.

Rory's head swivels like that possessed girl from *The Exorcist* until she's looking at him. "Sebastian is only the world's most famous wedding planner. He can turn a barn into a palace with only some tulle and fairy lights. You're very lucky Prince Arthur was able to secure him for this event."

Before anyone can say anything, Rory turns, gesturing for us to follow her as she hurries across the Grande Hall and off to the right, to the wing of the palace that contains the offices and board rooms. We walk briskly down the wide marble hallway, stopping at the end. Rory opens the white double doors and leads the way into the East Boardroom. "This space has been acquired by the planning team and will become nuptial central headquarters for the next six months. You'll hear us refer to it as NCH for short. Sebastian's big on acronyms, as he rarely has time to speak in full words. In fact, you should call him Baz instead of Sebastian. He doesn't have time to hear his entire name." She gestures for us to take a seat at the massive walnut table and then walks over to a counter and picks up a pile of packets. "You'll each get a packet. On page three is the list of acronyms you should memorize so you'll be able to follow the meetings."

My parents sit on either side of me on the side of the table that faces the wall of windows that overlook the meadow. My mother pulls out her phone and starts taking photos of the room. "This is where it all begins. These shots will be at the beginning of the wedding scrapbook. Rory, is it?"

Rory nods as she places a packet in front of my mother.

"Say cheese." My mum holds up her phone in front of her face, while Rory doesn't even bother to attempt a smile.

"Hmm, I don't think that one worked," my mum says.

"That's fine, Mum. We don't need a lot of pictures of the meeting."

"So, what's a guy have to do to get a cup of tea and a scone around here?" my dad asks, elbowing me in the ribs and winking in my direction. "This one says you make the best blueberry scones in Avonia, so I made sure to bring my appetite."

"You'd have to ask one of the palace staff," she says stiffly.

Four women and two men dressed in dark suits enter the room, briskly making their way around to the opposite side of the table and sitting down. I recognize them as assistants to the assistants of Arthur and King Winston. Damien, the king's right-hand man, who Arthur despises, walks in behind them and takes a seat as far from us as possible. The five of them open small white laptops and start tapping away on them without saying hello. Vincent follows them and greets us, then introduces us to the staff. A wave of relief washes over me as soon as I smell the blue cheese, knowing I'll have at least one ally on the other side of the table.

"Mmm, will it be a savory breakfast, then?" my father asks as he shakes Vincent's hand. "Smells like cheese of some sort."

"Will Arthur be joining us?" I say quickly, hoping Vincent won't know my father's referring to him.

Vincent smiles and walks around to the opposite side of the table, then sits next to a particularly surly-looking woman. "I'm afraid he's got a very busy schedule this morning, but he will be joining us for approximately eight minutes."

"Maybe he can get me a scone," my father mumbles.

My mother leans forward across me and hisses at him, "I told you to eat at home."

"Well, I've bloody well paid enough taxes to get a bite of breakfast, don't you think?"

"Of course you have, Ruben," Arthur says as he strides across the room toward us. I look up at him, both thrilled that he's here and mortified that he heard my father demanding scones.

Rory speaks into an earpiece. "The prince has arrived. You can bring Baz in now."

My mum shifts down one chair and pats the empty spot for Arthur. "Don't mind him. He's just a bit of a bear when he's hungry. Which he shouldn't be, because I told him to eat breakfast at home."

"It's no trouble at all," Arthur says. "I think we could all use a little something right about now."

Vincent stands without being asked and speaks into his walkie-talkie as he hurries out of the room, presumably ordering food for the meeting. Arthur sits next to me and rests his hand over top of mine, then gives me a kiss on the cheek. "You look beautiful this morning. Evi, Ruben, I'm so glad you both came to help sort out the wedding plans."

My dad slaps his checkbook on the table and opens it, revealing his Valcourt United football-themed checks. "I'm not much into the *frou-frou* details. I'm just here to pony up and eat."

Did I think I was mortified before? Because this is *so much worse.*

Arthur tilts his head and nods. "Ah, yes. There is the matter of who is paying for what, isn't there?"

"As father of the bride, I expect the bulk of the expenses will fall to me, but not to worry. We've been saving up for this." He winks at me. "We've got a nice-sized stash to marry her off with." He looks over at the aides on the other side of the table and points to me with his thumb. "Gotta get her out of the house at some point. She's damn near thirty."

A loud clapping sound comes from the doorway, and I turn to see two young men dressed in cream-coloured suits that seem to match what Rory is wearing, followed by a small man dressed in an ivory linen top and matching pants. He looks to be about forty years old and moves quickly to the head of the table. The entire time he walks, he speaks into his mobile phone. He ends the call by saying, "Done," then hangs up, looks us over, and smooths down the coif of perfectly-styled very black hair.

Rory points and assigns us titles, starting with Arthur. "Prince Arthur, groom, bride, M.O.B., D.O.B."

Sebastian's eyes fall on me for a long, very awkward moment. When he's finished assessing me, he says, "I see."

He then glances around the room and smiles. "Six months, people. The royal wedding of the century. Can't be done, they say? You just watch me."

Vincent returns followed by a line of servers pushing carts of fruit, baked goods, coffee, tea, and juices. Sebastian glances at them, sighs dramatically, and buries his face in one hand, at which point Rory jumps into action, standing up and hurrying toward the kitchen staff. "This is not the part of the meeting in which we eat. No one eats in front of Baz."

Vincent leans into Arthur's ear and whispers something. Arthur squeezes my hand. "I'm afraid I have to go, darling. Something quite urgent has come up." He stands. "Wonderful to meet you, Baz, everyone. I'm certain in your capable hands, we will find ourselves enjoying a most spectacular wedding."

Arthur then leans over my dad and puts one hand on his shoulder while holding his other out to shake it. "Let's you and I let them sort out the details, and once we know what the budget is, we'll talk money."

With that, he turns and goes, leaving me feeling like a toddler who's just had her blankie put in the washing machine. Baz instructs everyone to open their packets so we can begin the meeting. My dad leans over and murmurs in my ear, "Why can't we eat?"

Baz clears his throat and runs his tongue over his teeth while he stares down my dad. "Can we proceed?"

"Of course," I say quietly.

"You'll notice we're wearing ivory and cream today. This will be the theme of the wedding. Flowers, invitations, table cloths, napkins, chair covers—everything ivory and cream. This wedding will set a new standard in sophistication. Think opulent, think luxury, a true celebration of the achievement of being royal. Even the guests will be in ivory and cream. Only the king and Prince Arthur will provide the pop of colour."

"Oh, no, you can't be serious. You can't expect all the guests to go and buy ivory clothes when they've probably got perfectly good wedding clothes at home. Besides, think of how mucked up the children's clothes will be," my mum says, shaking her head. "Besides, Tessa loves cornflower blue. That's always been her favourite colour."

"Oh, has it?" Baz asks, sitting down, propping his arm up on his elbow, then resting his chin on his fist. Add the purple top hat, and he looks exactly like that meme of Gene Wilder from the original *Charlie and the Chocolate Factory*. "What else does Tessa like? Perhaps we could build the entire day around her favourite things?"

My mum completely misses the extreme sarcasm and beams at him. "She loves yellow lilies with orange tips, and she loves '90s dance music, her favourite meal is turkey with baby potatoes and lots of gravy, and she loves those little sausage rolls, you know, the ones you can get at the deli. Oh, and tiny weenies on toothpicks! Oh, and I saw the best little parting gift on Pinterest. We give each of the guests a baggie filled with jelly beans and attach a little tag that says, 'Thanks for bean here!'"

Baz wears an incredulous look on his face. "Rory, Ricky, Ryan, are you getting this all down?"

"Yes, Baz," they all say as they quickly start tapping away on their laptops.

"Good, because I'd hate it if we forgot the tiny weenies."

I rest my hand on my mum's forearm and give it a squeeze. She suddenly notices the look on his face and stops talking.

Baz continues, apparently finding time in his busy schedule to make fun of my mother. "What else? Should we go with a massive back yard barbecue theme? Perhaps have a bouncy castle for the kiddies, and maybe a big water balloon fight in front of the Abbey directly following the ceremony?"

I open my mouth to let him have it, but Vincent beats me to it, managing to make his point whilst remaining much more diplomatic than I would have. "Baz, I know you're in an incredible rush, and we were so fortunate to obtain your services on such short notice. Perhaps we could hear your plans for the wedding now so we don't keep you."

"Yes, please. Let's get on with it so we can eat already," my dad says, licking his lips and staring forlornly in the direction of the food carts.

Baz stands again and goes through the wedding day at breakneck speed. I'm shocked to see my entire day has been planned right down to the minute, starting at four-forty a.m., when I have to wake, and ending at ten-fifty-eight p.m., when Arthur and I will finish wishing the last of the guests goodbye. I stare down at the itinerary, realizing I'll spend four hours and fifty-two minutes in the receiving line. Not that I'm complaining, but dear God, I had no idea it could possibly be that long.

Once he's finished going over the itinerary, Baz informs both sides the guest lists will be required by the end of the week at the latest so we can move on to P2 of the N.P. (I looked it up: it means phase two of the nuptial preparation). Vincent then tells us our guests will need to fill out security check forms as soon as possible so they can be vetted.

"Oh dear," my mum says. "That means Uncle Carl won't be able to attend."

"And your nephew, Billy. Remember? He had that run-in with that stripper who said he—"

I panic, causing my voice to come out loud and squeaky. "Thank you, Vincent. Just get me the forms, and I'll sort it out." My entire body heats up with humiliation as the rest of the room breaks out into snickers. At least Arthur isn't here to find out about my love for tiny weenies and the criminal elements of my family.

Baz closes his packet, then looks at me. "I need the bride."

"Pardon me?" I ask.

"Stand," he says, gesturing wildly for me to walk over to him, as though that should have been perfectly clear in the first place.

I do as I'm told and make my way over to him at the head of the table, feeling completely self-conscious to have so many people staring at me while I walk in these heels. Oh, crap, how am I going to do this in front of millions of people if I can barely manage it in front of ten?

"That's what I thought." He looks down at Rory. "P and W."

She nods and types some notes.

"Excuse me?" I say, but they both ignore me because, apparently, this has nothing to do with me.

"Five and a half months will barely be enough time, but we'll do what we can," Rory says. "I'll see if Julie is free."

"Sorry, what is P and W?"

Rory rolls her eyes. "It's on page three."

I drop the courtesy smile I was wearing in favour of a 'don't fuck with me' look. "Please indulge me. I haven't had a chance to memorize the list yet."

I hear papers rustling behind me, then my mum pipes up, clearly excited to know the answer, "It says here 'P and W, posture and weight.'"

Baz lifts an eyebrow at me. "Will this be your wedding day weight, or do you intend to lose?"

"I don't know, I hadn't...I guess I was thinking of trying to firm up," I stammer.

"You need to decide now. If you can manage to shave off twenty before the wedding, I can get Ralphio to design your dress. Maybe. Not likely, but he owes me a favour. If you're not one to cooperate, however, I'll save the favour for someone who will."

"Cooperate?"

"Listen, here, mister," my dad says, clearly very hangry now. "She's perfect the way she is. If your designer only wants to make dresses for coat hangers, you can keep him."

I smile gratefully at my dad, who's too busy glaring at Sebastian to notice.

Baz ignores my father and turns to me. "This will be the single most important moment in the lives of any woman in your generation. The eyes of the entire world will be on you, but in spite of that fact, none of this is actually about you. It's about the fairy tale, the fantasy of the perfect couple. The handsome crown prince and his beautiful princess. Do you understand how important this is to the monarchy? *To Avonia? To women everywhere?* People need to be inspired, Teresa—"

"Tessa," my mum says.

"Whatever," Baz says, waving her off. "People need to be inspired. They also need to see the reason he chose *you*. It's the only way they can make sense of their pathetic lives. Do you understand?"

I say nothing, certain that my expression says I don't know what the hell he's talking about.

Baz sighs heavily, then goes on. "You have to be special. Spectacular. Better than every other woman on the planet. There has to be a *reason* for him to want to be with you. You can't be some ordinary woman. Because if you are nothing short of perfection, it leaves all the other ordinary women wondering, *Where is my prince? Why I am marrying this normal man who sits around all weekend watching football and drinking beer?* And if they do that, suddenly nothing will make sense to them anymore. It will lead to a general sense of dissatisfaction with their own ordinary lives, which will cause divorce rates to skyrocket, leading to all sorts of financial burden on the nation and the collapse of society as we know it."

"No pressure, though, right?" I say and laugh awkwardly.

Baz keeps his poker face in place, causing me to start to ramble. "Umm, well, okay. Sorry. I'm really quite...normal, I'm afraid. I'm in pretty good shape, I think. I like to run, but I also like to eat..."

"Yes, I can see that. But the good thing is, you've got potential. There's enough here to work with, and almost enough time. Follow the regimen my team will set out for you, and by the time the big day arrives, you might almost be able to fool most of the common people." He turns to Rory. "Twenty pounds will bring the waist in enough to make up for these child-birthing hips. I want tight arms. Ribs showing."

"Won't they be hidden by her dress?" My mum asks.

"No bloody way do I want her ribs showing." My father stands. "That's it. We're eating. Tessa, too. Come on, love, I'll fix you a plate."

Baz looks at me. "The decision is yours. But you must make it now."

I stare at him for a second, then hear myself say, "That's okay, Dad. I'm not hungry."

Baz almost smiles, then says, "Done," before turning and walking out the door while he places a call on his mobile phone.

What the fuck just happened?

****

"Ms. Sharpe, do you have a moment?" Vincent calls to me from down the hall just as my parents and I are about to leave.

I turn, knowing by his tone that whatever it is he needs to tell me, I'm not likely to want to hear it. I just want to get out of here after being publicly humiliated by a tiny man in cream- coloured linen.

"Certainly." I look at my parents and say, "You two go ahead. I'll see you at home."

My dad narrows his eyes at me. "Are you sure? We can stick around if you need us."

"That's okay, Dad. I can handle this." I give each of them a quick kiss on the cheek. "Mum needs to get to the cheese shop before they run out of Brie."

My mum's eyes light up. "I almost forgot, it's usually gone by noon. We'd better hurry, Ruben."

I watch them as they rush out the door, then follow Vincent to his office. Once we're settled inside, he offers me a water or tea.

"No, thank you. Even though those are both calorie-free options." I smile too wide in my attempt to act like what just happened didn't bother me.

Vincent doesn't smile back; instead, his expression is filled with empathy. "If you don't mind me saying, Ms. Sharpe, I think you look just lovely. And please don't worry about what Sebastian said. It's all a bunch of rubbish. If each wedding he planned didn't have far-reaching consequences beyond the actual ceremony and dinner, it would be much more difficult for him to go around being so pretentious."

I feel my body relax the slightest bit at Vincent's words. "I can see why Arthur likes you so much."

"Thank you, Miss."

"Can you do me a big favour?"

"Certainly." He picks up his pencil, ready to take notes.

"Could you call me Tessa? Or Tess is fine, too. I would just feel a lot more comfortable."

Vincent smiles at me. "I can see why Arthur likes you, Miss."

I laugh. "So, it's a 'no', then?"

"At the palace, we have very stringent protocols in place for a reason. Allowing ourselves to cross certain barriers can complicate things in a way which serves no one." He pauses for a moment, then says, "Having said that, I asked to speak with you because I think you could use my help. You're about to enter the very choppy waters of not only a royal wedding, but the royal life as well. And as you know, not everyone is in favour of this marriage."

I chuckle a little and shake my head. "That might be a bit of an understatement."

"Yes, well, better to understate it than put too much focus on what you can't change." Vincent stands and pours two glasses of water from a pitcher on an antique credenza behind his desk. He walks around and hands one to me, then returns to his seat. "What I'm about to tell you must remain between the two of us."

I nod, feeling my heart speed up a bit in anticipation of what it is he's about to say.

"Sebastian is a complete douche. He's a horrible little man with a Napoleon complex, and after this morning, I'm sorry I suggested him to Prince Arthur. Unfortunately, he truly is one of the only people who can pull something of this magnitude off in such a short period of time. Had you and the prince been more willing to allow for a more standard period of time, we wouldn't need him."

"Are you suggesting we postpone the wedding?"

"Not at all, Miss. What I'm suggesting is that we don't fill Arthur in on the details of today's meeting. You may have noticed he has a bit of a protective streak when it comes to you. Were he to hear about Sebastian's treatment of you today, he will fire him, which is not something we can afford to have happen unless you're willing to postpone."

"I'm not comfortable keeping things from Arthur, and I don't think you should suggest I do so."

"Ms. Sharpe, I know the prince better than anyone, including his own family. I'm not suggesting you make a habit of keeping things from him, but in this case, if your goal is to have the wedding in May, you would be acting against your own interests to tell him. A very small omission in sharing the events of one meeting will serve you much better in the long run. I know how badly Prince Arthur wants you back under the same roof, and I'm just trying to help make that happen as quickly as possible."

I stare at him for a moment. "I'll give it some thought. Thank you." Standing, I place my water glass on his desk and start for the door.

Vincent's voice stops me. "He's really only happy when you're here, Miss. And because I care for him very much, his happiness is really all that matters."

I nod and give him a small smile. "I feel exactly the same way."

EIGHT

Never Underestimate an Octogenarian in a Bright Pink Jogging Suit

Arthur

"There's been a slight change of plans, Your Highness," Vincent says, sliding into the back of the limo with me. "The French Ambassador will be at the meeting after all."

"Oh, Christ, is it still that LaPorte fellow?"

"I'm afraid so," he says. "I'll have to cancel your appearance at the shelter for abuse victims or your dinner with Ms. Sharpe. You won't be able to make it to both once he's finished talking."

I sigh, irritated that my day is about to be hijacked by the most long-winded man in all of Europe. "I can't very well be yet another man to let down the women at the shelter, can I?"

"Not really, sir."

"All right. I'll need a few minutes to call Tessa, then."

"Certainly." Vincent nods. "I'll need about four minutes to go over the prep for the meeting."

I glance at my watch, then dial her number.

She answers with, "How long do we have?" She's such a trouper. She never complains about my unavailability but makes the most of every second we have.

"Three minutes. How was Baz?"

"He'll definitely get the job done."

"Uh-oh, what happened?"

"What makes you think something happened?"

"Your tone and the vagueness of your answer." I turn to face the window, knowing Vincent will hear my end of the call anyway. At least I can pretend to be alone.

"It was just a bit of a challenge for my parents. They expected to have more say in the entire thing, I think. My mum, especially. She had all sorts of ideas, but I'm afraid none of them are going to fit with Baz's vision."

"Any that you wanted?"

"No, not really. I think it's best to let the expert make the decisions. I don't have the first clue about planning an event of this scale."

"You sure? Because it's your wedding, too."

"I'm sure, darling. Thirty seconds left. What did you call for?"

"You're going to hate me."

"You need to cancel tonight?"

"Yes. It was either you or I would have to skip out on the women's shelter."

"Oh, don't do that. They need your support more than I do."

"You're a good woman, Tessa Sharpe."

"I know. Time's up. I love you."

"You, too."

I hang up and sigh. "She really is wonderful."

"Of course, Your Highness."

I turn to Vincent, who hands me the prep package for the trade meeting. I flip it open, then say, "How can I get everyone else to see what I see in her?"

"I suspect they just have to spend a little time with her, sir." He points to the paper in front of me and says, "You'll want to pay particular attention to the section on water rights."

I nod and read the first few lines. "We should host a big bridal shower for her. Very soon, so she can win over all the ladies as soon as possible. That way, they can bring everyone else around long before the wedding."

I smile and nod, ignoring the urgency in Vincent's expression and the way he's pointing to the package. "I'll ask Arabella to host it. If she does it, they'll all come."

****

Twitter Feed, #BrookeIsBetter

IHateTessa: *Thank the good lord, the shock jogger beotch isn't preggers. Still hope for #BrookeIsBetter*

Kingslayer99: *@IHateTessa Hopefully, their yacht goes down at sea on the honeymoon and puts an end to the pair of them.*

IHateTessa: *Totally wrong, @kingslayer99! Prince Arthur is the bomb. Tessa's the only one who should go down with the ship.*

WeLoveTessa: *@IHateTessa Sod off. If anything, Arthur isn't worthy of her. #TessaIsTops*

I really need to stay off Twitter. That wasn't even a good comeback, and this really isn't good for my rage. I toss my phone onto the coffee table and lean back on the couch, considering going to bed early for a change instead of staying up half the night to argue with these half-wits.

I know I should be ignoring them, but the nation needs to know that more people than just me have a favourable opinion of the future queen. Although, when I really think about it, it may not be exactly true. Even my own family is split on their opinion of her. My father and sister versus Grandmum and me. I suppose I should start with them, shouldn't I?

My father's pretty much a lost cause, but I can work on my sister and bring her around. Her ego is still bruised from all the things Tessa wrote about our family in her Royal Watchdog days. In particular, I know she objects to the things Tessa wrote about me. I don't blame Arabella for how she feels, but I do hope that, in time, she will see my future wife for who she really is—a kind, caring, truthful person who has the best interests of our nation at heart.

If I can get Arabella to come around, others will soon follow. I stand suddenly, disturbing Dexter, who was fast asleep next to me, and hurry to the kitchen. I need to ask Arabella for a gigantic favour. And gigantic favours require gelato. I scoop out two big bowls of chocolate ice cream whilst trying to think of the best way to ask her to host Tessa's wedding shower. Even if she doesn't actually approve of Tessa, if she's willing to host the shower it will give the appearance that she's forgiven and forgotten.

I know it's going to be a tough sell, which means I'll likely find myself making my way down the hall with a variety of yummy treats many times over the next couple of weeks. Not that Arabella can be bought with food—it's just that this is our way of spending time together. I suppose we're not so different than other families in this way, but in our case we rarely share a meal together because of our schedules. So, we've developed a little ritual of eating junk food together late at night. But don't worry, my morning workouts more than make up for it.

I knock on the door to Arabella's apartment. A moment later, it swings open to reveal her in her robe, her face covered with green goo.

"Ooh! Gelato. Come in," she says, stepping aside.

"You've got a little something on your face."

"Hardy har har. What do you need from me?"

I hand her a bowl and follow her to the couch. "What do you mean? Can't I just want to hang out with my favourite sister?"

She flops down onto the couch. "Cut the shit, Arthur. You only bring food when you want something."

"That's because you're always gone, and by the time you come home again, I need something again. If you think of it, I really only ask for a few small favours a year."

Arabella rolls her eyes. "Out with it."

"Let's eat our ice cream first." I pick up my spoon and take a mouthful. "So, how was your trip?"

Arabella shrugs one shoulder. "Not worth talking about, actually."

"Uh-oh, trouble in paradise?"

"We broke up." She takes a scoop of ice cream on her spoon and pops it into her mouth, refusing to look at me.

"I'm sorry to hear that. You and Charles seemed so happy."

"Yes, I thought so, too. But it turns out he's only happy when he's seeing several women at once." Her eyes fill with tears, and she blinks quickly.

"What a complete tosser."

"Yes, well, my instincts for finding a good man are apparently shit."

"He's out there, and you'll find him. I promise." I pat her on the knee with one hand, in a very fatherly way. In a lot of ways, I have been a father to her, even though I'm only five years older. Our own father has never been much of a dad, so a lot of the more tender moments required of the job have fallen directly into my lap. "I suspect you'll have to kiss a few frogs yet before you find your prince. And if you keep putting that green shit all over your face, you should manage to find all your frogs quite quickly and get them the hell over with."

Arabella lets out a small laugh and wipes her eyes with her fingertips. "The thing is, I don't want to kiss any more frogs. I want what you've got—only with someone who isn't an awful person."

Urgh. She clearly isn't ready to forgive and forget. "Tessa's not..." No, just leave it. She's in pain. "You'll find the right man, I promise."

The timer goes off on Arabella's mobile phone. She plucks it off the coffee table and silences it. "Now, what is it you came to ask me for? I have to go scrub my face and take a shower."

"Nothing. I just wanted to see you." I stand and take both empty bowls, then walk to the door. "Goodnight. And don't worry about what's-his-fuck. You're absolutely perfect, and if he couldn't see that, it's only because of something completely wrong with him, not you."

****

"Are you feeling all right?" Tessa asks, sounding very distracted. She's in bed, the light from her mobile phone shining on her face. "You've been in there for so long, I was just about to come check on you."

Bugger. I know I really need to stop engaging in these Twitter battles, but I can't seem to help myself. I'm beginning to understand how Donald Trump feels. It's become somewhat of an addiction for me to defeat them at any cost, including missed time with the woman of my dreams who's finally been able to spend the night. Instead of making the most of it, I've been sitting on the counter in my bathroom with my phone in hand. "Never better. I just got caught up answering an email."

"At this hour? Surely, it could've waited till morning." There's a slight edge to her voice, which has been brought on by what I'm sure she perceives as a slight neglect of her this evening.

We only managed one round of naughty time before I got distracted by that stupid little ping on my phone. "Yes, I'm afraid it wouldn't wait. But I promise to make it up to you."

Tessa yawns loudly, and I know from that sound, there will be no round two tonight.

I don't like the idea of keeping things from her, but in this case, it really is for the best. "What are you reading at this late hour?"

"I've been foolishly watching a Twitter battle between the IHateTessa person and the WeLoveTessa people."

"Why would you do that?"

"Good question. It's all so middle school. Idiots, all of them."

"Even your WeLoveTessa person?" I do my best to sound neutral, even though I'm rather offended at being called an idiot.

"Even him. He just keeps fueling the fire. The smart thing to do would be to ignore these people."

"Hmm. I suppose. How do you know it's a he?"

"I don't, I guess. But there's a creepy quality about his admiration for me, so I assumed."

Creepy? "Women can't be creepy?"

"Not like this. I mean, it's nothing to worry about. I'm sure he's some gawky fifteen-year-old boy with food stuck in his braces. I'd show you his tweets, but I think reading the entire thread would bring out the caveman in you." She has a smile in her tone.

"Well, I'm sure he *or* she has your best interests at heart."

She shuts off her phone and puts it on the night stand. "I know, but I wish whoever it is would just stop already. He never even has anything intelligent to add to the conversation. Sub-par comebacks at best. Very lame."

Lifting her head off her pillow, Tessa gives me a light kiss on the lips—the kind that says, 'goodnight.' "If I'm going to have a knight in shining armor online, I'd much prefer a smart one. Like you."

I give a weak laugh. "Well, maybe I should log on secretly and come to your defense."

"Don't you dare waste your precious time like that. I'm very greedy, and I want whatever free time you've got to be spent with me."

****

I'm sitting at my desk, preparing for a call with the Prime Minister of Canada. Nice chap. Knows what it's like to be popular with women. There's a knock at my office door, and when I look up, I see my grandmother, dressed in a bright pink jogging suit, walking toward me.

"On your way to aquacize?"

"You don't get a body like this without working for it." She takes a seat across from me. "Twice a week to stay fit for the men."

"Well, if you're here to try to convince me to join you, I've already had my workout today. Besides, I really have no interest in staying fit for the men," I say with a smile.

"Now, that nice, smelly fellow of yours told me you wanted to see me."

"Yes. I was hoping you'd be hostess for a bridal shower for Tessa. You know, show the world this marriage has the family's blessing."

"Arabella turn you down?"

"She made her opinion known before I had a chance to ask."

Gran nods, then says, "Yes, of course I'll do it."

I let out a sigh of relief. "Good. And if you wouldn't mind, I'd prefer to let Tessa think Arabella is away rather than have her know she isn't showing up because she doesn't care for her."

"That's a huge mistake."

"I disagree. There's no point in upsetting Tessa unnecessarily."

"It's not unnecessary. She needs to know who her allies and foes are, for her own good."

"Arabella will come around. In the meantime, I'm just going to—"

"Try to create some pink, artificial version of the world?" Gran says, her tone full of sarcasm. "Why don't you just bubble wrap her and keep her in a locked room here at the palace?"

I set my jaw, preparing a counterargument, but Gran beats me to it.

"Don't give me that look, young man. You're dead wrong in the way you're going about this," she says. "You're going to have to accept the fact that she's an adult and can handle herself. To think otherwise would be not only foolish, but a miscalculation on your part. This type of archaic behaviour will grow very tiresome for her in short order."

"I'm not going to expose her to pain that can be avoided. That's not what you do when you love someone. You protect them."

"That may very well be, Arthur, and I know your motivations are pure in this regard. But I'm telling you she's not the type to put up with an overprotective man. She's a modern woman, and you're going to lose her if you aren't careful."

"Nonsense. What woman doesn't want to be taken care of?"

"There's a difference between taking care of someone when they're hurt and trying to hide the world from them."

I heave out a long sigh and pick up my pen, staring back down at the agreement before me. "Thank you for the advice, as always, Grandmum. But I assure you, I know what I'm doing."

"I don't think you do. You're trying to make up for something that happened a long time ago. Something that had nothing to do with you, even though you blame yourself."

"This is not about my mother." I keep my tone light, pretending the mention of her doesn't upset me, but knowing I don't have a snowball's chance in a hot oven at fooling my grandmother.

"Of course it is. Everything has been about her since she..." Her voice cracks, and I shut my eyes for a moment, wishing I had never asked her to host the bloody shower.

Grandmum continues. "Arthur, Tessa is not Cecily. Neither is Arabella—"

"Arabella is weak. She always has been, and when I step in, it's always because she needs me."

"That's bullshit. She's weak *because* you step in, but if you gave her a chance, you would see she's every bit as strong as you."

I shake my head. "She falls apart at the first sign of critici—"

"That's only because she's never had a chance to stand on her own two feet. Her big brother is constantly propping her up or standing in front of her when anything the slightest bit challenging comes her way. But this isn't about Arabella. It's about your bride-to-be."

"Whom I know far better than you. Tessa puts on a brave face, but underneath she's easily hurt."

"She might feel hurt, but she knows how to handle herself. You can't go your whole life being terrified she's going to take the same way out Cecily did. Tessa has more than proven her strength, so you need to just let that go, or you're going to lose her."

"Are you quite done? Because I have work to do."

My grandmother stands and taps her knuckles on my desk. "You can choose to ignore my advice, Arthur, but you do so at your own peril."

****

Email from me to Vincent:

RE: Bridal Shower of the Century

Vinnie, my pal,

Gran has agreed to host the bridal shower. Please arrange to have the catering and events team set everything up. If it can take place before Christmas, I think it would be best. Also, make sure there's a great variety of food, including meats baked in pastry shells. Her family seems to favour them.

A

Email from Vincent to Me:

RE: Bridal Shower of the Century

Very good, Your Highness. The catering coordinator has confirmed that along with the usual fare, there will be several trays of 'sausage rolls' to be brought in for the event.

Sincerely,

Vincent

NINE

Snack Envy & Unwanted Advice

Tessa

Text from Mum: *Tessa, it's your mum. Do you have a key? Dad and I are going to bed early to 'watch Netflix and chill.' That's what all the young people are doing these days, right?*

Email from Rory to Me:
RE: Choosing of the Dress
Tessa,

Your request to have Olivia Paul has been denied by Baz, as she is virtually unknown.

As per my previous email, Baz has managed to secure Ralphio, but you must meet with him by the end of this week in order to finalize these arrangements.

Baz wanted me to remind you that the dress sets the tone for the entire event, which is why it is imperative to have a seasoned designer assist in this regard. Baz will make himself available on Friday at 10 AM to help you choose the best dress for your body type. You would be wise to take him up on this offer.

Regards,
Rory

Email to Rory From Me:
RE: Choosing of the Dress
Dear Rory,

As per my first email on this matter I have already secured Ms. Paul's services, and having had excellent luck with her in the past, I feel very confident that she will provide me with the best dress for the occasion. In addition, the Royal Family, especially the Dowager, believe in using these types of events to provide up-and-coming artists with visibility, as an act of patronage.

I have a fitting scheduled with Ms. Paul on Thursday at five in the evening, to accommodate my work schedule. I will be happy to provide your team with sketches once they are completed.

Sincerely,
Tessa

Email to Me from Rory:
RE: RE: Choosing of the Dress
Baz will be most displeased.

****

"So, how's engaged sex?" Nikki asks, squeezing an unbelievable amount of honey into her coffee. "Is it incredible? I bet it's incredible."

"Could we hold off on discussing that particular topic until there are fewer people around?" I say as a large man jostles me out of the way so he can reach the creamer.

"Not really—I barely have any time with you these days, so I have to make the most of it. If I leave all the good stuff for the end, we'll never get to it." Nikki picks up her mug and her plate bearing a chocolate croissant and leads the way through the busy coffee shop to a table tucked away in the far corner, close to the fireplace.

I follow her, dodging customers as my mug of tea starts to burn my fingers. When we're seated, I stare longingly at Nikki's croissant, wishing I had ordered that instead of the fat-free, sugar-free, taste-free zucchini brownie. Xavier stands near the table facing the door, which means Nikki can stare freely at his arse.

"When we actually manage to have some time alone together, it's amazing." I take a bite of the brownie, only to discover it's exactly as boring as I thought it would be. "But between work, all the wedding prep, and trying to choose my charities, we barely see each other."

"*He* barely sees you? What about me?" Nikki says, taking a big bite of her croissant. She and Dr. McPerfect broke up a few weeks ago, and instead of me being ready with a bottle of wine and a carton of ice cream, I was on the solarium floor with Arthur.

"It's been, like, three weeks since I've laid eyes on you." Her words come out muffled as she talks. She wipes her mouth with her napkin and then gives me a thoughtful look. "You look sick or something. Like, a little pale, maybe. Are you all right?"

"Yes, I'm fine. Just a little stressed." And really frigging hungry.

Nikki nods and licks some chocolate off her fingers. "This is about your hate club and that fashion critic?"

My shoulders drop, and I sigh. "Yes."

"Fuckers. Every one of them."

"It's karma coming for me, isn't it?"

"Karma's a bunch of bullshit. If it were true, how come most Fortune 500 companies are run by sociopaths?"

"Good point." I have a sip of my tea, the liquid warming my insides. "The fashion critic I can handle. I mean, it just takes extra thought as to what to put on before I go out the door."

Nikki glances at my sweater, under which is a collared shirt done up to the top. She wrinkles up her nose. "Umm..."

"You don't like my outfit?"

"It's very...proper."

"I can't very well be dressing like a hooker."

"You never dressed like one before, but you *did* look like a woman in her twenties. Except that one pair of granny shoes."

"Okay, thanks, *friend*. Point taken." I sigh. "I'm just trying to polish myself up a bit. Is there anything so wrong with that?"

"No, but just don't polish yourself until there's no sign of the real you under that buttoned-up shirt." Tilting her head, she says, "I like Tessa 1.0 just fine. Now back up. You said you can handle the fashion critic, which means you're not handling the I Hate Tessa person as well."

"Not exactly. I can't seem to get it out of my head, you know? It's really awful to know someone you don't know hates you so much."

"Oh, shit." A look of understanding crosses Nikki's face, then she wipes it away.

"What?" My heartbeat picks up a bit.

"Nothing." She shoves another bite of croissant into her mouth.

"Seriously, you can't just say, 'Oh, shit' and leave me hanging."

Swallowing, she says, "What if it's someone you know? Like someone really high up in the Royal Family?"

"Oh, Christ, I never thought of that. What if it *is* someone I know? Like Arabella? Or the king?" I push the brownie away, suddenly feeling sick. "If that were the case, I don't think I'd want to know. I mean, how do you get past something like that?"

"It would make for very awkward family dinners."

"Wouldn't it?" I shake my head, hoping to shake the thought loose from my brain before it sticks. "It's not someone in Arthur's family. It's very likely some sad little troll with nothing better to do."

"Yup, you're right. It's just a troll. The smartest thing to do would be to stop looking at that Twitter feed. In fact, maybe just stay off social media altogether."

"Yes, that's exactly what I should do."

Nikki narrows her eyes a bit. "Which means it's the opposite of what you're actually going to do."

Nodding, I say, "But the entire time, I'll know you told me not to."

"That's why I love you," Nikki says with a laugh. She has a sip of her coffee and then leans in and nods toward Xavier, who's standing rather conspicuously about two feet from our table, watching the door. "But enough about you. I'm in serious need of a rebound. Have you found out if he's single yet?"

****

"How are the obituaries coming?" Hazel glides past my desk as she makes her way back to her office from the break room.

"Fine. As long as no one else dies today, we'll be all set for tomorrow's issue." I laugh a little at my tasteless joke.

It's a little after noon, and Hazel and I are the only ones still in the office, as the rest of the staff have gone out to eat. I bring a bagged lunch every day since I can't go out to eat with my workmates because the moment we leave the building, I'm fair game for photo ops.

I wouldn't want to go out today, anyway. A huge ice storm has hit most of southern Avonia, meaning the sidewalks and roads are nothing short of treacherous. I watch through the glass window as Hazel settles herself behind her desk. I really need to tell her I'm going to have to quit. She deserves to know. I'll tell her as soon as I finish this last announcement. I busy myself spell-checking the name of the Osborne family's new little girl, Destynie Maddisynne, who is destined to spend her entire life pronouncing and spelling her name out for people. Good luck with that, kiddo.

A few minutes later, I get up, stretch a little, and knock on Hazel's open door. "Can I talk to you for a minute?"

"Sure, come on in." She leans back in her chair and smiles at me.

"I need to tell you something."

"You're quitting?"

"How did you know?"

"The writing's been on the wall since you got engaged."

"I suppose it has." I fiddle with my ring, trying to push aside the yucky feeling in my stomach. "I wanted to give you plenty of time to replace me. I was thinking maybe I'd stay on until early spring, if that's okay."

"Of course it is. Stay on as long as you can. You'll be missed around here, you know."

"Thank you. I'll miss coming into work here, but I'll be doing a lot of charity work, so that will feel good as well."

"I'm sure it will." She gives me a small nod, then smiles. "You remind me of me when I was your age. Young, ambitious, the whole world at your feet. And like you, I fell in love with a powerful man with whom I had little in common."

Oh, dear, I don't like where this is going. "Arthur and I have a surprising amount in common, actually."

Hazel nods and makes a little *hmph* sound. "I'm sure you do; I was just talking about the very different upbringings. It was the same with my husband and me. And like you, we also got married very quickly. We were going to have the perfect, carefree marriage. Travel the world together, see everything, do everything, lazy Sundays in bed."

She smiles wistfully for a second. "He was offered a job in Paris, and we jumped at the chance even though it meant I had to give up my career. So, instead of reporting the news, I spent my mornings reading it while sitting at little cafés sipping coffee. I didn't have to worry about money for the first time in my life—no stress, only freedom. I took some cooking classes, and for a while everything was wonderful. He liked coming home to a hot meal and a wife who was starved for company because I hung on his every word."

"Well, I won't be cooking at least," I say with a little laugh.

She continues as though I haven't said anything. "It didn't take long before I was completely dependent on him. I was learning French, but I'd never been good at it, even in school. I had difficulty making friends because of the language barrier, and soon I had very few interests outside of my husband, which is not a healthy way for anyone with a brain to live.

"In the end, I could hardly stand myself—the endless talk of which colour curtains I should put up in the bedroom or what the spinach looked like at the market that day. I begged him to move back to Canada so I could work again, but he didn't want to give up his new life. He suggested a baby, and I considered it. I wanted it to be the answer, but in the end, I said no. He found a woman from his office who didn't mind giving herself up for him. They have four kids and six grandkids."

"I'm sorry. That sounds like it was very hard," I say.

"I'm over it." Hazel shrugs. "The thing is, when I see you and what you're about to do, it worries me because twenty years later the world hasn't changed one bit, even though we women like to think it has. Women still have to give up so much for love, and once the passion is gone, all those things that made you different and drew you together at the beginning end up pulling you apart."

"I'm not going to lose myself, Hazel. I know who I am."

"Do you? Because I can't see any way a woman wouldn't get completely lost in her husband's world if her husband is someone in Arthur's position."

I shake my head. "With all due respect, you don't know Arthur, and you don't know what we're like together. We need each other. We make each other better people, and that's not going to change after we're married." I stare at her, feeling very annoyed by her assumption that I'm going to end up exactly like her. "I know you're going to think I'm naïve, but Arthur fell in love with me because of who I am, because of the drive I have to succeed and how I keep him on his toes."

"Open your eyes, Tessa. If you marry him, something will have to give, and I have the feeling it will be you."

"I should get going."

"Sure." Hazel nods. "I didn't mean to upset you, Tessa. I'm just trying to help. I like you very much, and I think you have a lot of potential. I'd hate to see you exchange it for a sparkly tiara."

TEN

"Come here," said the spider to the fly...

Arthur

Text from me to Tessa: *What are you doing this afternoon/evening?*

Tessa: *I'll be at work until well after midnight. We go to press tonight and we need to report on the ice storm. Why? What's up?*

Me: *Damn. The cross-country skiing nationals had to be postponed so I find myself with twelve hours of free time. I thought maybe you could come over so I could keep you warm.*

Tessa: *Now I wish I hadn't asked. I'll be even more grumpy for the rest of the day knowing what I'm missing out on.*

Me: *Even more grumpy? What's wrong.*

Tessa: *I've had a big lecture from Hazel about the perils of marrying someone of a different class.*

Me: *Oh, Christ. What does she know?*

Tessa: *She did it and her husband fell out of love with her after the passion wore off.*

Me: *Well, that's because she started wearing floor-length sweater vests. Any man would struggle to maintain wood with that walking around all day.*

Tessa: *You're awful.*

Me: *Not awful. Just honest. Wait, how will you get home in this storm? The police are about to announce that they're shutting down the main roads.*

Tessa: *I'm walking to Nikki's. She's about two blocks from here.*

Me: *Will there be naked tickle fights?*

Tessa: *Umm, no.*

Me: *You sure? Because even if there's even a thirty percent chance, I'll strap on some skates and make my way over to her flat.*

Tessa: *Eye-rolling.*

Me: *And blushing, I'm sure. Don't worry about Hazel's cautionary tale. She doesn't know us. We're going to be amazing together.*

Tessa: *I know. It's just a little disheartening to know the rest of the kingdom can't see it.*

Me: *They'll get the idea in about thirty years or so.*

Tessa: *That soon?*

Me: *Sooner if you come over right now...*

I wait for two full minutes, but no answer comes, so I get up from my desk and make my way back to my apartment, strolling through the quiet halls of the palace, having sent the staff home hours ago so they wouldn't have to brave the icy roads during rush hour. Dexter, who has been sleeping on a large dog bed in my office, follows me down the hall. "Well, Dex, looks like it's just you and me tonight...and Chester, the fish, of course. Between you and me, he's not the best company. A little standoffish for the most part, but don't tell Tessa I said that."

We watch *Frozen Planet*, one of Dexter's favourite David Attenborough documentaries, until he falls asleep on the couch. I wander around my apartment, feed Chester a few flakes of his fish food even though Tessa has left strict instructions not to feed him more than once a day.

But come on. How's the little guy supposed to survive on such a small amount of food? I stare out the window. The freezing rain has given way to snow, which is now blanketing the meadow as it drifts and flutters from the sky.

Fuck, I'm bored.

Completely and utterly bored after only one hundred-eight minutes of unscheduled time to myself. I set off down the hall in search of my grandmother to see if she might be free for dinner. I knock and wait for a few seconds before the door is opened by none other than my old schoolmate and the woman everyone assumed I would one day marry, Lady Dr. Brooke Beddingfield.

"Arthur," she says, kissing me on both cheeks, "I was hoping I'd catch you today."

"Brooke, what are you doing here? I thought you were still in Zamunda."

"I got homesick and decided to come home early for Christmas." She steps aside, and I enter my grandmother's apartment, only to see her pulling on her cardigan.

"Everything okay, Gran?"

"Yes, dear. I'm just fine. Brooke, here, was just saving me a call to Dr. Griffin." There's something about the way she says it that sets off alarm bells in my head.

"Are you sure?"

"Yes, I'm quite healthy—aren't I, Brooke, dear?"

Brooke smiles. "The Princess Dowager is in remarkable shape for someone over eighty."

"Well, thank you for checking on her." I stare at my grandmother for a moment, then decide not to push the subject any further. Just because she's old, it doesn't mean I get to start treating her like a child. "Gran, the storm has given me a rare evening off, so I thought I would see if my favourite lady might be available to share a meal with me."

Grandmother rolls her eyes at me. "Liar. Your favourite lady must have turned you down for this evening."

"Well, yes, she has to work late, but that doesn't make my invitation any less sincere."

"Sure it does, but it doesn't matter anyway because I'm busy," Gran says. "I have a monthly poker game with some of the men who work in the garage. See if I can earn back some of the money we pay them."

She winks at Brooke, whose mouth drops open in shock. "Relax, Brooke—I'm only joking. I'll let them leave with most of their money."

"But I sent everyone home."

"Don't worry, *El Cheapo*. They're off the clock," Gran quips.

"I'm not cheap. I'm merely concerned for their safety."

"They're staying overnight in the staff quarters."

"Ah, I see," I say. "In that case, have fun. But not too much fun."

Gran waves off my comment, looking more than ready for me to stop hovering around like a helicopter grandson.

"If you're in need of a dinner companion, I find myself free this evening." Brooke smiles up at me and tosses her red hair over her shoulder. "Unless, of course, Tessa would mind us sharing a meal together. I wouldn't want to do anything to make her feel uncomfortable."

"Why would she mind me eating with an old friend? I assure you she's far too secure than to let something like that bother her." Hmm, then why am I getting an unsettled feeling in the pit of my stomach?

Brook grins. "Glad to hear it because, with your position and popularity, she'll have to get used to sharing you with the world."

"Won't be a problem, not for a woman like her," I say with a firm nod. There, that's better. As long as I talk about Tessa the entire time, this whole dinner will be completely above board. "Oh, I'm afraid you'll have to put up with my signature scrambled eggs."

"You mean you still haven't progressed past your first Gordon Ramsay lesson?" She laughs, closing her doctor's kit.

"He never came back, for some unknown reason."

"It's because you're a very slow learner, dear," says Gran. "And he knew he would end up calling you a donkey if he came back."

Brooke laughs and gives my gran a quick kiss on the cheek. "You're always such a delight, Princess Florence."

She crosses the room and hooks her arm into mine, an old habit of hers that I've always found a little bit awkward.

"Well, good luck tonight, Gran. Try not to clean them out completely. It's almost Christmas, after all."

"It would be quite rude of me to *let* them win. It's not a charity event. Now, out you go so I can have my pregame nap."

Brooke and I walk down the long hall, then take the lift to the main floor where the private kitchen is. The entire time, she chats about how much she misses everyone in Avonia and how different her life is now that she works for the Doctors of the World Foundation. She has dedicated her life to serving others and spends most of her days inoculating babies and young children and dealing with myriad health emergencies of those who can find their way to the clinic. I listen as I pull all the ingredients out of the fridge and start grating some cheese.

Brooke washes her hands and finds a knife and cutting board and begins to chop up some tomato while she talks. I try to focus on what she's saying, but part of me is troubled by Tessa's boss trying to talk her out of marrying me.

"Arthur? Arthur? Where is your mind this evening?"

"What? Sorry, Brooke. I'm afraid I'm just a little bit distracted."

"What's on your mind?" Brooke pulls a bottle of white wine out of the fridge and holds it up to me.

"Good idea. That will go nicely with the eggs." I open the drawer in which we keep the bottle opener, then slide it across the marble counter to her. She catches it deftly with one hand and makes quick work of the cork while I take two glasses down from the cupboard.

Once it's been poured, she holds her glass up to mine. "To old friends."

"To old friends." I nod, and we both take a sip.

She sucks back half the glass, then says, "Let's be really naughty."

Oh, bugger. I was afraid of this. "Pardon me?"

She gives me a sly smile. "Let's have toast with the eggs instead of salad."

I laugh, relieved she didn't just suggest we eat in the nude while she cups my crown jewels. "There's some bread in the bin over there."

"This feels like old times, doesn't it?"

"I don't recall us cooking together before." I take my phone out of my pocket to check for messages and see Tessa hasn't texted.

"Chemistry lab, remember? Or have you already forgotten first-year Chem at Oxford?" She laughs, touching my forearm.

"No, of course not. Professor Fumbledore..."

"With the long beard and round glasses..."

"Who never managed a sip of coffee without spilling on himself," I add.

Brooke laughs like I've just said the wittiest remark she's ever heard while I turn my attention to the stove.

She gets to work, humming a little before saying, "So, are you going to tell me, or do I have to guess?"

"Guess what?"

"What's on your mind."

"Oh, that. It's nothing. Just...work."

Brooke raises one eyebrow. "No, it's not. You're forgetting who you're talking to. I know all your secrets. Well, I used to, anyway." She smiles sadly and has another sip of her drink.

"Yes, I suppose you did."

"And have I ever told anyone any of them?"

"I assume not."

She glares for a moment, letting me know she doesn't appreciate my little quip.

"Fine, no. You've always been a very loyal friend." I turn and fire up the gas burner, then add some olive oil to the pan.

"And I always will be, no matter what. So you can tell me anything, Arthur. In fact, it might make you feel better."

"I'm fine, really. Very happy, in fact."

"Oh, come now. You have barely cracked a smile since I got here. You can't be that happy."

"It's nothing. Really. I'm just feeling a bit sorry for myself because I hardly ever see my fiancée."

The toaster pops, and Brooke sets to work buttering the bread. "I hope one of my dearest friends isn't being neglected by the love of his life."

"No, it's nothing like that. It's not like she's off gallivanting around the world with her friends or something."

"But she's not here either, is she?"

"No, she's not." I adjust the heat on the burner. "Tonight, she'll be at the office until the wee hours of the morning to help put out a rather thin publication that will be read by a handful of people before it's used to line birdcages."

Brooke laughs, the sound of it reminding me of a witch's cackle.

"Please forget I said that. It was very unkind of me. I only said it because it seems pointless for her to be working such long hours when she's going to quit shortly before the wedding." I stir the eggs, my chest tightening with guilt.

"I was wondering when she'd leave her job."

"We decided it was best to wait."

"Whatever for? I'd think she'd be absolutely snowed under getting ready for the wedding and her new life."

"She is, but Tessa was worried she'll look like a gold-digger if she leaves her job now."

A strange look crosses Brooke's face, but she covers it with a smile. "That makes sense. I'm sure many would think that."

"Anyway, none of it matters in the end. This is all temporary, and besides, Tessa and I are very much in love. Whatever comes our way, we'll manage to get through it together."

"I've never seen you backpedal so fast. It's only human to air your feelings about your significant other from time to time. In fact, it's not healthy for your relationship to keep everything bottled up inside."

"Is that your professional medical opinion?"

Brooks smiles and curls her hair around one finger. "Yes, it took me seven years of higher education to discover that little tidbit of wisdom. As a doctor who has your best interests at heart, I'm telling you, you need to talk."

"Yes, well, that may be true, but I'm not sure how Tessa would feel about me complaining to you when I really should be talking to her."

"It has to be a two-way street, Arthur. She can't expect to be engaged in a modern relationship in which she maintains a career that complicates *your* life and not allow you to have friends to talk to when you're upset about it."

I stir the eggs with more vigor than normal. "Her job doesn't complicate my life."

"Well, it certainly doesn't ease your burden in any way I can see," she says. She pauses for a moment, waiting for a response. I don't give her one.

I tip back the rest of my wine, then pour another before dishing up the eggs and the fried tomatoes.

When we're seated, she puts her hand on mine. "How about this? You air one grievance about your relationship, and I'll do the same."

I slide my hand out from under hers and pick up my fork. "I didn't know you had a boyfriend."

"I had to find one since you were never going to come around," she says, laughing even though I'm not entirely sure that was a joke. "He's an accountant for the Doctors of the World Foundation. It's a long-distance thing, though, since he's stationed in London."

"Wait a minute. He's in London, and you're *here* on your time off?"

"Things are very casual at the moment, but he'll be joining my family at Christmas for a couple of days."

"Is that what bothers you about him? You'd like it to be more serious?"

"No. To be completely honest, he's a little bit long-winded. And even for an accountant, he can be a bit dull. But he's a good man and a very good kisser, so I can overlook the rest." She takes a bite of the eggs, then makes an *mmm* sound. "Delicious, Arthur. I can see why you stick with this dish."

"Thank you."

She empties her wine, then picks up the bottle and tops us both off. "Now, you."

"You what?"

"You go. I told you my complaints about Evan. Your turn."

"I already did."

She raises one eyebrow. "You're no fun. You've only told me she has a career."

"Other than that, she's perfect."

"Nobody's perfect."

"She is."

Brooke makes a gagging face and points at her mouth with her index finger.

"No, seriously, she is."

"You know what's serious? The trouble you'll be in if you don't take off those blinders before the wedding. Couples fare much better when they're honest about each other's shortcomings from the start. It prevents the big letdown most people get when they finally acknowledge the other person is human."

"I know what her faults are, Brooke. I just don't feel the need to badmouth her."

"It's not badmouthing. It's just letting out a little of the buildup of frustration. Fine if you don't want to talk to me, but find someone to talk to. Have you spoken to Chaz lately? Maybe you'd feel better talking to him."

"He's been living in New York for the past couple of years since they moved to be near her family," I say, happy to change the subject. "As far as I know, they're doing quite well. Two kids already, and his law firm is killing it."

"Good for Chaz. But that still won't help you."

"I don't need help. I'm very happy."

"Okay, suit yourself." She shrugs. "You always have been a stubborn arse, never admitting when someone else might know what's good for you."

"All right, fine. I just wish the rest of the country would either accept our upcoming marriage or shut the hell up about it already. So what if she's a mechanic's daughter or a little accident-prone? She's a good person—strong and brave and kind, and she's going to make a wonderful queen one day."

"There. Was that so hard?" she asks, standing and making her way over to the island and getting out another bottle of wine. She uncorks it and brings it to the table without asking if I'd like more. Honestly, I don't even mind because I do want another drink. I'd like several, in fact.

Before I know it, I'm getting up to grab a third bottle of wine. Fuck it. Might as well make a night of it. I end up pouring my heart out about how difficult it is to be engaged to someone whose supporters hate me and who my supporters hate. I tell her about Hazel, and Phyllis and Daniel, the couple from the hospital, who warned us against marrying each other. I tell her about the #IHateTessa Twitter feed but stop short of mentioning the #BrookeIsBetter bit.

She listens intently, nodding and providing a surprising amount of sympathy for both Tessa and myself. "I have to admit, Arthur, I wasn't a fan at first. Not after all the things she wrote about you in her Royal Watchdog days. But if you say she's a good person, I believe it."

"Thank you. If only everyone else out there were like you. I can't even seem to get Arabella to give her a chance."

She puts her hand over mine. "She'll come around. You just need to give her time."

****

It's late by the time I walk Brooke to one of the guest rooms. I was going to send her home in a cab, but the police haven't opened the roads yet. My wine-soaked brain is attempting to set off warning signals of some sort, but I can't figure out what for. Or for what? What's the proper way to word that? The not-drunk way?

Fuck it. I'm drunk. "There you are, Lady Dr. Beddingfield. Your room. You should find everything you need." I bow, tipping forward slightly and bumping into her.

She laughs hysterically and grabs me, pulling me up to standing. Then her face grows serious and I know exactly what she's about to do. So, I back up two steps and say, "Sleep well."

"You, too."

I turn to stumble toward my room, but her voice stops me.

"Arthur, it really is nice to be with you again like this. I almost forgot how much fun we have together."

I stop and turn. "Me, too. I'm glad we had a chance to get caught up."

"If you ever need to talk, please know I'll always be here for you. In fact, I'll be here for whatever you need." Her face grows solemn. "Any time."

"Why, thank you, Madame," I say, putting on as formal a voice as possible to try to make light of what I know was a very serious offer.

"Can I tell you something?" Her gaze is intense, and I'm not sure I want to hear what she has to say, but I nod anyway.

"I'm worried that you and Tessa are rushing into this marriage without really knowing each other. You just have such different backgrounds, and it seems to me you have very different ideas about what you want out of this life. I just think you should slow down a bit, maybe."

I lean one hand against the wall to stop the hallway from spinning. "The date is already set. It's happening, and I'm absolutely thrilled about it."

"Are you?" She shakes her head a little bit. "I'm just trying to say—as a friend—that maybe you could find a reason to postpone the whole thing. Just to give yourself a little more time to be sure."

"No need, my friend." I spin on my heel and make my way toward my room, calling back to her, "We're very much in love."

A few minutes later, I flop onto my bed fully clothed and drop into a dead sleep, completely forgetting to text Tessa to say goodnight and tell her I love her.

****

Text from Brooke to Me: *I knocked on your door this morning, but you were either gone or still sleeping. I wanted to thank you for last night.*

Me: *I was probably working out already. Did you find a ride home?*

Brooke: *Yes, thanks. Always the gentleman. About my offer...that came out wrong. I only meant that I'd like to be here for you as a friend. Tessa, too. I'm sure she and I will become the best of friends as soon as we have a chance to get to know each other.*

Me: *I'm sure you will. She's amazing.*

Brooke: *Let's make sure we have some time together before I leave town. The three of us, I mean.*

Me: *Yes, let's.*

I stare at the exchange, wondering if her tone last night held her true intention or if her text today does. I suppose, in the end, it doesn't matter, does it? Even if she does have an interest in me, it's not mutual. She can wish we were a couple all she wants, it won't change anything. Not that she *does* wish it. But I suppose she might...

Text from Tessa to Me: *Hey, sweetie. Just getting up now. Was at the office until close to one a.m., so by the time I slid my way to Nikki's she was asleep.*

Me: *So, no naked tickle fights then?*

Her: *Haha. No. I'm not in the mood anyway. I'm super grouchy from all the crap at work lately. What'd you end up doing?*

Me: *Had some eggs and wine and went to bed, missing you horribly.*

Her: *You made eggs without me? That sucks. Now, I'm even more grumpy than ever.*

Me: *Come by now, I'll make you some and show you how much I missed you.*

Her: *I wish. Heading back to the office.*

Okay, so I know that was a perfect opportunity to tell her Brooke was here, but I'm not sure that's the type of thing you text to your fiancée when you don't have a chance to a) gauge her reaction, and b) explain. Plus, she did admit to being 'super grouchy', so, clearly, this isn't the time, and if there's one thing about making a relationship work, it's that timing is everything.

ELEVEN

The Toilet Paper Bride Champion

Tessa

It's Saturday morning, and I'm up with the sun, in spite of the fact that I worked until well after midnight last night. I lay in bed, staring at the cracked ceiling, wishing I could go back to sleep for another couple of hours but knowing it's not going to happen. I'm far too nervous to get any sleep at all. This afternoon, my bridal shower will take place in the small ballroom at the palace, hosted by the Princess Dowager Florence, much to my mother's chagrin. She was very disappointed to be *invited* to my bridal shower rather than *hosting* it.

To be honest, I don't want a shower at all. It's going to be awkward and uncomfortable to be in a room with two hundred—yes, that's right, two hundred—guests, one hundred and sixty-five of them I've never met before. Most of the ladies who will be attending would rather see Arthur marry Dexter than me, which kind of adds a special level of cringeworthy awkwardness to the event, don't you think?

At least I won't have to suffer through the uncomfortable act of opening gifts in front of everyone, having requested donations to the Avonian Literacy Foundation in lieu of presents.

I roll over and grab my phone off the night table and check for messages. There is one from Nikki I've been ignoring.

Text from Nikki: *What time should I be by to do your hair tomorrow morning? I'll need lots of time to get myself ready first for Xavier. Yum, yum. BTW, you're giving me a ride to the palace, yes?*

I haven't been able to bring myself to tell her I'll be having my hair done by the Princess Dowager's stylist today, having found it very difficult to turn down her kind offer. Princess Florence is really the only member of the royal family who approves of my relationship with Arthur, so I couldn't very well turn her down, even though Nikki will be very hurt when I tell her the truth. I stare at my phone for a moment, my gut churning and bubbling as I try to think of how to word my response back to her.

My dread of today's events makes me long for the days when the worst thing I had to suffer was a family dinner at my parents' house every few weeks. Now that I'm living with them full-time, it's like my life has turned into one long, endless Sunday family dinner, separated by the occasional break to go spend some time with Arthur.

Text from Me to Nikki: *Hey, Nikki, change of plans. I'll have to meet you at the palace. Don't worry about my hair. I got talked into letting the Princess Dowager's stylist do it so I need to be at the palace early.*

I hit send, then buried my head under the covers, wishing this day would just be over already. My stomach growls loudly, reminding me I'm still on this ridiculous pre-wedding diet, even though the logical part of my brain is telling me I don't need to. The terrified part of my brain keeps asking me what if Baz is right and I'm not spectacular enough as bride to the Crown Prince of Avonia, and it sets off a horrid chain of events for both single people and married couples around the nation?

That's just stupid, though, right? But still, since the first wedding planning session, I find myself panicking any time I eat something with a lot of calories, or a lot of fat, or a lot of calories and fat. I haven't had a bowl of crisps in weeks, and the last time I bought jelly babies for my nieces and nephews, it practically killed me to hand them over to them rather than scarf them all down in one sitting.

My stomach rumbles again, and I throw the covers off and go down to the kitchen in search of something nutritious and very bland since, besides rumbling, my gut is also churning with nervousness. I stand in front of the open fridge for a good two minutes before I decide to go with half a cup of fat-free yogurt and some berries, even though a big stack of pancakes and some sausages sound much better at the moment. How is it possible to feel sick to your stomach and starving at the same time?

Maybe that would be a good article for The Weekly Observer...*The Mystery Behind a Hearty Appetite When One is Nervous.* Oh no, that's crap. Good thing I'm on the announcements desk.

The sound of footsteps on the creaky stairs breaks my train of thought.

My mum walks into the kitchen in her bathrobe, her hair in rollers. "You're up early, Twinkle. Couldn't sleep again?" She plucks the kettle off the stove and fills it with water from the tap.

"I needed to be up early anyway. It's going to be a long day."

"Is that all you're eating?" She wrinkles her nose at my yogurt and shakes her head. "You're fine the way you are. If Arthur wanted some anorexic, he would've found one to marry."

"It's not for him. I just would like to have...toned arms for the wedding."

She raises one eyebrow at me, clearly not buying any of it. Luckily, she gets distracted. "Oh, I forgot to tell you, I'll be getting a ride with you over to the palace this morning so I can get a few things set up in the party room while you're getting your hair done." She smiles, looking far too excited for my comfort.

"Well, you're welcome to come along, but I'm pretty sure the staff has everything covered. You're meant to be a guest, so you can just relax and enjoy the afternoon."

"Oh, hog noodles. Those stuffy people won't have the first idea how to put on a proper bridal shower. I mean, really, *no gifts*? Everyone will be bored to tears."

My mother was not in favour of the no gifts idea. Even though Arthur already has enough of every household item to open his own Bed, Bath, & Beyond, my mother told me she's a bit miffed that we're taking away the chance for people to choose something nice to start me on the path to married life properly. But I probably shouldn't focus on that right now when she's just basically admitted she's planning what I'm sure will be some type of humiliating party games to play at the shower. "What exactly do you mean by a proper bridal shower?"

"Nope," she says, holding up one finger and shaking it at me. "I'm not saying a word. Otherwise, it will spoil the surprise."

"Mum, this is not our typical crowd. There will be almost two hundred guests—and they're not exactly the 'party game' type of people."

My mum waves her hand at me. "Everyone loves a good party game, Tessa. Even *rich* people. Now, I've hosted dozens of showers—both bridal and baby—so I know exactly what I'm doing. And since they won't let me bring any food, I can at least bring some fun."

My phone buzzes before I can continue to argue, and I look down to see Nikki's face on the screen. I cringe, then answer the phone. "Hi, Nikki."

"Are you seriously letting some eighty-five-year-old woman's stylist do your hair today? Do you know what a disaster that could be? You're likely to end up with your hair chopped off, dyed blue, and permed into tight curls."

"Well, let's hope not." I let out a weak laugh, hoping Nikki will start to find the whole thing funny as well, even though I can tell by her tone she's more than a little hurt. "Hey, you're up early."

"Yes, I got up extra early to get myself ready so I'd have enough time to do my best friend's hair for her bridal shower."

I get up and walk out of the kitchen, making my way to the bottom of the stairs while I talk on the phone. "I'm really sorry, Nikki. Obviously, I would much rather have you doing my hair than the Princess Dowager's stylist. But it was one of those situations where I didn't really feel like I could say no."

"Well, you could've told me sooner so I wouldn't have gotten up so early today."

Oh, fudge doodles. I've really managed to screw up the day already, haven't I? "You're right. One hundred percent right. There's no excuse for me not letting you know sooner, except I'm a bit of a coward who tends to put things off when I know I'm going to upset someone."

"No, that was the old Tessa, remember? The new Tessa deals with problems straight on."

"You're right. I am afraid I had a relapse, but it's over now, and I have a feeling I have a way to make this up to you..."

"Really?" Nikki asks, sounding intrigued, which is a huge improvement from pissed right off. "It better be good, because I'm very mad."

"What if I ask Xavier to swing by and pick you up after he drops me off at the palace?" I lower my voice so my parents won't hear me pimping out my bodyguard to my best friend. "It'll give you two a little bit of time alone together..."

"Can you tell him to pick me up without his shirt on?"

"I'm pretty sure that would constitute sexual harassment since I'm sort of his boss, in a strange way, and I'd be using my position of influence over him to allow you to ogle his body."

Nikki sighs dramatically. "Well, you're no fun."

"What if he drives you home after the party as well?"

"Now we're getting somewhere. We can consider this phase one of the 'make it up to Nikki' plan."

"Good, because I feel really bad about today, and there's definitely going to be a phase two coming." I pause, hoping she'll accept, but she waits me out. "And a phase three, of course."

She yawns loudly, then says, "All right, I'm glad we got that settled. I think I'm going to go back to bed for a couple of hours."

"You do that. Be ready by one-thirty for your escort to the palace."

"That sounds delightfully dirty."

"Well, it won't be, but at least there's the fantasy of it all."

"That ought to keep me going for a while."

"I hope so. But listen, you'll have to think of him like a stripper giving a lap dance. He can touch you, but you can't touch him. Otherwise, you're going to find yourself kicked out of the *Champagne Room*."

****

Text from Lars: *Can Nina bring Eugenia this afternoon? I know it says no kids on the invitation, but, she still won't take a bottle, and she feeds every hour, so Nina can't really leave the house without her.*

Text from Bram: *Can Irene come to the shower? We got back together last week and you know what a fan of the Royal Family she is. Oh, unless Prince Arthur will be there. If that's the case, I'm telling her 'no' whether she could come or not. Her crush on him goes beyond normal. I won't get into details but let's just say if I play along, everybody has a good time.*

Text from Rory, Assistant to Baz: *Tessa, Baz wants an update on your weight loss progress. You should be down five pounds by now. He wanted me to remind you not to overindulge today at your bridal shower, as every day counts right now. Also, you still haven't gotten back to me about the elocution and posture lessons. We should have started already.*

****

"You look very sophisticated, Tessa dear." The Princess Dowager smiles up at me and pats my cheek.

"Thank you." I stare at myself in the mirror for a moment, a little bit shocked to discover she's right. I *do* look sophisticated. And for what I paid for this bloody dress, I damn well better. I'm wearing a light blue Chanel dress with three-quarter-length sleeves. My hair is up in a French twist, and my make-up, for once in my life, could be described as impeccable. The dowager has lent me a string of pearls and matching earrings. "I hardly recognize myself right now."

"Yes, well for today that might be a good thing. The crowd you're about to meet will be hoping for you to fail. Your job is to show them you're every bit as good as them—which is true, by the way."

I turn from the mirror and beam at her, feeling as though she's the grandmum I never had. I blink quickly, feeling tears threatening my mascara.

The dowager gives a quizzical look in the direction of my chest, then reaches up one hand, tugs at the collar of my dress, and peeks down it. "Your breasts look rather small today. What happened to them?"

Well, nothing like having your fiancé's grandmum look down your top to stop you from feeling sentimental.

"I hope you haven't been starving yourself like so many ridiculous young women do these days before their weddings."

Before I can answer, she adjusts my bra through my dress, then stares for a moment at my chest. "Maybe it's just this bra, dear. We're going to have to take you shopping for some proper lingerie before the wedding."

She makes a little *tsk*ing sound as she walks away. "Either way, make sure you keep enough body fat so you can get pregnant. I want to meet my great-grandchildren before I kick off. Now let's get going. There are always a few bitches who show up early to these things, for some reason."

****

It's not the enormous Swarovski crystal chandelier you notice first when you walk into the ballroom, nor the beautifully laid-out tables with gold cutlery and matching gold trays stacked with finger sandwiches, dainty desserts, and expertly-arranged fruit platters. You certainly won't see (or hear, for that matter) the harpist sitting in the corner strumming her instrument, giving the space a heavenly feel. No, all these things pale in comparison to what catches your eye first.

It's the dozens of pyramids of toilet paper stacked on the floor, waiting for the guests to play 'Dress the Toilet Paper Bride' that you'll see. And it's my mum's voice barking orders that you'll hear.

"No, no! We won't want to start with the 'Groom in His Skivvies' game. No one's ready for that one right off the bat. It's more of an after a glass of punch game. Is that punch alcoholic? If not, I really think we would do well to find a couple bottles of vodka to pour in bowls to loosen things up a little."

Fuckity-fuck. My stomach lurches as I take in what's she's done in the time it took me to have my hair put up and some eye shadow swiped across my eyelids.

"Why the hell is there toilet paper stacked everywhere?" Princess Florence asks me.

"It's for a party game. I'll get rid of it." I sigh and start toward my mum, telling myself to stay calm even though I'm completely pissed at her.

On the drive over, I gave very specific instructions to my mother that none of the usual bridal shower icebreaker games were to be played. I almost believed she was going to listen to me, based on how earnest she seemed in her responses.

"Mum, could I speak with you for a moment, please?" I plaster a fake smile on my face, then remember to greet the rest of the staff, as well as Grace from next door, who has come early to help. "Hello, Grace, everyone. Thank you all so much for your help. Mum..." I do the 'come here' gesture with my finger, but she takes no notice and continues putting the final touches on what will go down as the tackiest royal bridal shower in history.

Before I manage to get to her, one of the pages announces the guests are arriving. I break out in a cold sweat, realizing my two worlds are about to collide in a most horrifying way.

Mum beams at me. "Goody!" She claps her hands together. "You look lovely, Twinkle, although that colour is a bit drab. Did you see that my cousin, Rose, is here already?"

Rose pops up from behind a table with a bag full of clothespins. "Hi, Tessa." She hurries over to me and gives me a big hug, squishing me against her ample bosom. "I thought since I've met the prince before, I would be the best one to come and help your mother get everything ready." She lowers her voice. "Although Grace from next door had to get in on this, too, of course." She rolls her eyes at me.

"Lovely to see you, Rose. Thanks so much for coming. Umm, if you don't mind me asking, what are the clothespins for?"

"Oh, never you mind!" my mum says. "You'll find out soon enough. Now, Grace, where's the veil? She needs to put it on before the people start coming in."

"Oh, no," I say, shaking my head quickly as I see Grace hurrying towards me, carrying a veil made from wrapping paper ribbon attached to an upside-down paper plate. "I've just had my hair done, and I think it would hurt the Princess Dowager's feelings if I—"

"Nonsense," says Mum. "Oh, as I live and breathe, it's the Princess Dowager herself." She rushes over toward her with her arms stretched out. "I didn't even see you there, you're so tiny in real life."

I watch the Princess Dowager stiffen as my mother bends over her for a long, awkward hug. I'm so distracted by this that Grace manages to get the wrapping paper veil secured to my head before I can stop her.

"I'm a huge fan of your family," my mum trills. "Not like Tessa, for a while there. She went over to the dark side, but I couldn't be more pleased that Arthur managed to bring her back around. Did you know that I have a very rare commemorative mug from your wedding?"

Vincent comes to Princess Florence's rescue, his voice filling the room. "May I present the Countess of Waterford, as well as her daughters, Denalda and Regina."

He looks at me as he motions for me to come stand near the entrance to the ballroom. It's clear from his expression that he's horrified by my veil. I give him a 'help me' look, but there's really nothing he can do at this point.

I make my way over to our first guests and curtsy awkwardly at them. "Pleasure to meet you."

They nod, very clearly trying not to laugh, then move on to saying hello to the Princess Dowager without speaking to me.

The next guest to be announced is none other than Lady Dr. Brooke Beddingfield, along with her mother and grandmother, who, by the way, are every bit as elegant and beautiful as Brooke, not to mention are aging like fine wine. Brooke gives me a kiss on both cheeks as though we're the best of friends, then says, "Oh, Tessa, you look positively hilarious! What a good sport you are."

My stomach decides now is the perfect time to join the conversation, growling loudly due to a lack of lunch. My cheeks heat up with embarrassment, and I raise my voice to try to hide the sound, but it's no use.

"My goodness, Tessa, was that your stomach growling? That didn't sound healthy at all."

"I forgot to eat lunch," I say as one of the other countesses catches Brooke's eye and waves her over, putting an end to our conversation.

Twenty minutes later, I'm still standing in the same spot, still saying the same thing as a stream of impeccably-dressed women enter the room, wide-eyed and whispering as they take in my mother's creation. The Princess Dowager, as the hostess, greets them first, then me, then my mum, then Cousin Rose, who gives each of them a clothespin and a piece of paper with the forbidden words on them (like bride, wedding, lingerie, etc.) and explains the game. For some strange reason, the ladies then make their way over to Brooke, and she greets them also. I strain my ears to hear what they're saying and catch little bits of their conversations, such as 'shocking' and 'should have been you' and 'what is he thinking,' and I hear Brooke's smooth voice repeating 'the heart wants what it wants.' I couldn't agree more. My heart wants to smash her in the teeth right about now. I wonder if there's some way to do that whilst maintaining a dignified air...

Under the pressure of greeting and trying to learn the names of close to two hundred new people, I have completely forgotten to find a way to have the toilet paper pyramids removed, and I've had no way to put a stop to whatever the hell else my mother is planning. My brain will only allow me to focus on a loop of horrible facts, starting with how much my toes are being pinched by these new heels, then moving on to the fact that I'm sweating so much that if I raise my arms, there will definitely be wet spots on my Chanel dress, to the fact that everyone here who's not related to me is in mourning for the fact that Arthur isn't marrying Brooke.

Finally, Nikki breezes into the room, dressed in a bright green vintage fifties dress, her hair a shocking platinum this week. Relief washes over me as I take in the sight of her. Finally, my best friend is here. She can help!

She curtsies very deeply in front of the dowager, then grins at me and winks. "Thanks for arranging my ride over here," she murmurs.

"I'm not going to get sued for sexual harassment, am I?"

"Oh, when I get started with him, there won't be any complaining, believe me." She runs her tongue over her teeth and makes a smacking sound with her lips.

"Nikki!" my mum calls. "Over here, sweetheart! You can help us get the games started."

I grip Nikki's arm. "You have to stop her. She's about to unleash an Abbott Lane Shower Hell on all these ladies and duchesses."

"It'll be fun," Nikki says, glancing around the room. "Besides, most of these women need to get the sticks out of their arses anyway."

"Please. They already think I'm a joke. Can you just—"

"Oh, toilet paper bride game! That's my favourite!" she says, hurrying over to my mum. "I get to be the bride in my group!"

There goes my one ally. Vincent walks over and tells us all the guests have arrived so we may proceed with the afternoon's activities. As much as I like Vincent, I wouldn't mind slapping that amused look off his face right about now.

He holds a microphone up for the Princess Dowager, who takes my arm and walks to the front of the room with me in tow. She clears her throat right into the microphone, then says, "Good afternoon, ladies. On behalf of the Langdon family, I would like to welcome you all and thank you for traveling from near and far to be here to help us celebrate the upcoming wedding of my only grandson, Arthur, to this lovely young woman next to me, Ms. Tessa Sharpe, who has been like a warm spring breeze throughout the palace these past months. Arabella couldn't be here today, as she is on a humanitarian mission in the south, but she sends her warm wishes to her sister-in-law-to-be."

Humanitarian mission? I saw her this morning in her workout gear.

Princess Florence continues. "So, please take the time to get to know Tessa today and in the coming weeks, as I promise you she's more than worthy of both your time and admiration. She will one day be a poised and wonderful queen with her eye on the needs of all the people—both big and small—of our nation."

I tear up a bit and whisper, "Thank you."

Just then, my mum grabs the microphone from Princess Florence's hand. "Hello!" she chirps. *Oh, dear God. Has she been into the punch already?* "For those of you who don't know me, I'm Evi Sharpe, Tessa's mum. I also want to thank you for coming today, and I wanted to say that our family is easily as excited as yours to be joining. I have always been a huge fan of the Royal Family, having amassed one of the most extensive collections of Royal Family commemorative dishes and knickknacks you'll ever find. So, we're sort of family already, in a way. Oh, but not in a strange, incestuous way."

I reach for my mum's arm and try to subtly pull it down so as to lower the mic away from her mouth, but she doesn't take the hint.

"Tessa's father can't be with us today—oh, not because he's died or is in jail, or anything horrible like that—he's just at home watching football because this is more of a ladies' thing. Anyway, on behalf of my husband, I wanted to say we couldn't be happier for Tessa to have found Arthur. We always knew she'd be a late bloomer and eventually she'd hit her stride and make something of herself. And she finally has. We never thought she'd make something this big of herself, mind you—I mean, my God, who ever thought she'd be queen one day? Not us, I can tell you. But she will be, as soon as...well...it's probably not polite to talk about that, is it?"

She pauses, and I open my mouth to speak, but tears fill her eyes as she keeps going. "Just imagine, someday I'm going to have a plate with my little girl's face on it in our buffet. Well, come spring already, I suppose." She beams up at me for a second while fanning tears out of her eyes, then says, "Anyway, that's enough sentimental words for today. Let's get on with the party! The Princess Dowager has been so kind as to provide all the refreshments, and I thought we'd better bring the fun! We've got loads of shower games planned, so get ready—"

"Gotcha, Evi!" Rose hollers, running at us with alarming speed. "You said 'shower,' so I get your clothespin!"

"Oh, so I did! I'll get it back, though! I always do!" My mum laughs into the mic. "First game is 'Dress the Bride.' Nobody can be in a group with someone at their own table. So, get up and find a stack of toilet paper in the room to stand by. No more than ten to a stack, now! Pick a group member to be the bride, and you've got ten minutes to make a gown out of all that toilet paper!"

A server walks by with a tray of Champagne, and I swipe two. I consider keeping both for myself, but then remember I'm 'sophisticated Tessa', who would certainly never double-fist booze at a bridal shower. I offer one to the dowager, who takes it with a grateful smile. "I hate these things," she says to me.

"Me, too," I say as Grace next door grabs me and hauls me to her group to be dressed.

By the time I'm draped in toilet paper, the Champagne has gone to my head, but not in a good way. In that horrible way when you haven't eaten in weeks and the bubbles make the room start to spin and make you feel hot and dizzy instead of light and airy. I look around at all the activity and the sour faces of so many of the guests here, and I begin to hate my mum for what she's done. She's made me even more of a laughingstock than I already was and ignored all my attempts to be elegant and sophisticated in the eyes of these hateful women. I glare at her as she finishes dressing Nikki, wishing she weren't here. A timer goes off, indicating that the game has thankfully ended, and the twenty brides are all lined up at the front of the room for judging. Of course, I end up standing next to Brooke, who somehow manages to pull off the toilet paper bride look as though it's Dolce and Gabbana. She looks so lovely and slim that I'm certain she'd outshine me in my real dress. Hate fills me as I watch her step out of the line to spin and laugh gaily for the crowd when it's her turn to be judged.

Of course, she wins the big prize for best bride, and I cringe as my mother walks over to her with the envelope containing her prize. Brooke opens it and smiles, looking delighted as she holds up a five dollar gift card for Krispy Kreme doughnuts. Somehow, my mum has managed to get the mic again. "Congratulations to the lovely Lady Dr. Brooke Beddingfield, who is not only so accomplished but is also the most beautiful toilet paper bride here today. Now, I think I hear some stomachs growling, particularly Tessa's. We'd better have a bite to eat so we can all hear each other over her stomach, and then we'll play a game we like to call *The Groom in His Skivvies*. You're gonna love it. It's hilarious." She drops the mic to her side and motions for everyone to go to the buffet table.

"Mum," I hiss. "Stop it now."

"What, Twinkle? Everybody's having a lovely time except you. I think you're just *hangry*. As soon as you have something to eat, you're going to feel much better. So, wipe that frown off your face and have a couple of sandwiches."

"You're humiliating me. This isn't fucking Abbott Lane, and these people are not our friends. This is the fucking palace. They don't dress people in toilet paper, and I don't want them sketching the future King of Avonia in his skivvies for a laugh. You've already made a joke of me today. The least you can do is spare him the humiliation."

The room goes dead silent, and I look up, suddenly realizing they've all heard what I've just said through the microphone that hangs at my mother's side. I glance around and see the shocked looks on the faces of everyone here, including the Princess Dowager.

But it's my mum's face that breaks my heart when I look back down at her. She has a phony smile plastered to her face even though I've hurt her feelings terribly. She just nods and says, "Let's get you something to eat."

****

I stand in the ladies' bathroom, unable to look at myself in the mirror as I unwind my toilet paper dress and remove my veil. If I could, I would hide in here until everyone goes home. But I know my time is limited before I need to make an appearance and try to salvage what's left of the party. The door swings open, and Brooke Beddingfield walks in. Of course. She looks at me, her face pulling into a sympathetic smile as she comes to stand next to me in front of the counters.

"I had the exact same idea. This toilet paper dress is getting rather warm." She starts to remove hers, her fingers delicately pulling at the tissue without ripping any of it.

"Yes." I give her a weak smile and continue working, hoping she'll finish quickly and just leave.

"Tessa, I've been hoping to find a chance to speak with you alone. I'm sure you must despise me, what with that awful *I Hate Tessa* Twitter account and that stupid *Brooke Is Better* hashtag—which I promise you I had nothing to do with. I only just found out about it a few days ago and am completely appalled. It must've upset you very much when you found out about it."

I nod and then ball up my dress and toss it into the garbage. "It's not ideal, I suppose, but I can't really expect much better, can I?"

"Yes, you most certainly can, Tessa," she says, reaching out and touching my arm. "As someone who would very much like to be your friend, I intend to do whatever I can to find out who is behind it and put a stop to it."

I stare at her for a moment, trying to process what she's saying and why exactly she's saying it. She reminds me of O.J. vowing to look for the real killer. "That's very kind of you, Brooke, but there's no need. The best thing to do is ignore it until they get bored and move on to someone else."

"Arthur said you were smart. He wasn't kidding. Well, even if we ignore those people, I'm going to help you find allies among the blue blood crowd. That is, if you'll allow me."

"Why would you do that?"

"Because Arthur is my dear friend, and I hope that you and I can be friends, too." She smiles kindly at me, and I almost find myself feeling comforted by her. "Besides, if he loves you, it means you must be an extraordinary woman."

I shake my head and look down at my feet, seeing some toilet paper stuck to my heel. "I haven't exactly been extraordinary today. Well, extraordinarily rude to my poor mum."

Brooke tilts her head. "Oh, Tessa, who could blame you? You're trying to present yourself as someone elegant, and your mum really didn't do you any favours today. Anyone could see why you'd snap."

"Still, it's no excuse," I say, digging around in my purse for my lipstick so I don't have to make eye contact with her in the mirror.

"Don't you worry about today. You'll have many more opportunities to shine in front of this stuck-up crowd. Plus, you'll have me in the background, selling them on you."

"Thanks. I appreciate it." I toss my lipstick back into my purse without having applied it, then start for the door. "I should get back to my guests."

Tears prick my eyes as I walk the hallway back to the ballroom. I fan them away and breathe deeply, ordering myself to calm down. I can cry later.

****

Everyone went home shortly after my meltdown, but not before a very quiet room of two hundred people listened to the soothing strumming of the harp whilst eating. The people at my table were especially silent, no one daring to look or talk to me, including Nikki, who sat next to my mum on the other side of the table. Every time I caught her eye, the look of disappointment on her face gutted me just a little bit more than the last time. I sat, picking at my food, my mind swirling as I relived the last twenty minutes of my life. I did my best not to notice all the guests slipping out without saying goodbye, and without me properly thanking them for coming. I knew I should get up and wish them off, but I simply could not bring myself to look any of them in the eye after how I had just acted. My mum got a ride home with Grace next door, who glared at me while she collected the unused prizes and put them in a big box.

Now, on the ride to drop off Nikki, I stare out the window at the grey sky, wishing I could take back those few horrible moments in which I proved to be very much lacking in character to everyone in that room. Nikki sits in the front seat with Xavier, and I doubt it's as much because she wants to sit with him as it is that she wants to be away from me. When we stop at her apartment, I get out of the car to say goodbye to her. "Well, thank you for coming."

"Sure." She fiddles with the clasp on her purse for a moment then looks up at me. "I'm not really sure who you are right now, Tessa. But whoever this is, she's not nice like my friend."

Tears fill my eyes, and I nod quickly. "I know. I don't know what was wrong with me back there."

"I don't mean just in the ballroom when you were swearing at your mum in front of hundreds of women. I mean lately, the past few months. You're just...different. You don't have time for the little people anymore. And if this is who you want to be, I guess I'll just have to be ready to let you go and be her."

"Is this about my hair? Because I've already explained that. I really didn't feel like I could say—"

"It's not about your hair. It's about the fact that I never see you. It's about the way you treated your mum, who was only trying to give you a proper, fun bridal shower. She just wanted to be a part of it all. And instead of embracing everything she was trying to do for you, you were cruel to her. The Tessa I love is never cruel, no matter what. I'm not sure I can be friends with this new you. "

"Please, Nikki. Don't say that. I know I was completely awful today. I'm under an unbelievable amount of stress right now, and I really need my best friend."

"Well, the people who love you need things too. This isn't just about you. It's about all of us losing our Tessa."

A cold blast of air hits, and I tighten my wool coat around me. "I can't be the same old Tessa anymore. I need to be better than her in every way."

Nikki shakes her head. "Arthur fell in love with the old Tessa. And I have a feeling he'll fall out of love with this new version once he gets to know her."

With that, Nikki opens the door to her building and walks inside, disappearing up the stairs. I stand on the sidewalk, wishing she was inviting me in right now to have a few glasses of wine so I could fill her in on every detail of my conversation with Brooke, then move on to a recap of the shower so we could laugh about some of the more snooty ladies at the party. But I was the snooty lady at the party today.

And nobody's laughing.

****

Text from Finn: *Heard about you blasting Mum today in front of a bunch of her idols. Wow, Tessa. Just wow.*

Text from Lars: *So...you okay or do you need me to spring for some therapy and/or meds for you? Nina said you turned into a total Bridezilla. Super disappointing, Tess. You better get your shit together or you'll end up alienating everyone who loves you. #MaybeBrookeisBetter*

Text from Hazel: *There are photos of your bridal shower on Instagram. Would have been a real boost to the paper if they'd been on our Twitter feed instead. #disappointed*

Text from Bram: *Thanks for letting Irene come to the shower today. She said you went psycho? WTF? You're supposed to be the nice one in the family.*

TWELVE

Socks Over Scepters

Arthur

Text from me to Tessa: *How's my best girl and why isn't she in bed with me right now?*

Tessa: *She's not worthy of the title so she went home where she can't do any more damage.*

Me: *I heard the shower didn't go exactly as planned. Come back so I can make you feel better.*

Tessa: *Thank you, but I really need to be alone right now. I'll call you tomorrow.*

Hmph. I look at Dexter. "That'll never do, will it, Dex?"

****

Twenty minutes later, I knock at the door to her parents' house. Xavier is chatting away at my driver, Ben, through the open window of the limo, having hopped out of the Tesla and informed me that the 'perimeter is secure' the moment we arrived.

I wait a bit, then knock again.

When no one answers, I text Tessa.

Mind letting me in? It's chilly out here and I may or may not have gourmet hot chocolate for you.

I stomp my feet, trying to keep them warm while I listen for the sound of her footsteps in the hall on the other side of the door. When she finally answers, she's dressed in her Sponge Bob pajama bottoms and bunny slippers, reminding me of the first night she was at my house. "Hello, sexy. You're looking adorable this evening."

"No, I'm not. I'm a total mess." She shakes her head and dissolves into tears, turning and walking back into the house.

I follow her, wishing I didn't have a hot chocolate in each hand so I could pull her into my arms. Shutting the door with my foot, I toe off my shoes and follow her to the television room, where she's clearly been on an *Outlanders* and celery binge. Celery? That's an odd choice.

She collapses onto the couch, pulling a big, fuzzy blanket onto her lap. "Don't marry me. I'm a horrible, horrible person."

I set the drinks down on the coffee table and seat myself next to her, wrapping an arm around her shoulder and pulling her close. Giving her a kiss on the forehead, I say, "No, you're not. You're the furthest thing from horrible. You just had a bad day is all. And given the circumstances, I think anyone would've cracked."

She lifts her head from off my shoulder and looks at me, her big green eyes filled with tears. "I was just awful. I humiliated myself and my mum when all she wanted to do was show everyone a good time."

"Don't be so hard on yourself. It's my fault, too. I never should've arranged the stupid bridal shower in the first place. It was a terrible idea putting you in a room with all those nasty women."

Tessa nods and sniffles. "That's true, actually. It was a terrible idea."

"I know. I don't know what I was thinking." I give her a little smile, hoping to cheer her up, but it doesn't work. "Where's your mum? I should really apologize to her."

"She left. Both my parents left while I was in the bath. They probably couldn't stand to be in the same house as their hateful daughter."

I gently tilt her head so it's resting on my shoulder, then rub her arm. "Don't say that. I'm sure they just had plans they forgot to tell you about. Besides, I don't think anyone can really blame you for losing it today, not with everything your mum was doing and saying about you."

"Even still, all I did today was prove that I have no class at all."

"That's ridiculous. So, you had a few sharp words for your mother. For God's sake, she had you dressed in something used to wipe your arse and was giving out gift cards for donuts."

"Oh, God, the Princess Dowager must be so disappointed with how I conducted myself."

"I doubt it. I'm sure she understood. She knows what kind of pressure you're under."

Tessa lifts her head off my shoulder. "What did she tell you?"

"Nothing. I haven't spoken to her this afternoon."

"Then who..." She tilts her head, a sudden look of understanding crossing her face.

I'm about to be in a lot of trouble, aren't I? "Brooke called me as soon as the shower ended."

Letting out a big puff of air, Tessa looks up at the ceiling, blinking quickly, clearly trying to stop herself from crying again. "Why would she do that?"

"Because we're friends. And just so you know, she would very much like to be your friend as well. In fact, when she phoned to tell me what happened, she told me to rush to your side with some hot chocolate and comfort."

"So, this was all *her* idea?"

"Yes, which should prove that she cares about your well-being."

"She and I are *not* friends, Arthur, no matter what she wants you to think."

"If you just give her a chance, I think you'll find she can be a very loyal ally to you. She may even be able to help you navigate this new life, since Arabella doesn't seem willing."

Tessa stares at me for a moment, and I know she's got something on the tip of her tongue that she's not sure she wants to say. "Arthur, be careful with Brooke. She has less-than-innocent motives when it comes to you."

"No, she doesn't. She has a boyfriend. An accountant from London. It sounds like things are quite serious between them." Okay, so I may have stretched the truth on that one just a wee bit, but it really will do no one any good if Tessa feels threatened by Brooke, especially when I have absolutely no interest in the good doctor in the first place.

"I think I need to be alone right now," Tessa says, rubbing her eyebrow in the way she does when she's really angry.

"I know you had a pisser of a day, but is it really a reason to ruin what is the rarest of occasions—us having an evening free together?"

Sighing, Tessa says, "I'm trying really hard not to start an argument right now, Arthur, but honestly, I'm at my wits' end, and your unflinching trust in Brooke isn't helping matters."

"Whatever Brooke's motives may be, I'm glad she called me so I could be here for you in spite of your disappearing act."

"Well, of course she would call you." Tessa stands and crosses the room, presumably to get away from me. "Today was a victory for her. She got to prove how much better she is than me. She even beat me at being a stupid toilet paper bride. *She* won the donut card, Arthur."

Women are a wee bit complicated, no? "I'll take you for donuts right now if that's what you want."

"It's not about the donuts!" she barks

"There's no need to raise your voice at me. I came over to help, but if you're not interested in feeling better, I'll leave so you can get back to sulking for the evening." I stand and stare at her for a long moment, waiting for her to stop me. She just stares at me until it's clear that she has no intention of changing her mind.

I give her little nod. "Goodnight, then." I stride to the door, then turn and call back to her, "Oh, and I've been overfeeding Chester, so he's almost out of food."

I walk out the front door and jog down the steps. Xavier, who is still standing on the sidewalk yakking at Ben, apparently impervious to the cold, stops talking when he sees me and his face falls. This is one of those moments in which I have to admit it truly sucks to be surrounded by staff twenty-four hours a day. He hurries to open the back door, but I beat him to it. I'm just about to climb in when Tessa's voice stops me.

"Arthur. I'm sorry. Can you just come back inside so we can talk?"

I turn and stare at her a moment, and the look on her face starts to dissolve my pride.

"Please?" she asks.

I nod and shut the door to the car, then follow her into the house. As soon as the door closes, she looks up at me, tears filling her eyes as it all come spilling out. "I'm fucking everything up, just like I knew I would. Everyone is mad at me, Nikki can barely stand to look at me, I've driven my parents away with my nastiness, your sister absolutely hates my guts. And you should have seen the look on Grace next door's face. Even Cousin Rose scoffed at me when she was leaving today. And I'm so fucking hungry, I can hardly stand it. I haven't eaten a proper meal in weeks, and to be completely honest, I basically hate everyone who's eating anything other than vegetables. And no matter how much I starve myself, I'm pretty sure I'm not going to be spectacular in the way the entire kingdom needs me to be when I walk down the aisle."

"What in the fuck are you talking about? Why are you starving yourself?"

"Because if I'm not an absolute stunner, the entire fabric of our society is going to fall apart and relationships everywhere will break down and the birthrate of Avonia will be reduced to nothing."

"Who in the hell told you that?"

"Baz." She sniffs. "And he's not wrong because, if I'm anything short of perfection, I'll never win over the people and they'll forever believe that I'm the biggest mistake you've ever made."

My blood fills with rage. "Baz! He's a tiny little dickhead with a Napoleon complex. Don't listen to a word he says. Let him sort out the catering for us and mail out the invitations, and let's be done with him."

Tessa shakes her head. "But what if he's right?"

"He's not. There's no 'what if' about it, so just forget him." Inside, I'm seething with a desire to find and kill Baz, but if I'm honest, I'm also a teeny bit pissed at Tessa for believing this shit. It takes every ounce of patience to manage my reaction. "You listen to me. Who are you marrying on May seventh?"

"You."

"That's right. *Me*. Not Baz or anyone else in the country. And I, for one, love you exactly the way you are. You're perfect."

"No, I'm not."

"To me, you are. Do you know what will happen to these gorgeous breasts of yours if you lose weight?"

"They'll shrink a little." She shrugs.

"Or even a lot possibly. Do you know how rare perfect tits are?"

She rolls her eyes in lieu of an answer.

"Unicorn-rare, so when you're gifted with a set like this, you don't mess with it."

She cracks a tiny smile, then shakes her head. "Idiot."

"Yes, I'm your idiot." Suddenly, I'm beginning to understand all the pressure Tessa has been operating under for these past few weeks. I pull her in tight for a long hug, inhaling the scent of her shampoo. "I can't believe all this has been rolling around in your head and you haven't told me. What does that say about me?"

"Nothing. It just says I wanted to handle it on my own so I wouldn't burden you with all this crap."

I pull back a bit and reach one hand up to touch her cheek. "Well, stop it already, because if we're going to have a life together, we're going to face a thousand Bazes. The only thing that's going to hold us together is if we talk and make damn well sure that the other one knows what's going on inside."

Tessa's face relaxes finally, and the look of panic leaves her eyes. She nods, tears spilling from her eyes that I wipe away with my thumbs. "We have to stick together, Tess. You and me, okay?"

"Okay."

"Good girl." I give her a gentle kiss on the lips. "Now let's get some pasta into you."

"Yes, please."

Half an hour later, we're seated at the island in her parents' kitchen, swirling spaghetti onto our forks, knees touching. Tessa is on her second bowl of pasta, and I'm more than a little impressed at how much she's managing to put away. "Christ, you really must have been starving. The pot's almost empty."

She just nods and shovels another forkful into her mouth, then has a sip of red wine.

"Feel better?" I ask when she's done.

"Much." She closes her eyes and smiles.

"Excellent, because I'm here to make you feel better, you know." I lean over and kiss her behind her ear.

"And you're so good at it."

"Yes, I bloody well am." I spin her stool to face me, then plant lingering kisses up her neck to that little spot that makes her lose her mind. She makes that moaning sound I knew was coming, then I pull her onto my lap. The look on her face tells me I'm about to get very, very lucky. It doesn't take long before our clothes are on the floor and she's on the counter with me in front of her, ready to go. The moment is cut short by the sound of the front door opening and the voices of her parents spilling down the hall.

"No, Evi, it was not 1984, it was 1982," Ruben says.

I panic and yank Tessa off the counter and onto the floor, then scramble to find my clothes. I've managed to get as far as one sock when her dad enters the kitchen. *Oh, fuck. Why the fuck did I start with a fucking sock?*

Tessa ducks down behind the counter while I stand like an idiot, covering my scepter with my shirt as her dad glares and balls up his fists. Evi is next, not noticing us at first, but clearly sounding irritated by her husband, who's blocking the doorway.

"Out of the way, you old poop. I want to make a tea."

She pushes past him, lets out a little yelp, then gives me a quick once-over. *Oh, shoot me now.*

Tessa, who has managed to get her bra on, tugs her shirt over her head and stands, saying, "Did you go out for dinner?"

Evi's face goes completely cold, and she says to me, "Tell your fiancée we were at Lars and Nina's."

She turns and leaves the room, followed by Ruben, who's muttering something about, "in my own bloody kitchen. Where I eat my food, no less."

THIRTEEN

Canned Christmas Muzak and Cinnabon Sweets

Tessa

"I should go," Arthur says as he scrambles to get the rest of his clothes on.

Disappointment fills my entire body. "I don't want you to."

"And yet, I must. You and your mum clearly need to have a big talk," he says, giving me a quick peck on the forehead, "And after what your parents just walked in on, I don't think I'll be able to face them for another few years."

"That couldn't have gone worse, could it have?"

Arthur sighs. "Not really. At least if we'd finished, we'd have *that* to feel good about."

I swat Arthur on the abdomen. "You're such a...man."

"Thanks. Now, go sort everything out with your mum. Maybe you can sneak over to my place later to finish what we started."

I nod and give him a light kiss on the lips, knowing that he's right, even though I wish he wasn't. "Okay. I'll see what I can do."

"I'll wait up for you."

We linger in the tiny foyer for a bit, missing each other already. When he opens the door, a blast of cold air rushes in. Reality.

I watch as his limo pulls away, then sigh and go find my mum. She's not in the TV room with my dad, so I know she's gone up to bed already. Dad looks up from the sports highlights when I walk into the room; his expression says everything he's thinking.

"I know. I'm going to go look for her to apologize."

"It better be a good one, mind you. You've gone and hurt her more than I've ever seen."

"I know."

When I knock on the door to their bedroom, I get no answer. I try again, then open it, quietly calling, "Mum, I came to apologize."

I see the shape of her lying in her bed, facing the other wall, but she doesn't move.

"Mum," I whisper. "Are you asleep?"

I wait for a long time before I give up. "I'm really sorry I treated you so badly today. I had no right to talk to you that way."

When she doesn't respond, I go back to my room and shut the door, crawling under the covers. I text Arthur and tell him not to wait up, then fall into a deep pasta coma.

****

"Is she still not talking to you?" Nikki asks as we examine some scarf and hat sets in Borgman's. She's agreed to a shopping date as phase two of the 'making it up to Nikki' plan.

I shake my head, running my fingertips along the soft wool. "Not a word. No texts. She hasn't even left one of those awful little notes on the kitchen counter."

"Wow. She must be really hurt." Nikki tries on a purple hat that clashes horrifyingly with her turquoise hair, then looks in the mirror and takes it off.

"Pretty sure that when she came and found Arthur and me...you know...it just made her think that the whole thing meant nothing to me."

"I can see why she'd come to that conclusion."

"Me, too, even though it wasn't that way at all." I turn the price tag over on a pair of leather gloves, then flip it back quickly, my cheeks warming at the fact that I can't afford to buy Christmas gifts for everyone on my list.

Xavier, who's standing a couple of feet behind me, tapping his foot to "Santa Baby," says, "Did you see the sales table over there? Forty percent off."

He points across the store and nods.

"Thanks, love." Nikki grins at him, then tugs me by the arm to take me over to check it out.

"Sometimes I think he can read my mind," I whisper. "It's a little creepy."

"I hope to God he can read mine." She glances back at him, then makes an 'mm-hmm' sound.

"Your mum would love this!" Nikki holds up a robin's-egg-blue cardigan.

I check the price, then shake my head. "She would, but my wallet won't. Too bad I couldn't have rented that Chanel dress for the shower." I sigh, suddenly feeling exhausted even though we've only been at the mall for twenty minutes. "Or I should have just wore one of my old dresses. The damn thing ended up covered in arse-wipe anyway."

She fixes me with a steely stare. "Try not to complain too loudly. You're going to be rich as sin in, like, five months."

"Sorry, I know I shouldn't be whining. It's just hard for me to wrap my head around that little possibility." We stroll in the direction of the store's exit, and as soon as we step out of the shop and into the crowded mall, "Santa Baby" gives way to canned Christmas Muzak.

"Possibility? What? Are you going to run out on him before the wedding?"

"No, but it's just hard for me to actually believe we're going to end up married, you know? I haven't exactly had the best luck with men up to now."

"Well, you hit the lotto this time." She points to The Gap, but I shake my head.

"Maybe I can postpone Christmas until June."

Nikki stops and looks at me for a moment, tilting her head like a curious kitten. "What's *really* wrong?"

"What do you mean? I've just been whining for the past half-hour."

"No, there's something else bugging you."

I raise one eyebrow. "You mean besides being broke, being stuck on the announcements desk, having my own personal hate club, having a mother who can barely look at me, and future in-laws who would love to see my head on a spike?"

"Yes, other than all those things. There's something else on your mind. Don't think I can't tell, bitch. Now out with it."

I glance behind me to see if Xavier is within hearing distance, then decide to go ahead and spill it. "I know I shouldn't let this get to me, I mean I really do know it. I know Arthur is absolutely in love with me, and this is totally crazy for me to worry about..."

"But..." Nikki says.

"But I have a really bad feeling about his friendship with Brooke Beddingfield."

We both stop in front of the Cinnabon without discussing it and get in line.

"Hmm. What has he told you about their relationship?"

"That they really are just old friends, and any speculation on their relationship turning into more is just that. Speculation. Oh, and he said he's never been attracted to gingers anyway."

"But that *particular ginger* is most certainly very much attracted to him," Nikki says.

"Right? It's totally obvious. And did you notice at the shower how everybody seemed to be giving her their condolences? It's like she was favoured to win the big beauty contest, and then some horrible hag with warts all over her nose won it instead."

"Who cares what those nasty witches think? As long as Arthur loves you, that's what counts."

A man breezes past and calls back, "Brooke's better!"

I freeze on the spot, and Nikki turns to go after him, but I grab her arm and hold her in place. "Not worth it."

"We can't just let him get away with that!"

"Sure, we can," I say. "The very worst thing we can do is acknowledge it in any way."

"People suck."

We get to the front of the line and order our cinnamon buns. Nikki turns to Xavier to see if he wants anything, and he quickly shakes his head no and then says, "Those rolls have eight hundred and eighty calories in them. It would take the average person over two hours of running to burn it off."

There's an audible groan amongst the people in line, and after we pay, I give them a sheepish look while Nikki and I walk away with our spoils.

"The thing is," I say as Nikki manages to snag an empty table for two. "It *does* matter what they think. If I can't get those people to approve of me, at least his own sister, eventually their opinions of me will start to erode Arthur's."

Nikki shakes her head while licking her fingers, having just swallowed an enormous bite. "You're not giving him enough credit. I mean, I don't know your man that well—which you need to fix, by the way—but I'd say he seems like someone who isn't likely to follow the crowd."

"You're right. I should stop worrying."

"Oh, no. I didn't mean you should stop worrying. When it comes to that Brooke bitch, *worry*."

****

We drop Nikki off at her flat an hour later, both of us having given up on Christmas shopping as soon as the crowd level hit what we call 'DEFCON 5' in which all the toddlers who need naps start to loudly protest the fact that they're still being dragged around in heavy wool coats and big boots while their mums 'pop into just one more shop, darling.' When we park in front of her place, she pats me on the knee. "Well, that was fun."

"No, it wasn't. I was a complete bore the entire time."

"True, but I'd rather be bored with you than having fun with anyone else."

"Aww, thanks, hon."

She smiles, and the look on her face says she has something in mind already. "Plus, I figured out phase three."

Uh-oh. I don't like the sound of this.

"You're going to agree to go on a proper hens' weekend before the wedding. Somewhere really fun, like London or maybe Vegas." Her eyes light up with excitement.

I open my mouth to turn her down, but she holds up one finger and presses it to my lips to stop me from talking. "Do not say no to this. I know Vegas is a stretch with the flight time and trying to get time off work, but please don't make me miss out on our last hoorah before you settle into domestic bliss. It's a once-in-a-lifetime thing, and because you've been such a shit friend lately, you pretty much owe it to me to do this. And I know, I know, you're broke. But that's what credit cards are for. You can just pay the minimum balance until after the wedding and then pay the whole thing off."

She keeps her finger over my mouth, so when I talk my words are muffled. "Nikki, I can't rack up an enormous credit card bill and expect Arthur to pay it for me."

"Sure you can." She finally drops her hand. "Besides, to him this will be nothing—a few hundred for airfare and your share of the hotel. He probably has that much in loose change under his couch cushions. And don't think he's not gonna go off and have some fabulous stag do with all the other dukes. They'll probably take a private jet to Vegas and spend the entire time making it rain cash at a strip club."

She opens the back door of the car and slides out before I can say anything, then leans her head back in and says, "It's going to be epic. Trust me."

I find myself smiling at the thought of an epic girls' weekend. "It might be kind of fun to go somewhere where nobody knows who I am for a couple of days."

"That's my girl!" Nikki slams the door before I can say anything else and hurries up the steps to her building.

I settle myself back into the seat, a sense of excitement coming over me at the thought of escaping my family, my job, and my troubles for an entire weekend. But then my mind wanders to work and the dress fittings and that whole fitting into the dress thing, and I realize I don't actually know if I'll even be able to find more than a few hours for a hens' night, let alone a whole weekend. Still, it would be nice...

My phone buzzes, and I see Hazel has sent me an email.

Tessa,

You will be pleased to know I'm pulling you off the announcements desk. The paper has been gifted thousands of photos from Paul Downey's widow. He was the official photographer for The Globe from 1972 through 2000. It's a rare find, indeed, but they're horribly disorganized, and I'll need you to go through them all and organize them by date, event, as well as importance.

I trust that you'll be able to complete this task before Christmas, as I'd like to use them in a 'Look Back' piece for New Years.

Best,
Hazel

I sigh loudly. "Xavier, can you please turn around and take me to the office?"

****

"This is Veronica Platt at the ABNC news desk with another edition of *Tessa Watch*. The future queen was seen browsing around at the mall today and dining on an enormous treat from Cinnabon. We'll have exclusive photos and footage, as well as fashion critic Nigel Wood, who joins us to analyze Ms. Sharpe's wardrobe choice right after headline news."

****

I walk through the door to my parents' home, dog-tired after another fourteen-hour day down at the paper. It's well after ten at night, and I'm surprised to see the light is on in the kitchen. I take my heels off, my toes breathing a sigh of relief to finally be able to fully stretch out, then make my way towards the kitchen with Mr. Whiskers wrapping himself around my ankles, begging for me to pick him up.

"Okay, here we go." I reach down, and the cat jumps into my arms and rubs his face against my cheek. When I round the corner, I see my mum sitting at the kitchen table, sipping some tea and staring out the window into the darkness.

"You're up late," I say, flopping into a chair across from her. I feel a pang in my heart when I look at her, because things have still not got back to normal since the wedding shower.

She gives me a slight nod and says, "Couldn't sleep."

We sit for a couple of minutes, listening to the second hand on the wall clock. All I want to do is drop into bed for twelve hours, but having a moment alone with my mum is a rare occurrence, so I decide it's better to make use of it than let the opportunity slip by. "Mum, about the wedding shower..."

She shakes her head. "It's fine, Tessa. We really don't need to talk about it."

"We *do* need to talk about it. I can't stand this horrible distance between us any longer." I reach out and touch her hand. "I'm so sorry for how I treated you that day. I had no right to talk to you like that, no matter how hungry I was."

"I'm not upset about that anymore, I promise. At first I was hurt, but now I'm just trying to learn to accept that I'm going to lose you." She blinks back tears.

"You're not going to lose me. I'll be living twenty minutes from here."

"Not true." She sighs. "When Lars got married, I knew I would lose him. You lose your sons when they get married because, when it comes to family, the woman always leads the way and she'll tend to lead it towards her own people. And the same thing happened with Noah. But I didn't mind because I always thought I would have my Tessa. I just assumed you would meet some nice young man, get married, maybe find a house a few blocks from here, have a couple children of your own, and raise them the way your father and I raised you." She smiles wistfully. "But over the last few weeks, I've come to realize that I'm going to lose you like I lost Lars and Noah."

"Oh, Mum..." A lump forms in my throat, choking out my words.

"No. It's okay. You can't help but be caught up in his family, in his way of doing things. It's how it has to be if you're going to survive your new life. And I'm happy for you. I truly am. You're going to get to live a life so much larger than anything I had imagined for you." Tears fill her eyes, and she reaches across the table and touches my cheek. "It's a good thing. Arthur is a very good man. But it means I need to let go of the dream I had for you since the first time I held you in my arms. Because you're going to trade it in for something so much better. I know it sounds silly but, in a strange way, I'm grieving."

Tears fill my eyes, and I nod quickly, holding her hand on my cheek. "It doesn't sound silly. The truth is, I'm terrified of all of this. There are moments when I wish Arthur was something else—a mechanic like Dad, or a pharmacist, or...anything else than what he is. I'm terrified I won't be able to become who I need to be. But I'm equally scared of becoming her and forgetting who I once was."

"Me, too."

Me, too? Isn't she supposed to tell me there's no way that'll happen, and I'll never change?

"I'm afraid you'll be walking a tight rope for your entire life, but one with great rewards along the way."

Well, that wasn't very comforting, now was it?

****

It's almost lunchtime on Thursday, and I'm standing in the boardroom at *The Weekly Observer* office, staring at the incredible mess I've made. Stacks of photographs cover every inch of the table, the chairs, and the floor, allowing me only a very small space in which to make my way around the table.

I've been working on this project for the last several days now, and there doesn't seem to be an end in sight. Trying to organize these first by year, then by subject is proving to be a hair- pulling experience. It doesn't help that my mind keeps wandering to the massive wedding preparation list I have waiting for me when I get off work every day. Unlike most brides, I need to familiarize myself with twelve different types of forks, spoons, and knives for any dining experience I should find myself in once Arthur and I are married. I also must learn to speak with the eloquence of Grace Kelly, and exactly how one learns to do that, I'm not sure. Then there's dress-fittings with Olivia Paul, finalizing the guest list for the big event, trying to tone my arms (I know, I know, but I still want toned arms), which requires more exercise than I can fit into my schedule. Oh, and I shouldn't forget that with Christmas quickly approaching, I need to find the perfect gifts for my future in-laws, who truly do have everything, on a budget that pretty much only allows for me to make macaroni jewelry for them.

I mean, honestly, what do you buy a woman like Princess Arabella, who can snap her fingers and have any designer in the world appear to make clothing for her? A pair of socks from Old Navy? And it's not like she can use kitchen gadgets or has any need for gardening tools or fancy loose teas.

I open the last box of photos and freeze, a slow smile spreading across my face. I may have just found a way to strike something off my list.

FOURTEEN

Waterloo

Arthur

Today is a day that will require the use of all my years of education and experience in both diplomacy and international relations. The Sharpes and Baz, the tiny, rude wedding planner, are coming back to the palace for the second wedding-planning session. Unbeknownst to Tessa, I'll be sitting in on the entire two-hour meeting to let that little dickhead know exactly how I feel about his suggestion that Tessa starve herself until the wedding.

There's also the matter of the financial aspect of the wedding. This, I shall have to approach lightly so as not to insult my future father-in-law, who has only slightly warmed up to me in the past few weeks. There is absolutely no way he will be able to afford even the booze tab, even if he bankrupted himself to do it. But since this is not exactly something you can say to another man, I shall have to find a way to get him off the hook for the cost of everything while keeping his dignity intact. Tricky business, this.

I collect my notebook and pen and make my way towards the nuptial planning headquarters at the far end of the palace. When I arrive, I see Tessa standing in the corner with her parents, engaged in what appears to be a very tense conversation. Her face lights up when she sees me, and I stride over to them." Good morning, Evi, Ruben."

I shake Ruben's hand and give Evi a kiss on the cheek, at which she blushes a deep red. I wink at Tessa, who I don't need to say good morning to because she spent the night last night for the first time in weeks.

"Artie, glad you're here," Ruben says, showing that, apparently, he's coming around. "We need to sort out how we'll split the cost on this whole thing."

"Yes, indeed. I received the budget earlier this morning from the planning team, so we should be able to figure that all out now."

"Excellent." He nods. "Hate having these things hang over my head. Mum's brought the checkbook in her purse."

"No, I haven't," Evi says. "You said you were bringing it."

"No, I didn't. I asked you to get it when I was on the way out to warm up the van."

"Is that what you were mumbling about while I was on the phone?"

"Well, you're the one who's always saying you can have three conversations at once and never miss a word."

"Not when I'm on the phone with Grace next door," Evi huffs.

Ruben throws his hands up in the air, then drops them to his sides. "Oh, bugger—now I'm going to have to drive all the way home and pick it up."

"No need, Ruben. None of the bills will be paid today anyway, and I believe my assistant, Vincent, has taken care of any deposits that were due already."

Ruben shakes a finger at me. "Now, don't go thinking you can sneak behind my back and pay for this whole affair. I intend to do my part."

"I know you do. You're a man of your word. But the thing is, it's hardly fair for us to split the costs evenly when my family's the one creating ninety-eight percent of the expenses. Plus, you've already paid more than your share of taxes over the years, so in a way, it's like you've been pre-paying for the wedding. What if—for now—you cover Tessa's dress, and then if we end up in a crunch later, we'll come to you for help?"

Ruben stares at me, and for one awful moment I think he's about to get very angry, but then he nods. "You make a good point, Arthur. All right. I'll cover the dress."

A loud clapping sound interrupts our conversation, and one of Baz's minions—the female one—calls out, "Baz is on his way in. Everyone, take your seats please. Let's be ready!"

Oh, I don't think so. Turning to Ruben, I smile. "Let's grab some scones before we sit down."

Ruben grins over at me, catching on immediately. In an act of shared defiance, we deliberately take our sweet time selecting a pastry.

Her voice grows louder. "Baz is coming down the hall. Please, take your seats."

"Sounds like she's starting to panic a little," Ruben says under his breath, giving me a sly grin.

"Well, selecting the right pastry is not a decision that can be rushed, now is it?"

The tall, skinny minion pipes up. "Your Highness, excuse me, but Baz has a very strict no eating rule during meetings."

Baz walks into the room just as he finishes saying this. He stops in his tracks and stares at us.

I give Baz a slight nod. "Yes, well, I have a strict 'always eat during wedding planning sessions' policy, and so does my future father-in-law here. And since we're footing the bill, I'm pretty sure we can do it."

Ruben chuckles a little as he balances two very gooey, enormous treats on a very small plate. By the time the two of us saunter over to the table and sit down, Baz seems to have developed a twitch in his jaw. He stands at the end of the table in front of the whiteboard, with a strange smile on his face. "Your Highness, I didn't realize you'd be joining us today."

"Wouldn't miss it for the world. I've cleared my entire morning." I pull a piece of the warm raspberry scone apart and pop it into my mouth with a grin.

"Okay, people. We're at the three-month mark. If you've bothered to read the packet, you'll know this is the most critical time in wedding planning. We've been through the invitation list, and we've got precisely two weeks to get them sent out. As it stands, we have fourteen-hundred guests on the groom's side and one hundred sixty-eight on the bride's side, although, as of this morning, eighteen more of those people don't look as though they'll pass the vetting process. Because invitations are mailed out ten weeks in advance, my entire team will be on this steadily for the next twelve days. Once we get past mail-out, this wedding is a go. There will be no stopping it at that point."

"Good," I say, "because we have no intention of stopping it."

Baz snaps his fingers, and the skinny minion immediately retrieves a bottle of water and hand towel from his bag. He hands it to his little boss, who dabs at his forehead, then takes a swig of water. "Okay. Guest list is done, so let's move along to the next item."

"The guest list is not settled," I say.

"What's that?"

"I've had a look at the reasons for rejecting many of the guests on the Sharpe side, and I reject your rejection."

Baz opens his mouth, shuts it, then opens it again. "You reject my...you can't reject my rejection. Each person has gone through an extremely thorough vetting process."

"I don't agree with your reasons. Forty-two of them have been cut because of their postal codes."

"Postal codes provide an accurate assessment of income level and can be extrapolated to infer the political stance. Those forty-two people will cause you problems. I can guarantee it."

I raise one eyebrow. "And I can guarantee that *not* including them will create even bigger problems for Mr. and Mrs. Sharpe, so I'm willing to take a bullet on this one."

"You very well might," he says with a smug smile.

"It's a risk I'm willing to take. Add them back to the list."

"Fine." Baz nods to the female minion. "The next item on the agenda is an update on the bride's weight issue, but I can see by looking that she's made very little progress so far." He wrinkles up his nose and stares down at her.

I slide my plate in front of her and say, "Darling, what say you finish this for me? I'm not as hungry as I thought I was."

Tessa grins over at me and takes a bite of the scone.

Baz nods. "Okay, I see what's happening here. She's gone whining to you about what I said, and now you're pretending she's perfect just the way she is so you won't have to be the bad guy. That's fine. You're paying me to be the bad guy so I can do the job." He turns to Tessa. "Put down the scone. "

"She'll do no such thing. She'll eat what she wants, when she wants. Tessa is absolute perfection exactly the way she is, and I won't have anyone—even the world's second foremost wedding planner—telling her she needs to starve herself."

"You're making a very big mistake, Your Highness." Baz closes his iPad case and makes to leave.

"No, you're the one making the big mistake. How long do you think it will take for me to convince all my single, rich, influential friends that you're incompetent?"

He stops where he is and glares at me.

"I *will* do it, Sebastian. My preference would, of course, be for us to resolve this little matter in a way that's satisfactory to me and to Tessa so that you continue your work. But if that's not possible, we'll gladly go in another direction."

I watch as his nostrils flare. He stares at me for a long moment, then opens his iPad case and says, "Item number three, final menu selection."

Oh, I am so getting lucky later...

****

"That." Pant. "Was." Pant. "Fucking amazing." I try to roll off Tessa, but she pulls me back down and kisses me some more. When she finally lets me go, I lie on my back and grab a tissue so I can dispose of my heir-stopper. "Uh-oh."

"What uh-oh?" she answers lazily.

"It's gone."

"What's gone? Your brain? Because mine is nowhere to be found at the moment." She sighs happily.

"The condom."

"What?" Tessa sits up quickly. "What do you mean it's gone?"

"You know how you kept me in there for more delicious snogging? I think by the end, I was...worn out and..."

"Oh, my God! Are you serious? It's still *in me*?"

"Yes, I believe so."

She reaches under the sheet and wiggles around for a moment, her tongue sticking out over her top lip. After waiting for what feels like an hour, I say, "Need some help?"

"No! Definitely not. I can get it."

I watch some more while she squirms and grunts a bit, then she finally goes very still. "It's lost."

"Lost? Well, it can't have gone far," I say with a slight chuckle. "Your arms just aren't long enough for you to retrieve it."

"Yes, I gathered that, thanks," she says, now with a slight edge to her voice.

"It's no problem. I can get it." I prop myself up on one elbow and turn on the bedside lamp.

"Shut it off! You can't go...digging around in there with the lights on."

"Well, I'm hardly going to find it in the dark."

"Nope, I can't let you do this. It's too embarrassing. Sorry."

"Would you rather I call one of the maids to help?"

She closes her eyes for a moment and breathes out loudly through her nose, reminding me of an angry bull. Not that I'd ever tell her that.

"Oh, fine. Just get it over with."

I sit up and tug at the sheet to pull it down, but she's got a firm grip on it.

"Do you really need to take the sheet off?"

"Have you forgotten I've spent many a happy hour down there?" I say, gesturing with my head.

"Yes, but not with the lights on...or for condom-removal purposes."

"And yet, the situation does require me to remove a condom, and I imagine you'd prefer me to do it sooner rather than later."

"Okay," she groans.

"Tell you what, cover your face with your hands so you don't have to watch," I say in a light tone as I move to the end of the bed. "Good God, your knees are really locked together."

"They do that at the gynecologist, too."

"Try to relax, Ms. Sharpe. I'll be in and out before you know it."

"That's what he said." She lets out a little laugh.

"Christ, I hope not," I mutter. "Tessa, please try to just let your knees fall to the sides."

I look up at her, and she has her arm slung over her eyes, her cheeks bright pink with embarrassment. Clearly, I'm going to have to ease the tension.

I put on my Attenborough tone and say, "The human male has his work cut out for him. Not only is he dealing with a very skittish female, but time is of the essence. He has just minutes to find the condom before the sperm escapes and impregnates the female. If he doesn't manage to unlock her knees, this could be the moment that sparks a tremendous scandal."

Tessa bursts out laughing, her legs finally relaxing.

Hmm, that was easy. Might as well keep going. "With the female now relaxed, he's in position to retrieve the all-important heir-stopper. He's going to have to go in with a gentle touch and a long reach in order to get the job done."

I keep talking while I do what I have to for another minute or so. Good God, that condom went very far up there. Oh, there it is. "And, jackpot! He's managed to find the elusive condom and will now dispose of all evidence, then open a bottle of Champagne so the pair can forget this awkward incident ever occurred in the first place."

Tessa pulls the sheet up around her. "You can probably knock off the Nature Channel thing now..."

"Righto."

FIFTEEN

Enchanted Castles at Christmas

Tessa

"You're skipping Christmas with your family?" Nikki says into the phone.

"Yes, and I can tell you my parents are none too pleased." I'm currently at my desk in a now empty office. Everyone else has gone for lunch, so I've managed to sneak in a phone call to Nikki.

"Arthur asked me to go to Didsbury to stay at the castle with his family for three days. I really need to get in some face time with Arabella."

"But still, Christmas?"

"I know. I feel horrible. My mum looked so hurt when I told her, but once I explained it, she understood. I think."

"Huh."

"I'm going to make it up to them. I'm making a big brunch on the twenty-seventh."

"Oh, the traditional two-days-after-Christmas-guilt-brunch. How lovely."

"Ha ha."

"Speaking of the hens' weekend, have you figured out when we can go so I can book flights?"

"We weren't—"

"Yes, I know, but if I don't bring it up, you never will," she says. "I can get us a crazy good deal if we go in March."

"Where, exactly, are we going?"

"I thought we said Ibiza."

"No one said Ibiza, which is a terrible idea, by the way."

"Come on. I need some sun and men who've had lots of sun so they have nicely tanned muscles for me to gawk at. The men in England are all so pale and covered up. We might as well just stay here if we're going to London."

"Ibiza is a total party island. Can we at least find somewhere not so...wild?"

"Okay, Granny. I'll see if we can book a river cruise down the Danube."

"Oh, God, you're really going to make this difficult for me, aren't you?"

"A little bit, yes. But you owe me, remember?"

"Owe you? For what?"

"Because you're too busy to hang out, and you're getting all princessy and stuff with your packed schedule and your dress designer and your delicious bodyguard. Tell him I said hi, by the way." She snaps her gum, making a loud popping sound into the phone. "Oh! I just realized Xavier will be coming with us, won't he?"

"No, I'm planning to leave him here. I can't exactly afford to spring for his ticket, and I don't expect Arthur to pay for his trip."

"Are you allowed to leave home without him?"

"Yes. Of course I can. No one outside of Avonia will recognize me, so I'll be quite safe."

"Too bad. Can you imagine him without his shirt on?"

"No, I can't. And I prefer not to." I quickly Google cheap flights to sunny destinations while I talk. "What about Monaco? It's supposed to be lovely there."

"Monaco is for rich, old people. We don't fit into either of those categories. Well, I don't. You, however..."

"I'm neither rich nor old," I say, feeling my hackles go up a bit at the accusation.

"You sure? Did you just hear how you answered me?" Nikki laughs, then puts on a very haughty voice. "I'm neither rich nor old."

"Oh, God, that really did sound..."

"Snooty?"

"I was going to say polished."

"Whatever label you put on it, you don't sound much like Tessa."

Bollocks. I'm about to give in, aren't I? "Fine. We'll go to Ibiza, but not to the nude beaches—and no raves."

"Yay!" she shrieks into the phone. "We're finally going to Spain!"

"And we're not doing one of those booze cruises."

"We can negotiate the terms when we get there."

"That's what I'm afraid of."

"Gotta run. My one o'clock is here."

****

Didsbury Castle is exactly as magical as I expected. It's over seven hundred years old, built from stone and made to last. One could fit at least twenty of this castle in Valcourt Palace, which still leaves it an impressive specimen of architecture. It's been refurnished many times over the centuries, but one thing remains the same—the incredible views of the sea and the shores to the north of the castle, and the gently-sloping meadows to the south. The land up here is vastly different than that near Valcourt. The hills roll to the south as far as the eye can see and, today, are blanketed in white snow with only the odd bare, frost-covered tree to break up the fields.

It's after lunch on Christmas Eve, and Arthur has just finished taking me on a tour of his favourite home. I haven't seen him so excited since the day we got engaged. He leads me quickly from room to room, telling me hilarious tales of his childhood much of which was spent here. We make our way through secret passageways (can you believe they have actual secret passageways?), from room to room while Arthur explains the difference between a palace and a castle.

As it turns out, a castle is built to provide protection in the event of an attack, whereas a palace is more of a luxurious home meant to impress. Unlike the palace, the castle has a homey feel with warm tones in the carpets, draperies and furniture, and is much more casual. Roaring fires have been lit in each of the enormous fireplaces to welcome us.

Dexter, who has made the trip with us in the limo, is fast asleep in front of the fire in the library, where we started and now are ending our tour. But I'm not here to learn about the secrets of Didsbury Castle or even to spend time with the love of my life. I have one objective—to make Arabella like me. Well, not make, more like *encourage* through my thoughtfulness and wit.

When I really think about it, I know it's a tall order. She's not likely going to warm up to me. But maybe, just maybe, by the end of the three days she'll hate me less. King Winston has elected to spend Christmas in Bali this year, having quietly left a few days ago. The dowager drove up with us and has gone to visit an old friend in the village. Arabella, who I suspect could not stomach the thought of making the trip with me, will be here any minute.

"So," I say, wrapping my arms around Arthur, "what's the traditional Langdon family way to spend Christmas Eve?"

"Christmas Eve dinner together, followed by heading into the village for midnight mass. What do the Sharpes do on Christmas Eve?"

"Scrabble tournament. Highly competitive, high-stakes, typically my one chance of the year to beat my brothers at anything."

"So, you fancy yourself quite the Scrabble master, do you?" Arthur grins.

"I'm pretty sure I could take you for a few dollars." I smile.

"I had something else in mind entirely." He gets that gleam in his eye, and I know what he's about to suggest.

"You're thinking strip Scrabble, aren't you?"

He pulls me to him and gives me a big kiss on the lips. "You know me so well."

A light cough coming from the direction of the door interrupts the moment. Arthur and I quickly drop our hands and turn to see who it is. Arabella gives us a little nod. "It looks like I'm interrupting."

"Of course you're not. Happy Christmas." Arthur crosses the room and gives her a big hug.

"Hi, Arabella. Happy Christmas." I try for a warm smile, but not wanting to overdo it, I narrow my lips causing the combination to come out looking like my dermatologist went overboard with the Botox. (Not that I've had Botox, or have a dermatologist, for that matter.) "We were just about to play some Scrabble. Would you like to join us?"

She gives me a hard look and then shakes her head. "I'm afraid I have some emails to return before dinner." With that, she turns and leaves.

I sigh, and my shoulders drop.

Arthur smiles at me. "Don't worry. She'll come around eventually."

"I hope so."

****

Dinner is served in the dining room, which is not to be mistaken for the dining hall, a massive room with a table that seats fifty. The dining *room* is much smaller, with a large stone fireplace currently decorated with Evergreen boughs and ivory pillar candles. Next to the fireplace sits the tallest Christmas tree I think I've ever seen. It stretches up almost to the ceiling and has been fully decorated with muted red and gold decorations prior to our arrival.

The Princess Dowager sits at the head of the table, while Arthur and I sit side-by-side to her right. Arabella is across from us, sucking back Moscow Mules like they're going out of style. The server, Mrs. Potts (yes, that's really her name, and yes, she does somewhat resemble a teapot in her build, but as far as I know does not have a son named Chip), brings out the first course, the traditional fish chowder and freshly baked rolls.

I polish off my pre-dinner wine and look around, wondering if it would be considered rude of me to serve myself another glass. I know I shouldn't, but I really am extraordinarily nervous to be sitting with Arabella again. We haven't spent this much time together since my first night at the palace, when I had only been invited so that Prince Arthur could try to impress my knickers off me and convince me to blog very nice things about the family.

Arthur squeezes my knee with his right hand to let me know he's here. I'm sure the tension coming off me is visible. I pick up my spoon and hold it the way they showed on that YouTube video, lightly resting it on the side of my index finger. I scoop away from me as I dip it in to the soup, then lift and delicately bring it towards my lips.

Mrs. Potts, who is quickly becoming my favourite person on the planet, comes back out and refills my wine. "How's the soup?" she asks.

"Delicious." I nod and thank her for the wine.

She sets another Moscow Mule in front of Arabella, then quickly surveys the table, gives a nod and turns to go, saying over her shoulder, "I thought it must be one of our better batches on account of how quiet it is in here."

When she leaves the room, her words hang in the air, forcing us to face the awkwardness between us.

"So, Arabella, do you have any trips planned over the next couple of months?" Arthur asks.

"No." Arabella dabs at the corners of her mouth with her napkin.

Princess Florence puts her spoon down and stares at her granddaughter for a moment. "You're not still holding a grudge, are you, my dear?"

Arabella shrugs and sips at her drink.

"Sulking is not a good look on you, darling. Neither is piss-drunk. Now, take that sceptre out of your keister and let's try and have a fun Christmas, shall we?"

I feel my cheeks glowing with embarrassment in that way that only happens when you're a child and you're over at a friend's house, and said friend gets in a massive amount of trouble from her parents because the two of you just polished off the last ten cookies in the jar. You know you're to blame as well, but they're only yelling at her, and you can't exactly do anything about it.

"You can't force me to like her," Arabella says quietly. She glances at me, but only for the briefest second before she continues eating her soup. I suddenly lose my appetite. Baz would be very pleased.

****

After dinner, the four of us make our way to the living room. There is another Christmas tree in this room, only this one resembles something a little more like what you would see in a more typical house. It's much shorter for one thing, so you wouldn't need a ladder to put the star on top. It's beautifully decorated, but interspersed are handmade decorations; when I examine them closer, I see that these were made by Arthur and Arabella as children. The sight warms my heart, and for the first time since I arrived, I think we may have more in common when it comes to celebrating Christmas than I originally thought.

Arthur, who was very quiet for most of the meal, announces that we should open our presents before we head into the village for mass. Arabella's eyes light up for a moment, then she seems to remember I'm here, and her face returns to its previous stoic look.

"Splendid idea," Princess Florence says, seating herself in an armchair next to the tree.

"I have a little something for each of you up in my room," I say, feeling my heart in my throat at the thought of giving Arabella her gift. She'll probably toss it in the fire even though it's taken me several hours to make.

"I'll be right back." I try to sound cheerful as I make my way to the door, but part of me wouldn't mind walking right out of the castle, getting in the car, and driving home to my parents' house. Imagine that. I'm *longing* to be with my family.

"Do you need help finding your room?" Arthur asks, following me to the hall.

"No, I'll be fine. I have an excellent sense of direction," I say, grinning because he knows nothing could be further from the truth.

He nods. "Yes, of course you do. Like right now, for instance. You do realize you're heading in the wrong direction?"

I laugh, spinning on my heel. "Obviously. I just wanted to make sure you knew." I lift my chin and start toward the stairs, calling over my shoulder, "See you in a minute!"

I get lost four times before I find my room and twice on the way back, which, if you ask me, is an improvement. My palms are sweating by the time I find the living room, and I hope no one notices the damp patches on the gift-wrapped boxes I'm about to distribute. Christ, I hope this works.

"There you are, dear." Princess Florence smiles up at me. "I was just about to send Arthur to look for you."

"No need. I always find my way, even if it takes me several wrong turns to begin with."

"That's the same for us all, I think," Princess Florence says.

I set my gifts under the tree and wipe my palms on my thighs as discreetly as possible.

"May I start?" Princess Florence says. "I've been waiting for weeks to give you your presents."

Arthur finds her gifts under the tree and hands one to Arabella and one to me, then sits beside me on the couch with his own. "What could this be?" he asks, rubbing his hands together with excitement.

Arabella, who has hers open already, says, "Oh, Gran!" Her face falls. "How to Catch and Keep Mr. Right?"

"You've had such bad luck, I thought this might be a bit of help for you. Now, you two. Go!"

I pull the wrapping off to reveal a book with a picture of a couple in bed on the cover, entitled, *A Working Wife's Guide to a Sizzling Sex Life*. "Oh, wow. Well, this is...thank you. It's very...very..."

"Don't mention it, dear. I know how hard it is for you young women to manage to keep all those balls in the air. This book will help you manage his." She hoots with laughter, and I find myself laughing with her.

When we're done, she turns to Arthur. "You, now. Don't be such a sissy. Open it."

"I'd rather not."

"Open it!" the Princess Dowager insists.

"Yes, Arthur, let's see what you got!" Arabella teases.

I poke him in the arm, getting in on the fun. "Stop being a sissy. Rip that paper off."

Arabella grins at me but then quickly scowls before looking back at Arthur.

Arthur swallows hard, then sighs as he rips the paper off. He shakes his head and says, "How on Earth did you turn into such a dirty old woman?"

Princess Florence snorts out a laugh. "What dirty? I'm just trying to be helpful."

"You most certainly are not. You're trying to embarrass us." He laughs.

"Read the title, Arthur!" Arabella insists. "What's your awful book called?"

"No, I don't think so."

I give him a light slap on the arm. "Read it out loud!"

"Fine. *A Man's Guide to Being a Lover and a Friend: Give Her What She Needs and Keep Her Coming Back for More.*"

"Ooh! I like the sound of that! Thank you, Princess Florence!" I say, trying to stifle a laugh.

"You're very welcome." She winks, and for the first time I feel the tiniest bit relaxed being in the same room as Arabella.

Arthur hands out his gifts next—a baby blue pashmina for his grandmother that he suggests will bring out her eyes, a set of noise-cancelling headphones for Arabella to take on flights, and for me a gorgeous full-length camel hair coat, something I've always wanted but never could afford. When it's Arabella's turn, she hands a gift bag to her grandmother and to Arthur, then mumbles, "I must've left Tessa's present back in Valcourt."

"That's all right, Arabella," I say, attempting a smile in spite of the pang in my chest. "You don't have to get me anything."

I watch as Arthur lifts a very smart cable-knit sweater from his gift bag, and Princess Florence opens a lovely set of bath salts.

"Well, mine are next, I guess," I say brightly. "They're nothing really. Just small."

I hand each of them my presents, then sit back down again on the couch. "It's better if you all open them at the same time. They're all the same. Well, sort of."

I glance between the three of them as they tear off the paper that took me an hour to wrap, then open the boxes.

"What's this?" Arthur asks, picking up the black album.

"I came across these photos at work. They were among hundreds of boxes of photos donated by Paul Downey's widow. I know you probably have thousands of photos, but I thought these, in particular, belonged with..." My voice trails off as I see tears in Arthur's eyes.

He's looking at a photo of himself as a little boy, holding his mother's hand while she smiles down at him. I hear a sob from the Princess Dowager, for whom I've collected an album of candid photos of her with her late husband and her son as a little boy.

"This is absolutely lovely, my dear," she says, smiling through her tears. "This must have taken you hours."

"Not too bad, really. My mum has an entire room devoted to scrapbooking, and she let me use her things."

I look at Arabella, who's wiping her eyes, her shoulders shaking. For her, I have dozens of photos of her mother, Queen Cecily, from the time she was engaged until her untimely death, only two months after Arabella was born. The last photo is a closeup of Cecily kissing Arabella on her forehead.

Arabella looks up at me and nods. "Thank you," she whispers. "I haven't seen any of these."

"You're welcome," I say. "I think you look just like her."

Arabella smiles and nods, then pats the album. "This is truly thoughtful, Tessa."

A warm glow spreads through me, and I know it's corny, but I really do believe miracles are possible, especially at Christmas. I look over Arthur's shoulder while he thumbs through his album, laughing at some photos and growing quiet at others.

"Look how young I was," Princess Florence says. "I almost forgot what perky bosoms I had back then."

****

It's been a long time since I've gone to midnight mass. We used to go when my Grandpa Seth was alive, but after we lost him, we slowly fell out of that tradition as a family. Sitting here now in the wooden pew at the front of the stone church, I have that same cozy, sleepy feeling I had when I was a child. The service is lovely, lit by candles only, with a choir of children who yawn in-between songs. The minister speaks of love and the meaning of Christmas and the importance of family to care for each other in this modern age. I rest my head on Arthur's shoulder a moment and close my eyes, coming dangerously close to falling asleep before I bolt upright.

When the service is over, we stay at the front while the people of the village come by and wish us a happy Christmas. It's a much more relaxed feel here in Didsbury, and the people feel more like friends than loyal subjects. Some of the young men even call Arthur by his first name, and later, when I asked him about it, he explains that these were his childhood friends who couldn't have cared less what his title was, only that he could hit the wicket with the best of them during cricket matches.

I stand back and watch as Arabella chats easily with some of the women, fawning over their little children and laughing about old stories. It's nearly two in the morning by the time we get back to the castle. Arthur and I make our way up the wide wooden staircase together, not caring to pretend we won't be spending the night in the same room.

Something has changed tonight, and it's not just an easing of tensions between Arabella and me. It's so much more. They've let me in further into the fold, sharing some tender and vulnerable moment I never thought I would see. A warm feeling fills my chest when I return in my mind to watching them pore over the albums I made, and us laughing and tearing up over their old memories. As I drift off to sleep in Arthur's arms, I'm filled with a sense of contentment I've never known before and hope never ends.

****

On Christmas morning we wake late, and when we wander downstairs, we're treated to the scents of an amazing breakfast that has been laid out in the dining room. The Princess Dowager is already seated at the table, and Arabella is standing at the side buffet, pouring herself a coffee, and my stomach twists a little as I wonder if she'll still have such a warm feeling toward me.

"Good morning, ladies," Arthur says.

Arabella turns and smiles, not just at him, but at me as well—and I feel myself relax a bit. After breakfast we linger at the table, chatting and laughing, the family clearly happy to have a day without anything scheduled.

Arabella turns to me, giving me a thoughtful look. "What do you do on Christmas Day normally?"

"Well, we open presents in the morning, and then we spend the afternoon relaxing. Our big meal is on Christmas Eve, so all the cooking is done come Christmas Day and we have a fridge full of leftovers for dinner. We usually stay in our pajamas well into the afternoon and watch Christmas movies."

Arabella's face lights up. "That sounds delightful. I've always wanted to watch *Miracle on 34th Street*."

"Ooh, it's one of my favourites."

"I think we've just booked our afternoon." Arabella nods and stands. "Arthur, I'm going to steal Tessa for the next couple of hours."

"Yes, well, just return her the way you found her." He gives me a kiss on the cheek before I get up to go. "I'm afraid I need some time to take care of a few emails, anyway. I'll join you later."

And so, in a way, I get my own Christmas miracle in the form of a future sister-in-law who doesn't despise me. We sit together on the sofa, snuggled up under big, cozy blankets, and watch the movie. When it's over, Arabella shuts the TV off and sighs. "I hope I can find a man like that someday."

I nod, not sure what to say.

She goes on. "I haven't exactly had good luck with men."

"Before I met your brother, I had a real knack for falling for the scummiest men. One of them actually cleaned out my bank account. The last one—the one who caused me to give up on men completely—ended our relationship by getting engaged to someone else after we'd been dating for close to a year. Oh, and then he fired me because he was my boss."

Arabella's eyes grow wide as she listens to my hard-luck history. "I had no idea. I just assumed you were the kind of girl who always had men chasing you."

I shake my head. "What would make you think that?"

"Because you're so pretty and outgoing. It seems to me men are attracted to women like that. They tend to find me rather aloof, I'm afraid."

"I suppose someone in your position would have to learn to be somewhat detached, but surely once a man gets to know you, he would see you're quite different underneath it all."

"I'm afraid I haven't found a man I've let past the wall," she says with a sigh. "Which, as it turns out, has been a good thing, because I seem to have that same knack that you do for choosing the wrong man."

"Well, that's just because there are so many shitty men out there. It's got nothing to do with you, I promise." I smile at her.

"You sound like Arthur. He told me I'm going to have to kiss a lot of frogs. It's not fair, really, as a prince he has women throwing themselves at him everywhere he goes. Princesses aren't so lucky. A lot of men find the money intimidating. It seems like they want a woman who needs them in that way, which I never will. Any time I meet a nice man who I could potentially fancy, I seem to manage to scare him off."

"Then you haven't met the right one yet. The right one will see behind the mask; if not immediately, he'll take the time to look beyond it."

"Is that what happened with you and Arthur? My brother's mask is even more well affixed than mine."

I smile, thinking of our first few days together, the immediate attraction I felt for him in spite of wanting to despise him. "I think so. I didn't want to fall in love with your brother. In fact, it was basically the worst thing that could've happened to me at the time. But once I caught a glimpse of who he really is, there was no going back."

"That's beautiful. I'm glad he found you."

"Me, too." I smile. "I mean, it's all sort of terrifying for me. I don't exactly fit into this world, but I'm going to keep trying because I know he's worth it."

"He is." She says with a nod. Then she gets a little gleam in her eye. "And as shocking as it is, so are you."

I laugh. "Oh, you really are Arthur's sister."

"I'll take that as a compliment."

"Good, because I didn't mean it in any other way."

Arabella turns her body toward me and curls her knees to her chest. "When did you know he was the right one for you?"

"Oh, that's a tricky one." I glance up at the ceiling, trying to recall the exact moment. And then it comes to me in one giant rush. "It was two weeks into our knowing each other. We went for a walk to your mother's grave, which is a very sad place to fall in love, I suppose. He didn't say very much about your mum, but I could feel the depth of his pain. I know this is going to sound crazy, but in an instant I knew who he was and how he had become *him*. The arrogance, the devil-may-care attitude, it all suddenly made sense. There was this incredible rush of feeling, like I wanted to protect him and love him and heal every one of his wounds all at once."

Arabella's face fills with emotion. "That's lovely, really."

A knock at the door interrupts, and when I turn my head, I see Arthur walking towards us. "I thought Christmas movies were supposed to have happy endings? You both look like you're ready to cry."

"We were talking about you," Arabella says.

"Well, that explains it." Arthur flops down on the couch next to me. "I'm a sorry case, aren't I?"

I reach over and tickle his abs with my fingers until he squirms. "Very, but I'll stick around anyway."

SIXTEEN

Slugs, Poo, and other Impolite Dinner Conversation

Arthur

On Boxing Day, the sun shines brightly against the blue sky as we ready ourselves to return to Valcourt. By the time we set off, it seems as though like Tessa and Arabella are old friends and it feels like all is right with the world. Grandmum is staying at the castle for another few days to visit friends. Arabella elected to get a ride with us back home, and the two of them have been having a grand time swapping stories and making fun of me along the way.

Arabella takes great pleasure in sharing a story about a time when I was ten and ended up with a slug on my arse when we went for a swim up in a pond just outside the village.

"I'll never forget it, as long as I live." Arabella laughs so hard, tears spring to her eyes. "This hideous slug pulsing away on his right butt cheek while Arthur screamed like a girl until our nanny managed to remove it with some salt."

"Oh, please! Don't try to pretend that you wouldn't have lost your mind had it been you," I say, poking Arabella on the shoulder. "Remember when you found a mouse in the stables and you got so frightened you threw up?"

I bust out laughing, and it takes me half a minute to realize I'm laughing alone. I stop and look at them. "What? Why isn't that one funny?"

Tessa stares at me with a poker face. "It's a mouse. That's not funny at all."

"Come on. It's hilarious. She threw up right on the poor little thing."

They both wrinkle up their noses at me and shake their heads a little. "Not funny," Arabella says. "Not funny at all, really."

"Yes, Arthur," Tessa adds, "you should really practice better judgment than that if you're going to be king someday."

I stare at them, shocked at how quickly the mood in the limo has changed and how fickle my audience has become. Then I notice a little gleam in Arabella's eyes, and when I glance back at Tessa, I see she's trying to stifle a laugh. "Are you two..."

They both burst out laughing, falling all over their seats as I sit stunned. I watch them for a moment as they giggle and say things like, 'Did you see his face just now? Hee hee.' 'Priceless. Oh, we got him good.'

"How is it possible that after only one day of hanging around together, *I'm* now on the outside, when I'm the entire reason the two of you know each other in the first place?"

Tessa shrugs. "Women are funny that way."

Arabella nods. "Sorry, brother—this is likely how it's going to be from now on, so you'll just have to get used to it."

I shake my head and mumble something about not wanting to get used to having my jewels busted on a regular basis, but inside I feel very pleased at how things have turned out.

As we near the city, Tessa sits up straight in her seat and says, "Arabella, you should come with us to my parents' house for dinner tonight. They've decided to have an extra meal tonight since I was away."

"Could I?" Arabella's eyes light up.

Oh, Christ. That's all I need, for Tessa's idiot brothers to be staring down Arabella's top while we pass the gravy. "She can only come if Bram has a girlfriend at the moment."

"Who's Bram?" Arabella says.

"He's my brother." Tessa rolls her eyes at me. "She would never be interested in him. She has far better taste than that, I can tell already."

"Don't be so sure."

****

An hour later, I find myself overruled and watch my sister, who has ended up sitting next to Finn, the youngest of the Sharpe boys, who is finishing architecture school this year. The way her cheeks turn red when he addresses her causes a sense of protective rage to simmer inside me as I try to maintain a conversation with her sister-in-law, Nina, who seems intent on explaining to me at great length the horrors of breastfeeding while one is suffering from mastitis.

"Sounds just awful," I say, trying not to look while she makes a circle with one finger around her right nipple to illustrate the extent of the infection. "I hope it goes away very soon. We should really try to find a cure for that. Maybe there's someone at the women's health foundation I could talk to."

"Would you?" Nina grins at me as though I'm a hero. "Noah, did you hear that? Arthur's going to find a cure for mastitis."

Noah raises one eyebrow. "Is he now? Have you been to medical school, then, Arthur?"

"No, I only meant—"

Lars pipes up from down at the end of the table. "Why exactly would you bother trying to find a cure for something we already know how to treat?"

"What's mastitis?" one of Tessa's nephews asks from the kiddie table.

"It's when a mum's breasts get all gooey when she's feeding her baby," one of the other kids answers.

"Jesus Christ, can we not talk about breastfeeding at the table?" Ruben says.

"Why not, Dad? It's the most natural thing in the world," Finn says, clearly trying to impress Arabella with his open-mindedness about women's health issues.

"That may be, but so is taking a poo, and we don't talk about that at dinner, now do we?" Ruben says, shutting down the conversation.

"Can you pass the sausage rolls?" Bram asks. "I don't think the lovely Princess Arabella has had a chance to try one yet."

"I offered her one earlier, but she doesn't like them," Finn says, an edge in his voice.

Oh, for fuck's sake. They're not both after her, are they? I try to get Tessa's attention so she can put a stop to this, but she's engaged in a very deep conversation with her mum, who wants to hear every detail of our reaction to the photo albums Tessa made for us.

Why exactly did I want Tessa and Arabella to be on good terms?

SEVENTEEN

One-Legged Men Should Not Dance on Bar Tops

Tessa

Email from Rory Stone, Assistant to Sebastian
RE: Elocution Instruction
Tessa,
I need you to contact me immediately regarding your elocution lessons. If you have not made arrangements to have someone from the palace provide you with instruction, you will need to book a date with me right away. I have very little time, but Sebastian has grave concerns in this regard, especially now that you have decided not to cooperate as far as your body mass index goes.
Yours,
Rory

Reply to Rory Stone
RE: RE: Elocution Instruction
Dear Rory,
Thank you for your interest in my elocution lessons. Please assure Sebastian that I am receiving intensive ongoing instruction via palace staff, in addition to my own research and careful study of the subject, so there is no need for me to take up your time.
Warmest wishes,
Tessa Sharpe

****

"What are you watching, Tessa?" My dad stands at the doorway to the television room, holding a beer, clearly wanting to watch football. It's Sunday afternoon, and I know there's a game on by now.

"*My Fair Lady*. You know, the one with Audrey Hepburn."

He seats himself on the couch next to me.

"I remember this one. I'm surprised you'd be interested in it, though." He cracks his beer open and takes a swig.

"It's research," I say, jotting down a note about posture that Professor Higgins gives Eliza Doolittle.

"For what?" my dad asks as he plants himself in his armchair.

"For being a princess. I'm supposed to be taking some princess classes, but I haven't had time, so I figured I'd cheat a little."

"Huh."

"*My Fair Lady*! Oh, why didn't you tell me this was on?" My mum hurries in and sits next to me on the couch.

We watch in silence for about twenty minutes. "Is he worth all this?" my dad says suddenly.

My head snaps back a little, and I turn to him. "Of course he is. He's incredible."

"He's just a man, like the rest of us," my dad says.

"Ruben, he's a *prince*," my mum cries. "Worth it?! She'll never have to even *think* about money again, let alone worry about it. She'll never have dishpan hands or dirt under her fingernails."

My dad shakes his head and stares at the telly. "Still seems to me that she's being asked to give up a lot for all of it."

A sense of righteous indignation comes over me. "Arthur hasn't asked me to do any of this. He hasn't asked me to change in any way. I'm doing this so I won't make a complete arse of myself wherever I go."

"Fair enough, then," my dad says with a small shrug. "Just don't go and get all dull on me, okay? You're an incredible girl. I'd hate to see those people steal your spark."

I swallow the lump that forms at the back of my throat. "I won't. I just want to learn enough so I can fit in with the blue bloods when I need to."

My dad nods. "Well, in that case, I suspect you'll need to do more than just watch this movie."

"Of course I will. I plan to re-watch *The Crown* next."

"That'll do it." He stands and pats me on the shoulder before he leaves the room. "Yup."

****

I've been spending a lot more time at the palace since Christmas, both as Arthur and Arabella's guest. Arabella has very kindly offered to coach me in elocution and posture and has patiently been going over the dos and don'ts of fine dining, which is a huge relief, since they don't really give the details on *The Crown*.

Today I'm in Arabella's apartment, and she's giving me a quick lesson on greeting visiting dignitaries before Arthur and I go out for dinner. I had no idea how complicated the simple act of saying hello could be, but it turns out there is a mind-boggling set of rules about where to stand and customs to follow, which cultures are insulted by bowing, and which are insulted by a lack of bowing, who should speak first (the answer is *never me*), and how to respond appropriately to a wide variety of greetings. With only two months until the wedding, I'm feeling a great deal of pressure to get all this straight.

"When all else fails, say nothing and smile." Arabella nods confidently. "You'll be fine."

"Have you ever seen me in public?"

Arabella laughs and pats my arm, reminding me of a young version of her grandmother. "You'll be fine. You may have the odd mishap, but who cares? It's endearing."

"Tell that to the #IHateTessa people."

"Oh, yes. I saw that. Awfully shitty, whoever they are. If only there was a way to stop them."

"We'd have to know who they are first." I sigh. "And the chances of doing that are slim to none."

She looks up at the ceiling for a moment, then says, "I wonder if that's true?"

"What?"

A knowing look crosses her face, and she says, "You leave it with me. I may have a way of figuring it out. Now, back to your posh lessons: I have some time this weekend. If you'd like, we could go over everything again."

"Oh, I wish I could, but my friend Nikki is taking me on a hens' weekend."

"Hens' weekend? I've never gone on one of those. Are they *so fun*? They sound so fun." She positively beams with excitement as she waits for my answer.

"Well, I've only been on one before, and it was a little bit on the wild side. We ended up in Amsterdam, and I'm afraid the bride-to-be lost her passport. Oh, and her virginity. Whoops!"

"Sounds delightful." The look on her face says what she's far too polite to allow to come out of her mouth. She would love to come along.

I'm torn, knowing Nikki is looking forward to having me all to herself without any of my new people to distract from our last hoorah together. But on the other hand, this sweet young princess is staring up at me, hoping to have a regular-girl experience for the first time in her life. As my future sister-in-law and new friend, I feel as though I can hardly say no. "You wouldn't be free this weekend to come along, would you?"

"Oh, no, I couldn't possibly impose. It just sounds like fun is all." She shakes her head and does her best not to look disappointed.

"You wouldn't be imposing. It would be wonderful to have you. I just have to check and see if we can get a plane ticket for you."

"Plane ticket? Where are you going?"

"If you can believe it, I've been talked into going to Ibiza."

"Oh, I love it there! You'll have the best time," she says, then her face grows serious. "Not to nag, but I'm assuming you've cleared this with Vincent and arranged to have your bodyguard with you?"

Oh, bugger. "No. I didn't think we'd need him since I don't think anyone will recognize me where we're going."

"They'll never let you go. Not without your bodyguard."

I suddenly feel quite hot and yucky. Nikki is counting on me to make this trip happen, and I can't afford to buy Xavier a ticket or pay for a hotel room for him. But Arabella's right. I can't exactly go alone. Vincent's words come back to me from the day they assigned Xavier to watch over me. *"Each addition to the Royal Family is both a blessing and a liability. Liability in the sense that, as human beings, you are vulnerable to attack or kidnapping. As the consort to the future king, you will be at especially high risk, even at this early stage of your relationship. If anyone wanted to get to the Royal Family, they could choose to do it through you, which is why you must never be without a security detail. To do otherwise would be a reckless and irresponsible affront to the family."*

My cheeks flush with humiliation at having to admit my financial status to a princess. No matter how close we've become over the past few weeks, I know she can't relate to what I'm about to say. "I'm afraid I didn't really think this through. I didn't ask Nikki to book him into the hotel, and I definitely can't afford to pay for him to come."

She gives me an understanding smile, even though I know she can't possibly know how this feels. "Not to worry. I'll book our private jet for you and get you an incredible deal on a nice hotel."

"No, I couldn't possibly ask you to do that."

"I want to do this for you, Tessa. Consider it a very belated Christmas gift."

"I'll only accept if you'll come with us."

Arabella's face lights up, and she claps her hands together. "Okay! I was hoping you'd ask again."

****

Text from Me to Nikki: *What are you doing right now? I need to have a chat.*

My phone rings immediately, and I answer.

"Let me guess, you need to cancel this weekend," Nikki says sulkily.

I can't blame her. In the past weeks, there have been a string of cancellations from my end, due to work or due to the wedding.

"Never," I say in my 'What? That's crazy talk' voice. "There's just a slight glitch with the plan. Turns out I'm not allowed to go anywhere without Xavier. The Royal Family would consider it a reckless and irresponsible act of defiance."

"Oh, well if Hottie McGuns has to come, that's okay by me. As long as you aren't cancelling—or worse—suggesting your new bestie, Arabella, comes with us."

"She's not my bestie. You are, and that's never going to change." My toes clench with trepidation. "But on that note, I may have just invited her."

"What? You promised it would be just the two of us."

"I know, and I'm very sorry. My plans for the weekend came up when she was giving me my posh lesson, and one thing led to another, and before I knew it, I was inviting her. Please don't be mad. If you were there, you would've seen that only an absolute bitch would have been able to resist."

"Sometimes life requires you to be an absolute bitch, Tessa."

"I know, I'm just not very good at it." I pause for a moment, and Nikki says nothing, which means she's totally pissed. "You'll really love her, I promise. She's very sweet and harmless and innocent. Think of it like an act of charity. I mean, just try to imagine that type of upbringing. She's probably never even tried a cigarette before. Her entire life has been carefully coordinated and controlled by other people. Plus, there's a particularly wonderful silver lining if she joined us."

"Which would be..."

"We get to take the family's private jet, and she'll set us up with an incredible deal on what I'm certain will be a fabulous hotel."

"You really should have led with that."

****

The flight to Ibiza is a little under two and a half hours. Just enough time for Arabella, Nikki, and me to polish off two bottles of Champagne while watching *Bridesmaids* on the big screen on the private jet. Traveling by private jet is nice, by the way. You don't have to suffer the humiliation of removing your shoes at security, because you don't even go through security. You just drive right up to the plane and then step aboard, and a very lovely flight attendant hands you a cold drink and a hot towel to freshen up.

The limo ride over to the airport was a little awkward, though, with me trying to bridge the gap between Nikki and Arabella, who have very little in common other than both being permanent fixtures in my life. It's strange the way that women can be territorial over their close friends, and Nikki is no exception. She greeted Arabella with a slight nod, then followed it up with the stink eye and mumbled a quick thank you for providing transportation.

But now that we've polished off two bottles of *Nicolas Feuillatte* Champagne the two seem to be in cahoots, insisting that we hit a nightclub as soon as we land instead of going to the hotel. Xavier and Arabella's bodyguard, an older man called Bellford, sit at the back of the plane. Every once in a while, I remember they're there listening to us laugh and ogle John Hamm and Chris O'Dowd.

When the plane touches down, I have a feeling I may be the one with the clearest head of the three of us. I decide a speech is in order, to ensure things don't get out of hand. I stand and sway a little while I hold up one finger at the girls. "Now, ladies, we're going to have a great time but not too wild. No public nudity, no men coming back to our hotel room, no getting arrested. I'm talking to you, Nik—"

"Boooorrrrring!" Arabella calls out.

Nikki makes a loud *pffft* sound at me and grabs Arabella by the arm. "She can be really dull at times. That's why she needs me." She stands and pulls Arabella up with her. They lean on each other as they stumble to the front of the plane.

Bellford hurries to catch up with her, muttering something that sounds like 'I'm too old for this shit.'

****

"This is Veronica Platt at the ABNC news desk, Sunday morning edition. Shocking news out of Ibiza this morning as Princess Arabella, Tessa Sharpe, and another unidentified Avonian citizen were arrested last night after an incident at a downtown nightclub. Giles Bigly has just arrived on-scene and has more on this story."

"Good morning, Veronica. I'm standing in front of *Amnesia*, considered one of the hottest nightclubs here on the island, where it appears things may have gotten very out of hand last night. With me now is Carlos Santos, a bartender who was on shift and witnessed the entire incident."

The camera pans out to include a very tired-looking man with black hair and a tight white T-shirt.

"Mr. Santos, tell us what happened last night."

"First, let me say I've been a bartender for over twelve years now, and I've never seen something like I did last night," he begins in a thick Spanish accent. "The three women came in with a group of about thirty people they apparently pick up off the streets as they are walking from their hotel. The one who they call the princess is buying drinks for everybody all evening. But the one with the pink hair, she is the crazy one. She make everybody dance, even the people who don't want to. Like, there is a man in the club with only one leg—she make him dance. She's a little bit scary, that one. She make all the men take off their shirts, even the one-legged man, who has a very good upper body, probably from, you know, trying to hold himself up on one leg. That's gotta be hard."

Giles nods smartly. "I'm sure it would be, but can you fast forward to the moment where things got really out of hand?"

"Yes, of course. The one they call the princess gets up on the bar, which happens, you know." Carlos shrugs. "And we let them, because they wearing skirts, so it's nice for us. Then the pink one gets up, too, and she pulls the one-legged man up, then her other friend—the blonde one—who has no business being on a bar. She cannot keep control of her legs and arms the way an adult should be able to do. So, they're dancing to a terrible song they make the DJ play. They sing along, screeching about holding on for one more day, I don't know, but they're singing loudly and dancing and the blonde one kicks the glasses off the bar and onto the floor.

"So, there is broken glass everywhere, and we try to tell them get down. We have to fix this, but then she loses her balance and knocks the man with the one leg off the bar and onto the floor with the broken glass. And remember, they take his shirt earlier so there's blood *everywhere*. People are screaming. The man with the one leg tries to get up, and it's just disgusting—his back now, okay..." Carlos winces and shakes his head.

"Then, one of the security guards that come in with the ladies—they're tall, big men with suits on so I know they're bodyguards—he tries to take the princess down off of the bar, but she say no. She don't want to go because her song is not over. You know how the ladies are about their songs.

"So, the pink-hair one jump on him and knocks him down onto the floor, and the glass cut his..." Carlos gestures behind himself with one hand. "...buttocks. We call the ambulance and have to shut everything down. My boss is angry because we kick everybody out and we can't make no more money. So, he say to the princess, 'You pay now for all the drinks you buy, and everything you break.' And then the princess say she don't got any money with her even though she's been buying drinks for the whole club all night. She say that the bodyguard who just leave in the ambulance has her money. So, we call the police and have them arrested."

"Thank you, Mr. Santos, for that very thorough account of the incident," Giles says. The camera pans back to him. "There you have it, Veronica. A bizarre turn of events last night that has us wondering if trouble will always follow Tessa Sharpe, even when she's queen one day."

The screen splits to show Veronica sitting behind the news desk on the left side and Giles standing in front of the club on the right. Veronica nods, looking very concerned. "Yes, Giles, one has to wonder. It brings to mind the whole Brooke is Better movement."

"Indeed. She certainly would never have been embroiled in this type of debacle." Giles nods.

"And Giles, this situation could have more serious implications on an international- relations level, could it not?"

"Yes. We have to remember that trade talks between Spain and Avonia have not gone well as of late, with the king having made some rather disparaging remarks about the Spanish Prime Minister a few months back. It seems as though some top-level government officials are seeing Princess Arabella's actions as an affront to Spain."

"Oh, dear. This is not good."

"No, it's not. It's likely why the princess and her two companions are still being held at this time, even though officials from the palace have made attempts to make reparations earlier this morning."

"Giles, I assume you'll have more on this as it unfolds."

"Yes, Veronica. I'll be heading to the police station as soon as I sign off to find out more."

"Excellent." The feed from Spain cuts off, and Veronica's face fills the entire screen. "Stay with us, because after this break we'll be joined by Nigel Wood for a full fashion critique of Princess Arabella and Tessa Sharpe's wardrobe choices last night."

EIGHTEEN

Girls Gone Wild & the Boring Boys Who Love Them

Arthur

Well, some stag do this turned out to be. Only three of my friends were able to make it for a weekend of hunting, drinking, and playing poker up at the castle. Timothy, an old mate from university, who has taken control of his father's shipping company in Ireland; Kyle, a duke from England, who is living off his parents' estate and basically has nothing to do ever; and my best friend, Chaz Williams, who I almost never get to see because he married an American and moved to New York so they can raise their children on McDonald's fries and super-sized sodas.

We had to skip out on the hunting because, apparently, it's not hunting season—so if we do go, we'd get slapped with some big fines and I'll be made out to be a monster by the animal rights people. So, we decided to start with a poker game first. Only, it turns out none of us are very good at poker, which makes for a rather dissatisfying time. If only Gran were here...

Next, we relive our uni days by walking all the way from the castle into the village to the pub so we can stumble our way home later. It takes just over an hour to get there on foot. By the time we reach the village, we've all remembered how utterly unenjoyable it is to go for a long walk on a cold, drizzly day. But at least on the walk home, we'll be too drunk and numb to notice the weather.

I open the old wooden door, feeling the rush of warm air and calling, "Let the fun begin, boys!"

I turn and shriek like a girl as a terrifying clown who's making balloon animals greets us with a creepy grin. The twenty or so children, who are running in circles and screaming (probably because they're scared and don't know why their idiot parents are just chatting and sipping pints when there's a clear and present danger in their midst), stop when I shriek and start laughing and pointing at me.

It turns out the pub is now used to host children's parties every Saturday afternoon. So, we end up next door at a little 'café, sipping tea and eating dainty sandwiches (which is all they serve at this time of day) while we wait for Ben to come pick us up.

Once we return to the castle, the group has a little more vigor, having now been fed and warmed with a nice cuppa.

Time to party!

We make ourselves comfortable in the living room in front of a roaring fire. I turn on the telly so we can watch football and then mix us up some strong drinks. It doesn't take long for the four of us to drift off to sleep, tired from the long walk and cold air. Mrs. Potts wakes me around dinner time.

"I didn't know if I should disturb you, but I'm afraid it's after eight p.m., and I'd like to go home soon."

Oh, God, we've been sleeping for over three hours.

"Okay, boys!" I stand and clap my hands. "Rally time! We've had tea. We've napped. Time to eat meat and drink our faces off!"

Timothy snorts as he opens his eyes, while Kyle mumbles for me to 'feck off.'

I jostle Chaz, who is snoring loudly. He jerks to sitting, shouting, "I wasn't sleeping, Janica! I was listening!"

Okaayyy...

****

By the time dinner ends, it's clear there's no fun to be had this weekend. Timothy spends the entire meal sexting his new girlfriend, then disappears to his room 'to get something.'

It's been close to an hour, and he hasn't returned, so I'm pretty sure I know what he's up to. Kyle's gone, having gone back to town to try his luck with the waitress at the 'café. It doesn't really matter anyway because I find myself distracted by another round of Twitter for Idiots, and after a few drinks, I end up spilling the beans to Chaz about what I've been doing with my non-existent free time.

"Seriously, Arthur?"

"I'm afraid so. I know I should delete the account, but I can't seem to bring myself to stop." I hand him my phone, relieved to have a friend as I unburden myself. "Look at this. Whoever it is, they keep digging up old pictures of Brooke and me."

He stares for a moment at a photo of us at a nightclub in Paris. His face lights up. "Oh, I remember that night. You took that little blonde back to your room."

"Umm, the Swiss one. Yes. Very fun."

Chaz's smile fades, and he holds the phone closer to his face. "Huh."

"What?"

"I took this picture."

"You can't have."

"I did. That's my thumb, there at the bottom. I remember Brooke teasing me about it."

My heart drops. "This means #IHateTessa is someone I know personally."

Chaz nods. "Has to be. I'd never post anything of you on social media, so they can't have gotten it off the Web."

"Shit. Could you have sent the pictures to anyone?"

"Well, yes, Brooke wanted all the photos of the trip—but it wouldn't be her, would it?"

I shake my head. "No, there's no way it's her. She'd never do something so cruel. Besides, there's never been anything between us. You know that."

"I don't know, Arthur—I think she's always carried a torch for you."

"She's got a boyfriend."

Chaz has a swig of whisky. "You're probably right. And even if she did want you, I can't see her being this brazen about it."

"Or this stupid. I mean, if she got caught, things wouldn't exactly end up with us together." I rub the back of my neck, wishing I was sober enough to figure this out. "But I'll still have to find a way to ask her. I'm going to see her next week. She'll be in Valcourt for her father's birthday."

"That'll be a bit awkward, no?"

"Just a bit. What a fucking mess." My phone pings, and we both look down at the screen to see that #IHateTessa has just called #WeLoveTessa a bunch of low-brow morons.

Covering his mouth with his hand, he tries to stifle a laugh, then lets it go. "You...ha ha ha...are in a very public fight with someone you know...ha ha ha...but you're both hiding behind secret identities."

He has a good long laugh while I stare at him, unable to find the humour in it. Deciding to change the topic, I ask, "How's married life?"

Chaz's face falls, and almost instantly he starts to sob uncontrollably. Well, fuck me, this took a quick turn.

"She's awful. Just awful. Always watching. Always judging. Always calling me 'darling.' 'Darling, that shirt doesn't go with those trousers. No more beer, darling, you're getting a bit of a 'dad bod.' Don't hold the baby like that, darling, you'll drop him." He shakes his head. "Do you know how many times I've dropped one of our children? Zero! Zero times! Well, that's not true. It's twice, actually, but both times he didn't get hurt."

Chaz looks at me with wild eyes. "Don't get married, Arthur. It's not worth the sex at the beginning."

Vincent, who has accompanied us to the castle but refuses to take part in any of our celebrations on the grounds of maintaining a professional relationship, sidles up to me while Chaz pours his heart out. I catch a whiff of him, then turn just as he's about to tap me on the shoulder.

"My apologies, sir. I don't mean to break up the party, but I'm afraid there is a rather urgent matter that requires your immediate attention."

Thank Christ.

****

Well, this is a total shit-show, isn't it? My bride-to-be, whom I've spent the past several months defending, has gone off and created a major scandal—and now I'm going to have to clean it up. If I'm honest, I'm rather pissed. I'm also a little envious they were actually having a wild weekend while I was suffering through the world's most boring stag do. I need new friends. I left without saying goodbye to Timothy, but not for lack of effort. When I approached his bedroom door, the sounds he was making told me it was better for me to just leave a note. Kyle, who struck out with the waitress, decided to stay behind with Chaz since I'm heading directly to the Prime Minister's residence, followed by the police station, then straight back home. As soon as I said I needed to leave for Ibiza, Chaz started shaking his head furiously. "No way. There's no way I can go there without risking a divorce."

And that would be bad, because...?

I manage to sleep on the two-hour drive back to Valcourt, then once on the plane I shower, shave, and drink an entire pot of coffee to help sober me up for when the plane touches down. Whoever said that worked was full of shit, by the way. I'm now wide awake with my head spinning a bit. It's very early in the morning when I arrive at the Prime Minister's home, bearing a case of the finest Avonian ice wine from the north country.

Camera crews, who have obviously been alerted to my plans, wait outside the grounds of his house and surround the limo, taking photos and motioning for me to roll down the window as the gate slowly opens. Once inside, I'm asked to wait in a formal sitting room while the Prime Minister takes his sweet time finishing his breakfast. It's a little show of power, but not one that bothers me, because I would do the same were I in his position.

Our meeting is brief, and although it starts out tense, I manage to ease the situation by relating to him as a parent. Even though I don't have children of my own, I play the whole irritated older brother bit, which works like a charm. We discuss how far apart our two nations are in the trade agreement, and I assure him we've found some room to move. By the time he walks me to the door, he's giving me advice about having a strong hand when it comes to the youngsters and keeping them in line. He walks outside with me, and we stand together, smiling for the cameras. The reporters shout questions about Arabella and Tessa, but I ignore them, saying useless things like, 'I'm happy to have met with the Prime Minister today,' and 'the people of Spain will always hold a special place in my heart.'

The media circus at the police station is far worse. As I get out of the car, it occurs to me this story is likely going to follow us for decades to come, and my mood starts to sour. I wave to Giles Bigly from ABNC, who's standing by, ready to get his story. Ollie keeps the reporters at bay while I stride up the steps to the police station. I'm immediately greeted by the Inspector. "I'll take you back to see the prisoners."

Prisoners. You mean my sister, my future queen, and her best friend? "Thank you."

Xavier stands guard just outside the cell. His face lights up when he sees me, and I wonder how he can possibly be so full of energy when he's very likely been standing for over twelve hours straight. He must be on something, no? Like perhaps he mixes uppers with his steroids?

I find the three women huddled together on a single cot. Nikki is passed out, face down on the pillow, while Tessa stares down at the floor, chewing on her lip, her eye make-up spread all over the tops of her cheeks, and her hair absolutely wild. Arabella, whose eyes are swollen and red, shakes her head and mutters, "Fuckity-fuck."

"Good morning, ladies. How's your hens' weekend been so far? I trust it's been relaxing."

Arabella and Tessa jump up and start exclaiming their excitement to see me, quickly followed by explanations, apologies, and statements about how this isn't their fault.

"Are you furious?" Tessa asks. "I would totally understand if you were furious."

"Well, I would say this weekend could have gone a lot better. For starters, I could still be at Didsbury at my own stag do instead of spending the night en route so I could spring you from the hoosegow. Or perhaps, if you had busted up a club in a country with which Avonia is *not* in the middle of tense trade negotiations, that would have been preferable. Or say, if you hadn't busted up a club *at all*...also good. Alternatively, you could have skipped the bit where you put two men in the hospital. That would have been a much more pleasing way to end the weekend."

Tessa covers her mouth with one hand. "Oh, my God. I'm so sorry, Arthur. I had no idea things would get so out of hand."

"It's my fault completely," Arabella says. "I'm the one who was trying to prove I could be just as wild as anyone else."

Tessa turns to her. "No, it's my fault. I'm the one who broke all the glasses."

"But that's just because you're clumsy." Arabella turns to me. "She didn't mean to kick all those glasses off the bar top. I *meant* to get very drunk and buy booze for the entire nightclub. Have you heard anything at all about how that one-legged man is doing? And Bellford?"

"Bellford will be fine. Pretty sure the one-legged chap is going to sue us and win."

Tessa reaches through the bars and grips my hand with hers. "I feel just awful. I've ruined your weekend and embarrassed you horribly."

"Not to mention you've embarrassed yourself yet again." I shake my head. "Honestly, Tessa, it's like you just invite trouble wherever you go. And it could so easily be avoided if you would just *think*."

As soon as the words are out of my mouth, I regret them. Tessa looks like I've just slapped her in the face. Xavier clears his throat. When I look at him, he gestures with his head toward the door, where the Inspector is standing, listening to everything. Bollocks.

****

"I'm Veronica Platt at the ABNC news desk. At the top of the hour, security footage has been released of the now infamous *Amnesia* night club incident, which ended with Princess Arabella, Tessa Sharpe, and one other companion being arrested by the Spanish police. We'll have the video for you next, but first, do you know the signs that your hamster may be having a heart attack? It's trickier to spot than you might think."

****

The plane ride home is tense, to say the least. Arabella and Nikki shower first. Unfortunately for Tessa, they use up all the water in the tank, leaving her with only some wipes with which to get all the nightclub and jail cell evidence off her. I can tell by the look on her face this hasn't helped her mood. My sister and Nikki then go straight to sleep in the bed at the back of the plane, leaving Tessa in the main cabin with me and the bodyguards, as well as Vincent and two other assistants, Mary and Stephen, with whom I'm sitting as we try to find areas in the trade agreement we can adjust in Spain's favour, but every option comes with issues that will negatively affect Avonian businesses. This would be difficult enough were my head not pounding and my heart not aching.

Whenever I glance over at Tessa, who is sitting alone by the window, she's staring out at the sky, no expression on her face. As angry as I am, I also want to comfort her. I know she didn't mean for any of this to happen, and when I think about how harsh I was, my gut aches.

About an hour into the trip, I can't take it anymore. I need to go talk to her. I excuse myself and make my way over to her.

"Mind if I sit with you?" I ask, hoping she'll say yes.

She shrugs one shoulder without looking at me, so I lower myself into the seat next to her.

"I owe you an apology."

"Yes, you do."

"I was wrong to speak to you the way I did." I place my hand over hers, but she pulls it away and tucks it under her leg. "Tess, please look at me. I'm truly very sorry. Can we just forget about that and move on?"

"Just forget that you called me stupid in front of your sister and Xavier and some Spanish policeman?" Her voice is devoid of emotion, and she keeps her gaze out the window at the pouring rain.

"I didn't mean it that way; I meant—"

"That you can call me clumsy and foolish, then just say, 'Sorry, shouldn't have been a total arse to you, let's move on?'"

"Don't put words in my mouth. Arabella's the one who called you clumsy." I suddenly become aware of the silence throughout the rest of the cabin, and I lower my voice. "I don't understand why this has to be a big fight between us. You made a mess of things. I wasn't exactly gracious about having to clean it up. I'm apologizing for that. I would think you would understand why I was upset and accept my apology."

"Well, you thought wrong, *Your Highness*. In case you weren't aware, I'm not one of your employees. You can't just say whatever the hell you want to me and expect me to smile and take it. If I'm to be your wife, I won't be lectured like a child."

Out of the corner of my eye, I see Ollie and Xavier trying to make themselves appear very small in their seats. "Please lower your voice."

Tessa's head snaps back. "Did you seriously just order me to lower my voice right after I told you you can't lecture me?"

"You do realize you're actually lecturing me about lecturing you?"

My phone rings. It's the office of the Minister of Finance. Tessa hardens her gaze. "Do not pick that up."

Honestly, I had no intention of picking it up until she told me not to, but something about her tone brought out the defiance in me. I lift the phone to my ear. "Peter, I have a feeling I know what this is about."

"Just read your changes to the trade agreement. I need to go over them with you."

"No problem. I've got nothing but time."

NINETEEN

Emergency Meeting Fails

Tessa

Text from Mum: *Tessa, it's your mother. Call me as soon as you get back to Avonia. Your father and I are beside ourselves with worry. Oh, and have yourself checked for lice before you come back home. Grace next door said those Spanish jails are famous for lice.*

Text from Noah: *I can't believe you went on your hens' weekend without inviting Nina. She's very hurt, although she's pretending to be glad since you wound up in jail. Your invitation to join her ladies book club has now been officially rescinded (so there is a silver lining to everything). Is Arthur still planning to marry you after causing an international incident? Let me know as soon as possible, because if the wedding's off I can get really cheap flights to Disney World that week but I have to buy them right away.*

Email from Hazel
RE: Behind the Scenes Look at Spanish Prison Nightmare
Dear Tessa,
Are you all right, dear? If so, please call me as soon as your plane touches down. There has got to be an exclusive for us here.
Yours,
Hazel

Email from Me to Hazel
RE: Behind the Scenes Look at Spanish Prison Nightmare
Dear Hazel,
We weren't exactly in a Spanish prison, but rather a holding cell in the police station. It was very clean and not uncomfortable, really. The officers were most accommodating and, in fact, offered us water, tea, and breakfast this morning. Although I would love to offer an exclusive to The Weekly Observer *on this weekend's events, I'm afraid it's more likely that the palace will put out an official statement and no further mention will be made of this weekend publicly.*
Thank you in advance for your understanding on this matter,
Tessa

Email from Hazel
RE: RE: Behind the Scenes Look at Spanish Prison Nightmare
Phew! So glad to hear that you're okay and weren't violated or otherwise abused. Please ensure the Palace Officials that The Weekly Observer *will be most cooperative in allowing an advanced read of any article on the matter.*

****

Well, this is just perfect. The one time that the king is actually in town is right when I'm not only completely exhausted and extremely hung over, but I've also gone and caused an international incident. Arthur (who I may or may not ever speak to again, I'm not sure), Arabella, and I are in the back of the limo heading toward the palace after having dropped Nikki off at her flat. I would've given my favourite pair of Jimmy Choos (well, my only pair, really) to stay at Nikki's so I could pass out on the couch for about forty hours or so. Instead, I'm listening to one side of a very tense conversation between Arthur and the king's chief adviser, Damien.

"You will do no such thing." Pause. "No." Pause. "Absolutely not. They will not be dressed down." Pause. "Out of the question." Pause. "This is nothing like Harry." Pause.

"First of all, they're not twenty years old—they're grown women. Second, you'll note none of them was wearing a Nazi uniform." Pause. "We're just about at the palace. I'll see you in a few minutes."

Gratitude edges out some of my anger as I listen to him defend us. When he hangs up, I say, "Thank you."

Arthur looks at me with disdain. "I'm merely trying to avoid further embarrassment."

So, I guess we're not about to make up after all.

Sighing, Arthur says, "Here's what we're going to do. Tessa, Ben will take you home as soon as he drops us off. Arabella, just go straight to your apartment. I'll deal with this and let you know how it turns out."

"Umm, no," I say. "I caused the problem. I should bloody well fix it, or no one in that palace will ever respect me again."

Arthur shakes his head. "I'm afraid that ship may have sailed."

"Arthur!" Arabella says. "That was an unkind thing to say."

"Well, excuse me," he snaps. "But I'm a little out of patience at the moment. You've made a mess. The best thing you can do is allow me to manage the situation from here on out."

The limo stops in front of the palace, and Arthur pushes the intercom button. "Ben, please take Ms. Sharpe home."

I lean over him and say, "No, thank you, Ben. That won't be necessary."

Arthur and I glare at each other, then I say, "I broke it. *I'll* fix it."

"No, you won't. I promise you, you will only make it much worse," he says. "There's a certain way of handling these situations, and I don't have the time to school you on it before we walk in there."

"*No, I won't?*" My voice rises. "Did you just tell me what I was going to do?"

"Quite the opposite. I told you what you aren't going to do."

"Same thing."

"If you think it's the same, then you really don't belong in that meeting."

Arabella gasps. "How dare you talk to Tessa this way?!"

He doesn't even bother to look at her but keeps his eyes on me while he says, "I've traveled all the way from the northern tip of Avonia to Ibiza and back today, leaving my friends behind. I've groveled to the Prime Minister of Spain. The one thing I'm asking you to do is to stay out of it and let me handle it for you."

"And that's the one thing I can't let you do. I know how to apologize, I know how to keep my mouth shut, and I know how to agree to whatever is needed in order to control some of the damage." I set my jaw. "Now, I'm not going to stand behind you while you fight my battles, so if you don't mind, please get out of my way."

"It's your funeral."

"Fine. Bring on the bagpipes."

****

In hindsight, insisting on attending the meeting wasn't the smartest of the choices I've made. Things didn't go quite the way I had hoped. I had expected to be able to make a humble and heartfelt apology to the king in the presence of a couple of his advisors, have him accept, then leave triumphant. Instead, I walked into a room of over thirty people in suits, several of whom serve on the public relations team, and none of whom would address me directly. I then sat through lengthy security footage of the entire incident which caused me to feel quite nauseated, at which point I began burping loudly and repeatedly. The next humiliating twenty minutes were spent watching various news reports from around the globe, including translations of what the Spanish media had to say on the matter. And I don't think I have to tell you that none of it was even the slightest bit flattering. Apparently, I have earned a new nickname—'The Countess of Catastrophes'—for obvious reasons.

Oh, and it turns out a bookie in Monte Carlo has set up a pool giving three to one odds that Arthur and I will break up before the wedding, and four to one odds that Arthur will end up married to Brooke. They've had so many people betting, their website crashed, so that's lovely to hear.

Arthur, who was so pissed about me insisting on attending, barely looked at me when the entire humiliating meeting was over. He walked me as far as his office, keeping an unusually wide distance between us, then told me that he needed to go straight to work to put the final touches on the trade deal with Spain, so he trusted I could show myself out.

I'm now in the staff washroom, standing in front of the long counter, staring at the disaster that is me in the mirror, hoping no one else comes in. I need to collect myself so I won't start bawling the moment I get in the car with Xavier. In a matter of a few hours, I've managed to horribly injure an already physically disabled man, humiliate myself, start an international scandal, and piss off my fiancé beyond measure.

The door opens, and in walks none other than Brooke Beddingfield. Well, isn't that the cherry on top of my shit sundae?

"Tessa, I was hoping I'd run into you." She rushes over and gives me a hug, clearly just so I can smell her amazingly delicious perfume that she probably bottles herself. "You poor, poor girl. I can't believe what bad luck you've got."

"Oh, hi Brooke." I pull back and nod. "Yes, it's been quite the weekend."

"I can tell just by looking at you that you've been through hell. You should be home in bed."

"Thanks, yeah. I'm going home now, actually."

"Good. Go lie down. Rest. Replenish those fluids." She turns to the mirror, sets her Yves Saint Laurent Classic handbag on the counter, then fixes hairs that are not now nor ever will be out of place. "I can't even imagine the pressure you must be under. The entire world watching you, waiting for you to succeed or fail. How are you coping with it all?"

"Apparently not that well." I put some soap on my hands, turn on the tap, then immediately regret it. Why didn't I just walk out? "What are you doing in town?"

"It's my dad's birthday. The big six-oh. I'm throwing him a huge party." She gives me a dazzling smile, then her expression morphs back to sympathy. "But this has got to be so hard for the two of you. The media scrutiny, those ridiculous Twitter battles, and now *this*. It must wear on you both terribly. Arthur tried to deny it when I slept over, but I finally managed to get him talking about his many concerns. I really let him unload, you know? So important. But then, in the end, he said there's no point in worrying about things you can't change. He said, 'Yes, it's true that Tessa will always be a mechanic's daughter, and probably also very accident-prone, but it doesn't mean she's not a good person.'"

I turn off the tap and dry my hands on a towel, my entire body going numb as I listen to her speak. I'm trying to process all the shitty things she's saying, but there are just too many of them, and I'm struggling to figure out what to focus on first. The part about her staying the night comes to mind immediately. "I'm sorry, when exactly did you stay over?"

Brooke gasps and puts a hand over her mouth. "Oh, dear, I'm afraid I've spoken out of turn. I just assumed Arthur would tell you that we were stranded together during the ice storm."

"It must've slipped his mind," I say, turning the tap back on and starting to wash my hands again so I don't have to make eye contact. The hands again? Really, Tessa? She's going to think you have OCD. "We're both just so busy all the time."

"I'm sure that's why."

When I glance up at her, she's giving me a smug grin that I wouldn't mind slapping off her beautiful face. "Anyway, please don't be angry with him. I'm afraid we had too much wine, and he just really needed to unburden himself about some of the stresses that come along with getting married. He doesn't really have a lot of people he can talk to about something so intimate, and he knows he can trust me."

"Well, that's a great comfort for me, Brooke. Arthur needs true friends." Oh, I think my posh lessons are paying off because what I really meant was 'go fuck yourself.'

"Well, I should really run. I'm here to see if Winston will bring his bagpipes to the party. He has such the hidden talent, doesn't he?" She gives herself a quick once-over, presumably finding everything perfectly perfect, then plucks her bag off the counter. "And don't worry about this silly scandal. It'll blow over. Just keep reminding yourself how lucky you are to have landed Arthur. He's beyond the whole package—gorgeous, refined, athletic, intelligent, *future king*. And as if that weren't enough, he makes the most delicious eggs I've ever had."

"Yup. That's him," I bark as the door swings closed behind her.

So much for calming down. When I walked in I was teary, and now I've added ragey to the mix. *Breathe, Tessa, breathe.*

****

I know I should go home. I do. I should walk out the front door, go home, shower for about two hours, then sleep for twenty so I'll calm down enough to discuss this whole thing rationally with Arthur. But sometimes a girl's so angry, she storms past her fiancé's assistants to his assistant, then past his assistant, and marches right into his office, bringing hell with her.

Arthur, who is sitting at his desk, looking very busy and important, glances up at me without a smile. "I thought you'd have left by now."

My legs carry me to his desk with a sense of purpose. "I was on my way out when I ran into Brooke. I thought I should swing by your office and tell you that I'm not going to look the other way while you carry on with Dr. I'm-So-Perfect."

"Carry on...? What are you talking about?" His face fills with confusion.

Oh, he's good at the lying. He might even be 'hashtag better than Barrett' at it.

I tilt my head and stare at him from under my eyebrows. "I'm talking about your little sleepover. You remember, the one with the cooking of the eggs and the drinking of the wine?"

The door closes behind me, and I realize Vincent must have done it. I cringe internally with embarrassment, then get right back to being furious.

Arthur's mouth falls open. Busted. "I can—"

Holding up one finger, I hiss, "Oh, do not say it. Don't you dare say you can explain, because I've got that little speech memorized from my days with Barrett." I put on a mocking tone and say, "'We're just friends. Nothing happened. It didn't mean anything.'"

Arthur's tone remains even and calm, which only serves to irritate the shit out of me right now. "We *are* just old friends, and nothing *did* happen."

"Oh, something happened all right," I spit out. "You got wasted and told her how terrible it is to be getting married to a commoner."

Arthur closes his eyes for a second and purses his lips. "I never said that. I was just talking about the Internet trolls."

"You didn't say the bit about me being an accident-prone mechanic's daughter?"

"Yes, but that's out of context."

"What could possibly be the right context for that?" I shout. "You know what? Don't answer that. It really doesn't matter because I'm not going to be with someone who lies to me."

"Now, wait. I didn't lie—"

"You just didn't tell me, right? *Totally different.*" Sarcasm drips from my tongue. I turn on my heel and start for the door.

"Where are you going?"

"Back where I belong."

****

Instead of going home, where I know the press will be waiting, I have Xavier drive me to Nikki's. I stand on the sidewalk and push the buzzer, holding it for over a minute before I hear her voice. "This better be life or death."

My voice cracks. "It's me. Let me in."

When I get to her flat on the second floor, I dissolve.

Nikki, who's in her jammies already, doesn't say anything, but just wraps her arms around me and lets me sob for a minute. When I feel like I can talk, I pull back and make my way to the couch to sit down.

"Did you guys break up?"

I shake my head. "No, but I think we're going to."

"Oh, hon. I take it the meeting didn't go well?"

"It was awful. Humiliating on so many levels. Arthur wouldn't even look at me the entire time, so everyone there knows he's furious with me." I sniffle, and Nikki hurries over to the kitchen to retrieve a box of tissues.

"As if that weren't bad enough, when I was leaving, that witch, Brooke Beddingfield, showed up at the palace—looking and smelling perfect, of course. She told me she slept over at the palace during the ice storm and she and Arthur got really drunk and he 'unburdened' himself about how stressed out he is to be marrying someone so far out of his class, which is just really shitty on so many levels."

"Wait. Back up. That's too much information to process. They had a sleepover?"

"Apparently."

"Like a sleepover with naked tickle fights sort of sleepover, or she just happened to have slept in one of the five thousand bedrooms at the palace?"

"It's five hundred, and I don't know. Either way, he kept it from me and I'm pissed." My stomach clenches at the thought of them doing anything naked. I take a deep breath and let it out. "I don't think I can marry him, Nikki. Not if he's going around telling people like her that he's having second thoughts about me. It's just such a betrayal." My voice cracks. "And you know the worst part? He made her *eggs*, Nikki. Eggs."

"Umm, of everything you've just told me, that doesn't seem like the worst part to me."

"You don't get it. That's *our* thing. His and mine. He makes these delicious eggs, and I pretend it's the only reason I'm with him. But now that's ruined because he made them for her."

"Ahh...and he kept it from you."

"And he kept it from me."

"Is it possible *she's* lying?"

"At this point I'd say anything is possible, but she definitely stayed the night—and I know without a doubt he lied about it." I sigh. "Oh, shit, I just realized something. Remember how he's been on his phone at all hours for the past few months? All secretive?"

"That son of a bitch. If he's messing around on you, I'm going to slice off his jewels with my thinning scissors. Hand to God."

TWENTY

Where's Dr. Phil When You Need Him?

Arthur

"You idiot." Arabella's voice cuts into a rather satisfying dream in which I've just saved Tessa from a hippo (considered the most dangerous animal in all of Africa, you know) and she was about to thank me.

"Wake up!"

I open my eyes. "Nice to see you, too."

"If you cost me the chance at having Tessa as my sister-in-law, I will *never* forgive you." Arabella whips the curtains open, and a blinding light causes me to wince.

"Wow, when you change your mind about someone, you really change your mind."

"Don't think you can distract me, you arse."

"Arse? That's hardly fair."

"It's more than fair. Now get up, get dressed, and go fix what you broke before it's too late."

"We had a little disagreement. It's hardly a deal-breaker, so leave me alone." I roll over and pull the covers over my head. "I've had almost no sleep over the past two days."

"How can you think of sleep at a time like this? You're about to lose the love of your life."

"Wait. How did you know about any of this? Did Tessa call you?"

"No. I heard from one of the staff this morning."

I raise one eyebrow. Arabella lifts her chin. "I'll never tell, so don't bother. Did you really sleep with Brooke?"

"No. Of course not," I snap. "She got caught here during the ice storm. She was here examining Grandmum. I made her some dinner. We had a few laughs. I walked her to one of the guest rooms. End of story."

"You *cooked* for her?"

"Why is that such a big deal to you women? I had let the staff go already, so someone needed to make dinner."

"I don't like it. It's too cozy."

"What was I supposed to do? Turn her out onto the street?" Giving up on sleep, I start to get up, but Arabella covers her eyes with her hands and shrieks.

"Don't get up!"

"Right." I'm naked. Almost forgot. "Please wait in the living room until I've had a chance to put on some clothes."

"Fine." She nods, then leaves, with Dexter trailing behind her.

I lay back, staring at the ceiling and wishing I could just go back to sleep. Instead, I grumble as I force myself out of bed and throw on some sweatpants and a T-shirt. By the time I walk out into the living room, she and Dex are in a full-on lovefest, with him licking her cheek while she rubs behind his ears. When she sees me, she glares.

"I know I should have told her at the time, but she wasn't exactly in the best mood the next day, so I put it off."

"For three months?"

Sighing, I grab a bottle of water from the mini-fridge. "This really is none of your business. You do realize that?"

"It bloody well is. Tessa's the best thing that's happened to this family in a long time, and I'm not going to just sit back and watch you mess it up."

"I tried to apologize. She wasn't ready to hear it, but I'm sure if I give her a day to cool off she'll come around."

"So, you just left it like that? 'Sorry, babe, come on by when you're ready to forgive me?'"

"First of all, I never call her 'babe.' Second, she wouldn't let me get a word in edgewise, then she stormed off. In case you didn't notice she was a bit out of sorts yesterday, so the smart move was to just let her go. Third, this truly is None. Of. Your. Business. Now, if you'll excuse me, I need to go in search of a coffee."

"No, what you need to do is go in search of your fiancée."

"Relax. She'll probably wake up this morning, realize she overreacted, and it'll all be sorted out by lunch."

"Doubt it. I think you really stepped in it this time."

"Thanks, Dr. Phil, but I don't require your advice on women."

****

Apparently, I do need advice on women, because it's been two days and I haven't heard a word from Tessa. I've texted, called, and emailed, but I'm getting nothing. Now I'm starting to get a little mad. The media is having a field day with the scandal, with the *Amnesia* security footage playing around the clock. The Spanish Trade Agreement is also setting off waves in the financial district, and I'm thanking my lucky stars that the referendum about whether to oust the Royal Family isn't happening now, because I'm certain we'd lose. I've never had so many angry phone calls in my life.

The top trending topic on Twitter since Sunday is #BrookeIsBetter, which shows no signs of slowing down. Things are getting really vicious now. Whoever he is has created meme with a photo of Brooke and me on top and a picture of Tessa kicking that chap onto the floor on the bottom. The caption is "Why go for the sublime when you can choose the ridiculous?"

It's been retweeted eight thousand times now.

My phone rings, and I see it's Chaz. "Hello, Chaz, how's the world treating you?"

"For once, better than you."

"You've been watching the news."

"I've been watching the Twitter feed. You figure out who it is yet?"

"No. I haven't had a chance to even think about it with the whole Spain scandal debacle."

"I suppose not. You and Tessa all right?"

"Not exactly."

"I'm sorry to hear that. I hope things will clear up."

"At this point, I wouldn't bet my crown jewels on it. Can I call you later? I'm just heading into a meeting."

"Keep your eyes open. Whoever it is, is probably right under your nose."

TWENTY-ONE

Divorcees in Short Skirts

Tessa

It's been three days since I stormed out on Arthur, and each day is a little worse than the last. I think it's over. I meant, it really has to be over, doesn't it? I stare down at my "Break Up or Make Up Sheet" that sits on my desk.

Break Up:

He was very cross with/unacceptably rude to me about the nightclub incident. I don't want to be trapped in a marriage with a man who will speak to me that way.

He has kept a big secret from me for months, which means he may be keeping more or will do so again in the future.

The secret has to do with a sleepover with a very beautiful woman who clearly wants to get her hands on his scepter.

He's secretly texting at all hours, and I'm pretty sure it must be Brooke (or some other beautiful opportunist).

How did he know where Brooke was supposed to be?

Any break-up list bearing the word secret more than twice proves grounds for a break-up.

All signs point to an affair.

If it looks like a duck and quacks like a duck...

He has misgivings about marrying a mechanic's daughter and someone so accident-prone.

I'm themed paper napkins, and he's silk linens and gold cutlery.

I will never belong in his world, no matter how long or how hard I try.

Make Up:

He has been trying to reach me for the past seventy-two hours to sort this out, which means he's worried, which is a good sign that he cares (even though it doesn't excuse his behaviour).

He may be telling the truth about Brooke that nothing happened and he has no interest in her. If this is the case, it would be horrific to end our relationship over something that, in the big scheme of things, is quite small.

I've never felt more alive or loved than when I'm with him.

I can't imagine having a day's happiness without him.

But if he's a lying, cheating sack of crap with a crown, I'll never have a day's happiness with him...

****

"Tessa! Arthur's here!" my dad calls up the stairs.

Dammit. My heart pounds wildly in my chest as I throw off the covers. I was already in bed in my Sponge Bob pajamas, even though it's only seven in the evening. I glance at myself in the mirror. I cannot see him like this. I'm a total mess.

"Tessa! Do you hear me?" my dad hollers. "Your boyfriend is here."

I open the door a crack and hear my mum's voice coming from the bottom of the stairs. "She's up in bed already, I'm afraid. She's been a bit of a Grumpy Gus since her trip."

I strain my ears, but I can't make out what Arthur's saying to her. Hurrying to my closet, I flip through my clothes, looking for a dress or jeans or something. But it's too late. There's a gentle knock at the door.

"Tessa, it's me. I'd very much like to see you."

My shoulders droop, and I look at the door, only to see him pushing it open with one finger. Why does he have to look so freaking handsome? He's all sexy casual in his jeans and dress shirt, while I'm all bad breath and wild hair and...Sponge Bobbish.

He leans against the door jamb and gives me a sad smile. "Even when angry, yours is the face I want to look at above all others."

I force myself not to smile. "What are you doing here?"

He glances at the bed, and I know he's thinking about whether he can come in. "I was hoping you'd be ready to hear me out. It's been over three days."

"Well, I'm still very angry and confused." Folding my arms across my chest, I shrug one shoulder. "And I'm not really taking visitors at the moment."

"Ah, I see."

"You know, coming over without warning gives you a very unfair advantage." I wave one hand up and down at him. "You're all well-put-together and...and clean, and I'm in angry pajama mode."

"I didn't show up uninvited because I wanted an advantage. I just couldn't wait another minute to see you."

"Don't say that." I tear up a little, feeling my stone heart start to warm. "I'm trying very hard to stay angry at you."

"I deserve that. Let me come in so you can yell at me and tell me what an arsehole I am."

Rolling my eyes, I say, "Fine. Shut the door. My parents are likely going to eavesdrop otherwise."

Arthur walks in and closes the door, making the tiny space feel even smaller. I cross the room, avoiding him, then sit on the floor and lean my back against my bed, tucking my knees to my chest to hide. A moment later, I feel the warmth of his body against my arm as he seats himself next to me.

"Nothing happened. I promise." His voice is slow and gentle. The scent of him is intoxicating. He smells like leather and aftershave and home.

I'm so overcome by his nearness, I can't speak.

"And nothing will ever happen between us. I've never particularly been a fan of gingers," he says, nudging me with his shoulder.

I give him a look that says he's not the least bit funny.

He nods. "Not the right time for that joke, I see."

"Not really." I shake my head and fix my gaze on the purple shag wall-to-wall carpet, wishing we were doing this anywhere but here. "The thing is, I don't know if I can trust you, which is pretty important if we're going to be married."

"I should have told you. I had every intention of telling you, in fact, but the next morning when we texted, you were so upset I'd made eggs for dinner without you that I didn't think it wise to tell you I made them for another woman. I can see now my logic was faulty."

"Very. I would've been really pissed, but at least I would have known you'd be honest with me."

"You're right. It was cowardly, and it was a mistake. One I won't make again. But you need to know I only kept it from you to protect you."

"That's rich," I scoff.

"It's true. I can't bear the thought of having you upset or disappointed by anyone, least of all me. I want every day of your life to be easy and fun and wonderful. Is that so bad?"

"Yes, it is. It's unrealistic. And it's patronizing. It's like you don't think I can handle being an adult."

"That's not true. I just want to shield you from anything and everything bad in the world. I think a lot of women would find that endearing."

"Then you should marry one of them." I run my fingers through the shag carpet. This carpet is who I am. I'm a purple shag and costume jewelry, not tapestries and tiaras. "You should marry Brooke. She wouldn't have to cram for being a lady by watching Audrey Hepburn movies, and she'd certainly never lose a condom up her wooha. Although, if she did, she would undoubtedly be able to free it herself using a combination of her elegant long arms, delicate fingers and, I'm sure, superior control over her vajayjay muscles. She probably would love to be patronized by you. You could travel the globe together, inoculating babies and being dazzling."

"Jealousy doesn't suit you."

"Maybe not, but jealousy is the only thing that's going to protect me from getting hurt right now because it reminds me that you're not to be trusted."

He reaches out and runs his fingertips over my left hand. "If I wanted her, I could have her. But you're the one wearing my ring, not Brooke. That should count for something, shouldn't it?"

"Yes, it should." I sigh heavily. "Is she the one you're texting at all hours?"

"What? No. I haven't been texting anyone."

"Then what are you doing on the phone all the time? Who are you chatting with if it's not Brooke?"

"If you don't mind, I'd rather not say. It would only upset you, and I'd rather avoid that."

I groan. "Oh, God, are we back here again?"

"If I tell you, there's also a very good chance you'll think I'm a complete and utter fool, in which case you won't want to marry me anyway."

"I'd rather be with a fool than a cheat."

"I'm not cheating on you. Never have. Never would."

"Words aren't enough."

"I'm afraid words are all I can give. There's no way to prove an affair that hasn't happened."

There's a knock at the door, and my mum's muffled voice says, "I've brought you some lemon tarts and tea."

"No, thank you, Mum," I call.

"Oh, are you two lovebirds in the middle of something? I'll leave the tea outside the door."

"Thank you," I bark.

I wait a second to hear her footsteps on the stairs, but there's no sound. Then another light knock. "If you're decent, I'd just as soon leave the tray in the room, or Mr. Whiskers'll get into the tarts."

"Fine!" I say.

The doorknob turns, and my mum peers in, carrying the tray in one hand. "Loves sweets, that one. Odd for a cat, really."

She walks in and stares at us for a moment. Her face falls a little. "Oh, dear. You two look like the sky is falling. What could possibly be so wrong?"

Neither of us says anything, so she sets the tray down in front of us on the floor. Oh, Christ, she's using the Royal

Family tea set, which means King Winston is smirking up at me now from the side of the cups.

My mum pats both of us on the ankles before standing. "Young love can be volatile, I know. Ruben and I used to have the loudest rows when we were first together. Oh, how we went on and on over the silliest things. But then, in the end, we'd realize how ridiculous it all was, and we'd make up and things would be wonderful again, and usually nine months later we'd have another boy."

I shudder at the thought of them 'making up,' which I've caught a glimpse of recently and haven't managed to scrub from my brain. "I assure you this isn't silly, Mum."

"It never is when you're in the middle of it. You can only see it for what it is when it's over." She smiles and nods reassuringly. "That's when you get a glimpse of the big picture, which is all that really matters. Marriage means you stay together and work it out, no matter what the problem. So, have some tea and something to eat, because by the looks of things, you have quite the long talk ahead of you."

"Thank you, Evi," Arthur says. "That's very kind of you."

"You're more than welcome, my dear boy." She turns to go, then stops. "Tessa, did I ever tell you about our old neighbour, Doreen the divorcee?"

"Mum—"

"She used to fancy your father. Drove me nuts when he'd even say hi to her. She used to come by in low-cut tops and short skirts and ask him to do little jobs for her. 'Evi, can I borrow Ruben's big man hands again? I can't get this jar open.'" My mum snorts, clearly still miffed at Doreen. "Wasn't his fault, though. He was quite the hottie back then. Your dad never strayed, even though he couldn't help but give her a second look. I mean, you couldn't really help it, those big knockers just out on display—"

"Mum," I say in a warning tone.

"Sorry. Anyway, eventually, she found a plumber who was happy to help her with all her odd jobs."

My mum opens the door and mutters something about being sure that didn't last long, then she turns and says,

"There's always going to be a Doreen, Tessa. Whether you let her get in the way of your happiness is completely up to you."

With that she shuts the door, leaving us alone with our tea and tarts. Arthur turns to me with a question in his eyes. He lowers his voice. "Was she listening at the door?"

"Anything is possible around here."

Neither of us touches the tray, and if I had to guess, I'd say Arthur feels every bit as sick as I do at the moment.

"I realized while my mum was talking that it doesn't really matter what you've been doing on your phone."

"It doesn't?" His voice lifts with hope, which kind of breaks my heart.

"We're not meant to be together, Arthur. We've been fighting so hard to make this work, but it just won't."

"Don't say that. We're perfect for each other, and you bloody well know it." He reaches out and places his hand over mine. "I know we've been having some difficulties, but that's to be expected. Weddings generally cause couples a great deal of stress, but once we get it over with, we'll be fine."

"Did you hear what you just said? Once we get it over with? That's not how you should feel about your wedding day."

"Isn't it? I'm a man. Men generally are more enthusiastic about the wedding night and the bit about spending your life with the right woman than the actual wedding. And in our case, it's just this massive production that really has very little to do with us as individuals and everything to do with obligation and tradition and international relations."

"That's true. You could literally have an instruction manual with 'insert bride here.'"

"Not if I'm the groom. There's only one bride for me."

Against my better judgment, I look up at him and nearly melt into his eyes. They're full of adoration and love, but I can't believe it. Not if I'm going to survive. "Those are nice words."

"But they mean very little."

"I believe that *you believe* I'm the right woman for you. But I'm afraid you're wrong."

He narrows his eyes at me. "I'm not *wrong*. I know what I want."

"Sometimes what you want and what you *should have* are very different things. I'll never fit into your world, Arthur. I'll never be graceful or sophisticated, and I'll never be happy to sit back and let my husband handle everything for me while I stay safely tucked away in the background, blissfully unaware of anything negative happening in the world."

Arthur runs a hand through his sandy-blond hair. "Good God, I don't want to put you in some little box. I just don't want anyone to ever hurt you."

"You hurt me when you lied. And you hurt me when you let Brooke have the satisfaction of being the one to tell me the truth. She's probably had a field day with that one." I put on a very posh accent. "You should have seen the look on her face. She had no clue I'd spent the night."

Arthur's voice tightens. "Brooke's not like that. She's not a gossip. She's a good person."

I let out a long sigh. "Please don't defend her to me. She wants to be your wife, Arthur. It's as plain as the nose on my face. She'll do whatever she has to do to make that happen."

"She's not like that."

"Then why did she come find me so she could stir up trouble between us?"

"She said she assumed I would've told you."

I rest my chin on my knees. "So, you talked to her about this?"

"Of course I did. I had to find out what she said to you."

"Do you have any idea how humiliating that is for me?"

"About as humiliating as me having my fiancée storm into my office and yell at me in front of my staff?"

My head throbs with confusion and anger and hurt. "So, you were trying to get me back?"

"No. I was trying to prepare myself for dealing with you. In case you're not aware, you're not exactly reasonable when you're upset."

"So, this is my fault now?"

"Jesus Christ. You manage to twist everything I say in the most hideous of ways." He stands and walks toward the door, then turns back to me. "I came here to apologize and beg you to forgive me and to reassure you that I never have, am not now, nor will ever be interested in sleeping with Brooke Beddingfield, or any other woman for that matter. But every word just seems to deepen the hole I'm in. Maybe I should just go. You can call me when you're ready to work this out."

A desperate desire to get up, rush to him, and wrap my arms around his neck comes over me, but I know I can't. I stay where I am on the floor, forcing my feet to remain rooted. "We should call off the wedding."

The words hang in the air for a horribly long moment. When Arthur finally speaks, his voice is too calm. "Call it off as in postpone, or call it off as in call the whole thing off?"

"The second one," I whisper. "We're just too different, Arthur. I love you, but that won't be enough. I can never be the woman you want me to be."

"Don't say that. This is just a silly fight." Arthur's voice cracks, and he clears his throat. "She's our Doreen. She'll move on to some plumber any day now, and we'll laugh about it."

"It's not just about Doreen. There's no way to make this work," I say, shaking my head. "It's the truth. We need to accept it."

"I'm not going to beg you, Tessa."

"I don't want you to beg." I stare down at my left hand for a moment, then pull the ring off before I can change my mind. "I want you to be happy, Arthur. You'll never find happiness with me."

I place the ring in his hand and close his fingers around it, then open the door and walk to the bathroom, closing the door behind me before he has a chance to say anything else. Leaning against the door, I hear his footsteps on the creaky stairs, then him wishing my parents a good night.

Then he's gone.

TWENTY-TWO

Chester, the Ring-Bearing Betta Fish

Arthur

Have you ever had the wind knocked out of your lungs? Like, really knocked out so you're left gasping for air and making that strange honking sound? That's me right now. Not the humiliating honking sound, but the feeling of losing the very air I breathe. I have never felt hollow before. Well, once I suppose, when I lost my mum, but it was so long ago that it's a foggy memory now. I sit in the back of the limo, clutching the engagement ring in my folded palm so tightly, the diamonds cut into my skin. Ollie and Ben know what just happened. My face gave it away. Thankfully, they've said nothing to me.

As we near the palace, lit up against the dark night sky, I want to go anywhere but inside that building. It's home, yes, but in many ways it's a prison of obligation and expectation that has held me captive since birth.

But when I found Tessa, it was as though my world opened and there would always be freedom and laughter and love waiting for me at the end of each day, even within those walls. Everything suddenly made sense, and for the first time I didn't mind the future that lay before me. I looked forward to it because I had the right woman with whom to share it. When I went to see her a mere hour ago, I thought I could make everything all right. I assumed we'd argue, she'd believe me, and then we'd end up very quietly making up at least once. But I never expected this.

Ben pulls in behind the palace, and I get out, not waiting for him to open the door. I thank him and Ollie, then jog up the steps. Inside, my legs wobble under the weight of what has just happened. I start for the vault to return the ring but end up back in my apartment instead, sitting on the couch, staring at it while Dexter nudges me for some pets.

"Now what, Dexter?"

****

It's been two weeks since we've seen or spoken with each other. I told myself I wouldn't beg, and I haven't. But now I'm starting to question the sanity of that declaration. I mean, if a little begging is the difference between a lifetime of love and spending the rest of it without her, maybe I should swallow my pride...

I stare at my mobile phone. Hmm. Still no messages from her. I push the button on my intercom, and Vincent answers.

"I need you to send me a test text."

"Again, sir?"

"Yes, again. There's definitely something wrong with my phone."

Vincent clears his throat. "Perhaps you should just try calling her."

"What? Do you think this has something to do with...no, no. I'm just very certain this phone isn't receiving all incoming messages," I say, my face burning with humiliation.

My cell makes a loud ping, and I look down to see a text from Vincent.

If you say so, Prince Arthur.

"Did you get it?" Vincent asks.

"No, nothing. See?"

"Are you quite certain? I distinctly heard a ping," he says. "Perhaps I could order a lovely bouquet of roses to send her? Or some chocolates from Bernard Thebault's shop?"

"Oh, just got the text now. That will be all, thank you."

****

Shock. That's the way to call her bluff. I'll tell her we need to announce the cancellation of the wedding, and she'll come running back.

Text from Me to Tessa: *I need to speak with you.*

Her: *You can call me now. Everyone else has gone for lunch so the office is empty.*

I dial her number and hold the phone to my ear, my heart in my throat as I wait for her to pick up.

"Hi." Her voice gives nothing away.

"Hi, how've you been?"

"Surviving. You?"

"Same." I swallow the urge to launch into a ten-minute monologue on how much I miss her. "I was wondering if we could meet somewhere. We need to sort out how to handle the break-up in the media."

"Oh. Right," she says. "I don't think meeting in person is such a good idea. Can we do it over the phone?"

"Of course." But then I can't look at your lovely face again.

"I guess we need to draft up some sort of official statement about canceling the wedding."

Dammit. That didn't work at all. *She's* the one who brought it up. "Yes. I could have Vincent do it...if it's too difficult."

"Maybe that would be for the best. I'm sure he'll know just how to phrase it."

"He will."

"Just promise me one thing."

"Anything."

"No mention of 'conscious uncoupling,'" she says with a hint of a joke in her voice.

I smile, and for a moment it feels like we're us again. "Are you quite sure? I was thinking of calling Gwyneth to help find the most obnoxious phrase possible."

Tessa laughs, and the sound nearly breaks me.

"Is there anything else?"

"Yes." Let's get back together and have a palace full of children and live happily ever after. "Shall I have someone drop off Chester at your house? He misses you terribly."

"How can you tell?"

"He used the little blue rocks on the bottom of his bowl to spell out your name."

Tessa rewards me with another loud laugh. Hope ripples through me until she speaks again. "Would you mind keeping him? Or maybe Troy could take him. I'm afraid Mr. Whiskers will turn him into a snack."

"He can stay here. I just didn't want to get sued for custody."

No laugh. That might have been offside. I said I wouldn't beg, but hearing her voice is too much. I have to try. "Tess, this doesn't have to be—"

"My workmates are just getting back," she says. "So, if there's nothing else, I should let you go."

"Righto. Nothing else." Except that I won't ever stop loving you.

****

"Your Highness, I'm afraid Baz is here," Vincent says.

"Who?" I look up from the paragraph I've been reading over and over.

"Sebastian. The wedding planner."

"Oh Christ. What does he want?"

"It seems Ms. Sharpe won't return his team's correspondence. He's quite annoyed, actually."

Sighing, I put my pen down. "Show him in."

Vincent nods and starts to leave, then stops. "Is there anything I should know, Your Highness? About the wedding?"

I pick up my pen and look back down at the agreement. "Oh, yes. It's off."

There is a long pause before Vincent says, "Very good, sir." His tone doesn't match his words.

A moment later, Baz rushes into my office. "Why does he always wreak of Parmesan?"

"I hadn't noticed." I gesture for him to take a seat.

He sits down and gives me a skeptical look.

"You needed to see me?"

"When you've been in the business for as long as I have, you develop a nose for trouble. Small things others wouldn't notice that don't escape your attention."

"The wedding is off."

"Off as in postponed, or off as in it's never going to happen?"

"The second one."

"And you didn't think maybe I should know?"

"I was hoping for a different result."

"And that isn't going to happen?"

"I'm afraid not, so if there's nothing else, I really have a lot of work this morning. I can have Vincent show you out."

"So, I'll start the dismantling process?"

"Sure, whatever you want to call it."

"Are you making an official statement, or should I?"

"I'll take care of it. For now, say nothing."

He gets up and shakes his head. "Can't say I'm surprised. Marrying down only works if it's one or two rungs on the ladder. Not if you have to climb down a mountain to find your bride."

The look on my face sends him scurrying out the door, leaving me alone with this awful feeling that has followed me everywhere. I stand and walk to the window, staring out at the city across the river. Somewhere over there is the woman I love, and the fact that I don't know where she is, what she's doing, or how she's feeling might very well kill me.

Unable to take being in my office for another minute, I decide to go for a nice, long run. As I pass by Vincent's desk, I stop.

"Cancel my next two hours. I need to get out for a while."

"Very good, Your Highness."

I pick up a gold-plated paperweight on his desk and fiddle with it, trying to force the words out of my mouth. "Also, I'll need you to draft up an official statement canceling the wedding."

He freezes for the slightest moment, then quickly recovers, saying, "Yes, of course. I'll have it for you when you get back."

"Excellent. Thank you." I place the paperweight back down and walk away without looking at him.

****

I seat myself at the conference table and put my phone on my lap so I can keep an eye on the Twitter feed. Damien sits directly across from me, Vincent to my left, my father at the head of the table. Several other assistants and advisors fill the other chairs. My father, who is drinking tea for once, has a sip, then turns to Damien, who is too busy on his phone to notice the glare he's getting.

My phone buzzes, and I see it's a shitty tweet from @IHateTessa. *It's been days since The Countess of Catastrophes has done anything stupid. Let's see how long she can keep up this streak. #BrookeIsBetter*

Father clears his throat, and Damien snaps to attention. "Yes, let's get started. We need to discuss the many objections to this agreement with Spain. It's imperative we find a way to offset..."

His words float to the background as I think of a retort. Trying to be as subtle as possible, I type: *@IHateTessa At least she knows how to have fun. You probably haven't left your mother's basement in years. #TessaIsTops*

I press the tweet button, then return my attention to my father, who is saying, "...if we give a tax break to the wool exporters, we'll have to offer one to the..."

Ping. The sound comes from Damien's phone. He immediately looks down, shakes his head, and starts to type.

I watch for a moment as he finishes whatever he's typing, then feel my phone buzz. Looking down I see a tweet: *@WeLoveTessa Oh, yes, she's accomplished so much. Her idiocy has caused serious problems for the wool exporters. Likely that the gov't will have to provide tax breaks now.*

That twatwaffle! He is so getting fired. I stare him down for a moment, then type one word: *Busted* and press tweet.

Damien's phone pings, and he looks down at it, his face blanching. When he looks back up at me, I run my tongue over my teeth while I think of what to do with him.

My father, who has clearly figured out that some of the students aren't paying attention in class, says, "I'm trying to run a kingdom here, so if you two wouldn't mind not fucking around, it would be greatly appreciated."

Ignoring my father, I stare at Damien, then say, "Give me your phone now."

"I will not."

"You will. That is property of the Royal Family."

"Arthur, he doesn't have to give it to you. It's enough that he shuts it off for the rest of the meeting," Father says. He then turns to Damien. "Honestly, I'd expect this kind of malarkey from one of Arthur's staff, but not you."

"Hand it over. Now." I stretch my arm out, but Damien clutches his phone to his chest.

"Arthur, what is this about?" my father asks.

"It's him. He's @IHateTessa."

"Don't be absurd. Damien's been in my employ for over twenty years. He would never do something so foolish."

"But he did, and he is."

"Oh, for fuck's sake. Hand him the bloody phone, Damien, so you can prove him wrong and we can get this bloody meeting over with."

Damien sighs and looks at my father. "There's no point. He's right."

Holy shit, I'm right! I don't know whether to be happy I've solved the mystery or leap over the table and choke the life out of him. I glance at my father, whose mouth is hanging agape in a most un-regal way. "Why would you?"

"I thought you wanted me to, Your Majesty. You said it yourself, 'She'll bring down the monarchy with her ridiculous antics.' I couldn't allow that. I thought if there was enough public pressure, the prince would call it off. Or perhaps Ms. Sharpe would have the sense to do it, but it would seem her lack of shame knows no bounds."

I turn to Ollie. "Please strip Damien of his keys and security passes and escort him out of the palace immediately."

Ollie walks over and stands behind Damien's chair. Damien looks at my father. "You can't let him do this. I was only trying to protect the family."

My father shakes his head. "I never meant for you to do anything like this. Do you know what kind of scandal you'd have brought on the family if the media caught wind of this?"

"I didn't think anyone would find out, Your Majesty. And no one would have, had your son not been doing the exact same thing."

"It's entirely different," I say, feeling more than a little sheepish. "I was defending the future queen."

"Arthur, you've been engaged in his insanity?" Father asks.

"I have, although I'm not proud of it."

Shaking his head, he says, "I'm going to have to live forever, because I think it'll take that long for you to grow up." He nods at Ollie. "Please escort Damien out."

"Wait," I say, holding up my hand. "I need to know who you got the photos from."

Damien glares at me. "I'm not inclined to say."

My father raises one eyebrow. "Then I'm not inclined to give you a good reference."

Damien closes his eyes for a moment, then says, "Lady Beddingfield."

"Brooke?!" I ask, my gut twisting with betrayal.

"Her mother. Dr. Beddingfield had no idea."

I won't go into this bit because Damien starts to plead, and it's all rather pathetic. Instead, I'll skip forward a bit to when Vincent and I return to my office after the meeting.

"Will there be anything else, Your Highness?"

"No, thank you, Vincent. I'll see you tomorrow."

"If I may ask...all the trips to the washroom?"

"Tweeting. Told you there was nothing wrong with my prostate."

"I'm glad to hear it, Your Highness."

****

"Your Highness, wake up."

A waft of bleu cheese and coffee causes me to wince. I groan and roll over, remembering this is the day we'll officially announce that the wedding is off, which will undoubtedly spark a frenzy of media speculation and a flurry of celebratory tweets from the IHateTessa people. Let the unending humiliation begin. "I'm not going to work out today, Vincent. Please tell Ollie not to wait for me."

"I'm afraid you need to get up, Your Highness. It's your grandmum." Something in his tone brings me to life. I sit up without warning my dehydrated, hungover brain, and it pounds in defiance.

"What happened?"

"She's been taken to the hospital. It's her heart."

I get up and rub my eyes, not caring that I'm nude in front of Vincent. He's seen it before. He turns and sets the tray on the night table, then pours me a coffee while I hurry to the en suite to wash up. "Is it serious?"

What a daft question. Of course, it's serious. She's been taken to the bloody hospital. She never goes near a hospital if she can help it. Gran says it's the best place to get really ill.

"We don't have much information yet, but she's in stable condition."

Two minutes later, I'm in a suit, knowing I'll be expected to look and act the part of the future ruler. Strong. Stoic. In control. None of which I feel at the moment.

Vincent hands me the mug and two Advil.

"How did you know I'm hungover?"

"The empty beer bottles lined up on your coffee table."

"Right. Thanks for the pick-me-up."

"Of course. Princess Arabella is also dressing. She'll meet you at the front entrance so you can ride over together."

I nod and hurry off. "Is Troy here yet?"

"I'm afraid not."

"Will you—"

"Yes. I'll watch Dexter until he arrives."

"Thank you. Not sure what I'd do without you."

The entire ride to the hospital is a blur. Arabella fights tears and stares out the window while my brain pounds, not letting words of comfort and hope through to my tongue. All I really want to do is call Tessa so she can be by my side right now. I've never needed anyone more than I do her, now.

Arabella clears her throat. "Will Tessa meet us there?"

I shake my head. "Things are not exactly good between us at the moment."

I stare out the window but can feel her eyes on me.

"Define 'not exactly good.'"

"The ring is sitting at the bottom of Chester's fish bowl right now."

"Oh, Arthur. Should I be sorry for you or angry with you?"

"Both."

The car stops behind the hospital, and Ollie gets out, along with Bellford, Arabella's guard, who is now back on duty, having recovered from his Ibiza arse injury. They get out, and Ollie goes inside while Bellford opens the back door for us. One of my grandmother's attendants meets us and walks us to the cardiac and stroke ward without a word of information or comfort. We're taken to an empty hospital room and told that Gran is having tests done. Arabella takes my hand. I squeeze hers to let her know I'm here for her before I lead her to the only chair in the room and gesture for her to take a seat. I stand next to her, waiting and hoping.

In a lot of ways, Gran has been more of a parent to us than our own father. She's always there with a snarky comment and some sage advice, but praise, too. And love. So much love.

We wait in silence for what could be five minutes or two hours. Finally, the door swings open and Gran is wheeled in on a bed. She looks so pale, I can almost see through her skin. Her hands are bruised and have IV needles bandaged to them.

She opens her eyes and purses her lips when she sees us. "Oh, for God's sake. Don't look so distraught. It's just a mild heart attack."

After the orderly parks her bed and leaves, Arabella breaks down in loud sobs as she stands and hurries to Gran's side. I go with her and brush my hand along Gran's cheek. "You're cold. Let me call for more blankets."

I push the call button on the wall.

"Thank you." Her voice is weak, and she closes her eyes for another moment. "Arabella, really, dear. You need to pull it together, child. There's a very handsome doctor I want you to meet, and you mustn't have a blotchy, puffy face."

Arabella lets out a surprised laugh. "Okay. I'll stop. It's just that you look so small and fragile."

"I am small and fragile. I'm eighty-four."

I smile down at her. "At least you haven't lost your spunk."

"And I won't. Not even after the surgery."

"Surgery?" Arabella asks, tearing up again. "You said it was a mild heart attack."

"I lied. It's more of a ninety-percent blockage in three of my arteries."

"You knew something was wrong, didn't you? That's why you had Brooke examine you."

Grandmother nods. "Yes, but it shouldn't come as a surprise to anyone. I'm positively ancient. And I'm addicted to fish and chips."

I chuckle in spite of myself. "When are they doing the surgery?"

"In a couple of hours." Her bravado falters ever so slightly, and I bend down and give her a long kiss on her forehead.

"Don't get all mushy. I'll be fine."

"I hope so," I answer, and I'm not ashamed to say I had to whisper it.

TWENTY-THREE

Mr. Whiskers Strikes Again

Tessa

"Tessa, get up, Twinkle."

"I don't want to," I say, stuffing my face into my pillow, my stomach lurching as I realize it's been fourteen days and ten hours since Arthur walked out of my life forever. Other than the one phone call, we haven't spoken, texted, emailed, or snapped each other the entire time. Each day starts with a kick to the gut as reality sets in.

"But you must. You've got an appointment with that nice Olivia for your final dress fitting."

Shit. She's right. I have to go. Olivia's expecting the final five hundred dollar payment on the dress I'll never wear. I lay there for another minute, listening as my mum swipes through my closet looking for an appropriate outfit.

"I'm surprised you and Arthur haven't sorted this out yet. You young people these days don't seem to have the fortitude to fix your problems. It's quite disappointing, really."

"Please, not now." I sit up and swing my legs over the side of the bed.

"Whatever it is, it can't be that bad."

"Yes, it can."

"Did he cheat on you?"

"No."

"Did you cheat on him?"

"No."

"Is he cruel?"

"No, of course not."

"Is he bad in the sack?"

"Mum!"

"No, I suppose not."

"I don't want to talk about it. I should have a shower."

"Yes, you're getting a bit ripe," she says, opening the window to let the early morning spring air into the room. "Breakfast is on the table, so hurry along before Mr. Whiskers helps himself."

As soon as the door shuts, I dissolve into tears, shocked at how things have gotten as far as they have. I know it's for the best. Really, I do. It's just hard to work out why sometimes things that are 'for the best' hurt like hell.

****

Xavier is waiting when my mum and I walk out the front door. Each morning I expect to find that he's no longer here, but so far he remains, his usual smile fixed in place. "Good morning, ladies! Spring is finally here. I see your tulips are coming up, Mrs. S. Very nice."

Mum blushes. "Thank you, dear."

He opens the door for us. "Mine are still barely peeking through the ground. What kind of fertilizer do you use?"

Their conversation fades into the background as my mind takes over. I wonder if he knows but he's just very good at pretending. I wonder if they all know already at the palace. They must. The thought makes my stomach churn because soon the entire nation will know and I'll forever be known as the woman who couldn't keep her Prince Charming. But who cares what they think, really? They never liked me anyway.

My phone buzzes, and I pull it out of my purse, my heart pounding in hopes that it's Arthur.

Text from Nikki: *It's my day off. Any chance you can come over so we can order curry and watch cheesy movies?*

Me: *I'm on my way to a very ironic dress fitting, then straight to the office.*

Nikki: *Damn. Any word from your man?*

Me: *Thankfully, no.*

Nikki: *Sigh. You sure that this is what you want? I mean he's super hot and crazy rich and really fun.*

Me: *He's also a liar and possibly a cheat.*

Nikki: *I almost think he's got so much going for him that I'd be willing to overlook that if I were you.*

****

"There's our beautiful bride!" Olivia claps her hands and hurries across the airy loft that is both her home and studio.

I smile, hoping I look convincing. "Olivia, lovely to see you."

"The dress is all ready for you in the change room." She turns to my mum. "Can I get you a tea or a water, Mrs. Sharpe?"

"No, don't fuss over me. I'm fine."

I hurry to the change room so I can get this over with. I undress and carefully take the gown off the hanger, then step into it.

"Let me know when you're ready for me to do up the buttons!" Olivia calls.

I put my hands into the long lace sleeves and pull them up to my shoulders, keeping my head down. I do not want to see the final product. Not now.

"You ready, Tessa?"

I pull the curtain to the side and nod, then turn so my back is to her. My hair is swept up off my neck so it won't be in her way. I feel the tug and pull as she makes quick work of the buttons that go all the way up the back of the bodice.

"How are you going to do your hair?"

"Um, up, I think. I'm not quite sure."

"Oh, yes. You look lovely with your hair up. But also with it down. It falls so beautifully around your shoulders," she remarks. Olivia stares at my face in the mirror, then says, "Are you all right, Tessa? You don't seem like yourself today."

"Oh, I'm just tired."

"You must be so busy. I can't even imagine everything that goes into planning a royal wedding."

I laugh awkwardly. "I couldn't have imagined it before either."

When she finishes, she pats me on the upper arms and says, "Gorgeous. Let's go make your mum cry."

I step out of the dressing room and out onto the circular white rug. My mum sits on an armchair and tears up immediately when she sees me. I do the same.

"You're a vision." She stands and walks over to me. "An absolute angel. Arthur's heart is going to stop when he sees you."

No it won't, because he won't ever see me in this.

She reaches out and lifts my chin so I have to look in the mirror. The woman staring back at me is unrecognizable. The dress is perfect for a future queen—a delicate lace fitted bodice with long sleeves and a full skirt with a simple but long train. But it's not perfect for me. This is someone else's dress, and Arthur is someone else's groom.

I'm no princess. I'm just a girl who fooled herself into believing fairy tales are real. But they aren't, and even if they were, mine would have ended two weeks ago.

****

"Can I see it?" Poppy, who needed to come home from school at lunch today due to a fever, follows me up the stairs as I lug the dress that has been carefully tucked into a garment bag.

"I'm not supposed to take it out of the bag in case it gets ripped or otherwise damaged. It's very delicate."

"Puleeaasse? I won't touch it, I promise."

"No, Poppy. I really can't. Not right now, okay?" My words come out louder than I mean, and she shrinks a little.

"I'm sorry. I didn't mean to raise my voice. I'm just a little stressed."

"Are you turning into a Bridezilla? Tabitha said you'd probably go all crazy before the wedding."

"I'm not...I promise not to turn into a Bridezilla. I just have a lot on my mind, and I have to get to work. I took the morning off, but if I don't hurry up, my boss is going to fire me." My arm aches under the weight of the dress. I really should have stuck with the upper body routine Xavier set out for me.

"Are you going to keep your job after you get married to Prince Arthur? Mum says it's ridiculous that you think you're going to keep working. She said your job as a princess will keep you so busy that you won't have time to work. Plus, it's silly for you to bring home a tiny paycheck to the palace when your husband is sinfully rich."

"Oh, did she say all that?"

"Yup. And Dad agreed." Poppy nods her little head up and down, looking very much like her mother at the moment. "But he may have just been saying 'mmmhmm, yes, dear' without really listening to her. He was watching cricket on his phone at the time."

"Okay, well, thank you, Poppy. I'd better hang this up and head out the door."

My dad appears at the bottom of the staircase. "Poppy, what are you doing off the couch, love? Grandmum said I'm to keep you lying down until your fever's gone."

Poppy sighs and turns, letting her shoulders droop as she clomps down the stairs, now reminding me very much of me.

I walk into my room and wrench open the closet door. Where the fuck am I supposed to keep a dress this big? I mean, seriously, I'd have to remove every article of clothing in my closet to get it in there. Glancing at the clock, I realize I don't have time to figure this out right now. I lay the garment bag on my bed, then shut the door to my room firmly. As I hurry out the front door, I call, "Bye, everyone! Leave the door to my room shut so Mr. Whiskers won't get at my dress!"

****

"Tessa! There you are!" Hazel's voice curves around the glass wall of her office and smacks me in the face.

I hover over my chair, not sure if I should finish sitting down at my desk or get back up. Sitting sounds good. "Sorry, the dress fitting took longer than I expected."

"Forget that. What can you tell me about the Princess Dowager?"

"Umm, she was born in Belgium, actually, but moved here when she was six. She still heads up over fifty charities, and she's really quite funny when you get to know her."

"No, not her history. Her *condition*." Hazel walks out of her office and comes to stand in front of me.

"What condition?"

"Don't pretend you don't know."

"Know what?"

Hazel gives me a sly smile. "Oh, you're good. I'd almost think you haven't heard."

"Heard what?"

"Oh, fine, if you don't want to say anything, you could just at least just say that instead of playing dumb."

"I'm not playing." There's a distinct edge to my voice that I shouldn't use with my boss. "What happened to Princess Florence?" I stand.

"She was taken to the hospital early this morning. No one knows why."

I grab my purse off my desk. "I have to go."

"Text me as soon as you know anything! I want the lead on this!" Hazel calls.

****

Xavier, who's sitting in a chair facing the lift, closes this month's edition of *Extreme Health Magazine* and stands.

I push the down button to the lift and dig around in my purse for my mobile. "We need to get to the hospital straightaway."

"Oh, good. I hoped you'd decide to go see her."

"You knew?" I ask, irritation flooding through me. "Wait, of course you knew. You know everything that goes on, don't you?"

Xavier's face gives nothing away. "It's best to act as though we aren't aware of the personal lives of the family. It's the only way anyone can feel comfortable being guarded."

"Well, you could have told me *this*." The door opens, and we get on together, riding down in silence.

When we reach the main floor, Xavier steps off ahead of me, holding his arm back as he always does to keep me from getting off before he's had a chance to survey the area. I push past him and rush to the door. I'm done waiting patiently.

****

By the time we arrive at the hospital, I'm a mess, not sure if I should go in or stay out. I texted Arabella on the way but haven't gotten a response. What if no one in the family wants me there? What if they refuse to let me in to see Princess Florence? Or worse, kick me out? What if she didn't make it?

I force my legs to keep moving in the direction of the front desk, trying to swallow my fear.

"Ms. Sharpe. This way."

I turn and see Vincent's kind face. "Oh, Vincent, thank God. I just heard. Is she going to be all right?"

"I'll let the family fill you in on the details as they see fit."

As they see fit? Hmph. "Thank you."

When we reach a door marked private, Vincent knocks gently. The door swings open to reveal Arthur standing directly in front of us, looking a little disheveled even though he's dressed impeccably. His mouth drops open when he sees me.

"I'm sorry. I probably shouldn't have come. If you want me to go, I will."

"No, I'm glad you're here." He steps aside to let me in to what I now see is a small waiting room with two love seats and a television. "She's in surgery. Triple bypass."

Arabella is sitting on one of the love seats. She gets up and comes to me, hugging me tightly and sobbing on my shoulder. I wrap my arms around her and rub her back with one hand. "She'll be okay. She's the toughest person I know."

"She is, isn't she?" Arabella pulls back and wipes her eyes.

She sits down, and I sit next to her, needing to keep a physical distance between myself and Arthur. It hurts just to look at him. Arthur's eyebrows knit together when he sees I've decided to sit with his sister, but then he seems to accept it. We sit, the ticking of the wall clock filling the empty space, each click of the second hand bringing another small measure of worry.

After a long time, Arabella says, "I think I'm going to go home so I can shower and rest a bit."

"Okay," Arthur says with a little nod.

"Thank you for coming, Tessa." She pats me on the leg and gives me a long look, filled with meaning. "I hope you'll be here when I return."

"Me, too."

As soon as she's gone, I glance at Arthur and see he's staring at me. He nods, his eyes glistening. "Thank you."

"There's nowhere else I'd want to be."

"I know." His voice is somber. "And I know this doesn't change how you feel."

"Good. I wasn't sure how to say that." I give him a sad smile. "There's a danger in these situations to let the emotion of the moment take over."

"Don't worry. I won't allow that," he says. "But would you mind terribly if we sit next to each other anyway?"

I stand, nodding, my eyes filling with tears as I cross the room to him. I settle myself on the loveseat, then take his hand. He squeezes it tight, then winds his fingers through mine, and it almost breaks my heart to feel the familiar, beautiful warmth of his skin. I lean my head on his shoulder and let silent tears fall. Tears for Princess Florence, tears for Arthur and all he's lost, tears for me and what I'm giving up. I feel Arthur's head resting on mine, and we stay like this for a long time, just breathing together and feeling what the moment holds.

The sky has grown dark by the time I wake. I'm tucked in Arthur's arms, and by the calm rhythm of his breath, I know he's asleep. I don't dare move, even though my right leg has gone all tingly. I won't disturb him for fear that this will be the last time we'll wake up together. I want to stay right here in his arms forever, but I know any minute someone will come through that door and this will end.

He stirs a little and pulls me closer, making a small sound. I lay against him, listening to his heartbeat against my ear. I know this heart. It will someday beat for someone else, and I think that might just about kill me when it happens. All too soon, he wakes and sits up a bit, moving me with him. I let go and sit up straight.

"Sorry for the unauthorized cuddling," he says. "Habit."

"No need to apologize. It might have been me who started it."

"I miss everything about you, Tessa."

"Arthur, please," I whisper.

He looks down at me, his eyes filled with pain. "Please, what?"

The door swings open, and light fills the room. A tall man in scrubs walks into the room, looking tired but smiling. "I'm Doctor Philps."

Arthur and I stand to greet him, squeezing each other's hands.

"The surgery went better than can be expected with someone of the Princess Dowager's advanced age. She's a real fighter. She remained stable long enough for us to clear out all the blockages and is doing remarkably well."

Arthur lets out a long breath. "Thank you. That's wonderful news."

Dr. Philps nods. "She'll be in recovery for the next couple of hours, but then you can see her."

He leaves us alone, and Arthur lets go of my hand so he can take his phone out of his suit jacket. "I should let Arabella know."

"Yes, and I'm sure you need to draft an official statement."

Nodding, Arthur says, "Yes, of course."

"I'll go so you can get to it." I stop myself from giving him a goodbye kiss, then turn to leave.

"Tessa?"

When I look back at him, his face is full of meaning.

"It's best if I go." I force myself to open the door and turn down the hall and out of his life forever.

****

Silent tears slide down my cheeks the entire ride home. I smell like him, and I don't even want to shower again because I can't bear the thought of allowing even the smallest hint of Arthur down the drain. Maybe we could make this work, after all. It just felt so right when we were together today—like all my doubts disappeared when it was just the two of us.

"You okay, Tessa?" Xavier asks from the driver's seat.

I nod and try to smile, looking in the rear-view mirror to meet his gaze. "No," I whisper.

"I know," he says. "But at least the Princess Dowager will be. That's the important thing."

"Yes, it is."

What if I'm making the worst mistake of my life? What if we could build a wonderful life together? I stare out the window at the moon and say a silent prayer for a sign. Something, anything, that will tell me what I should do.

****

My mum greets me as soon as I come up the front steps of the house, her face full of sorrow.

"It's okay. She'll pull through, Mum."

"I heard on the radio. It's not that." She swallows, a guilty look on her face.

I close my eyes, not wanting to hear whatever is coming at me next.

"Poppy wanted to see your dress, so she snuck up when we thought she was asleep."

"That's okay. I'm sure it's fine." I shrug. "Did she have sticky fingers or something?"

"She left the bag open...and then she left the door open," she says sheepishly.

I freeze, already angry at what I know has happened. "Mr. Whiskers?"

"I'm so sorry. He had an absolute heyday in there. It was like he was filled with rage at that dress for some reason."

I slide my shoes off and start slowly up the stairs without saying anything.

"Do you want something to eat? I could heat up some leftover lamb stew."

"No, thanks."

Mum's voice follows me up to the top floor. "Poppy feels just terrible about it, too. She made you a drawing to apologize."

"That's nice." I go into my room and shut the door. I don't bother to turn on the light or check out the damage to the dress. In the end, it doesn't matter. There won't be a wedding anyway. I just won't be able to sell it and get some of my parents' money back for them. I tug at the shreds of dress and the garment bag, pushing them onto the floor before I crawl under the covers, fully-clothed. I wanted a sign, and there couldn't be one clearer than a shredded wedding dress.

TWENTY-FOUR

All-Knowing Grandmothers

Arthur

It's mid-morning by the time I make it back to the hospital to see Gran. Last night when I saw her, she was sleeping soundly the entire time, so I left without being able to speak with her. When I arrive at her room, it's so full of flower arrangements, it's hard for me to find my dear, sweet, snarky little Grandmum. But when I do, she's already sitting up, reading the newspaper.

"How are you feeling?" I say, giving her a light kiss on the cheek.

She smiles up at me. "I'd be much better if they'd let me go home already. The food here is atrocious."

"I'll have your meals brought to you from the palace."

"That would be lovely, thank you." Her face grows serious. "Now, what's this shit about you canceling the wedding?"

"Where did you hear that? The official announcement won't be made until this afternoon."

"I have my sources. It's a good thing I needed emergency heart surgery, so it could be put off until I could talk you out of it."

"You don't need to worry about that right now, Gran. You need to stay calm."

"Then you'd better start talking, or I swear I'll have another heart attack just to spite you."

"You would, wouldn't you?" I let a half-grin escape my lips, then I sigh, remembering that Tessa and I are over. "I'm afraid Tessa has come to the decision that she does not wish to marry me." My tone is formal and distant. I could just as easily be giving the weather report. "It wasn't my choice, but I must respect her wishes."

My grandmother's ice blue eyes fix on me. "What did you do?"

"Why must I have done anything?"

She raises one eyebrow at me. "You're a man. Men tend to bugger things up."

"I kept something from her that I shouldn't have. I also was a little harsh with her about that whole night club incident. I also refused to answer when she asked for a full explanation of something I've been doing—but it was for her own protection."

"Oh, Arthur, come here." She gestures with one finger. "Closer, dear."

When I lean down over her bed, she reaches up and slaps my cheek. I pull back, straightening up out of reach. "Ouch. That was hardly necessary."

"That's to remind you to stop being a chauvinist."

"I'm not—"

"You certainly are. You're doing exactly what I warned you about, and you can see where it's gotten you. So go find her, tell her the truth, then stop trying to hide the world from her!"

"I can't." I shake my head. "I told her I wouldn't beg."

"So bloody what?"

"So, I have to have my pride."

"Bollocks. That's just a cowardly excuse. If a little begging is the difference between a lifetime of happiness with the right woman and being alone like a fool, it's time to strap on some kneepads."

The door opens, and Brooke walks in, wearing a lab coat over her dress. "Hi. I came as soon as I heard." She hurries over to my grandmum and gives her a kiss on each cheek.

My gut tightens as I watch her, and I wonder if she was in on the whole #BrookeIsBetter thing the entire time. "You came? From Africa?"

She nods and smiles back at me. "Of course I did. You left that message that you wanted to see me as soon as possible, and I tried but couldn't reach you. Then when I heard about the Princess Dowager, I realized what it was about and rushed straight to the airport."

"I don't think you do know what this is about."

Her smile fades.

"Brooke, we need to talk."

TWENTY-FIVE

T-Minus Two Hours

Tessa

"Tessa? Has Arthur found you yet?" Princess Florence is propped up in the hospital bed, her tiny Yorkie on her lap. Talk about different rules for royals.

"Um, no. I came alone. I wanted to see you and make sure you're doing all right."

"Oh, this? It's nothing, I just needed to come in for a little cleaning." She gestures to the chair next to the bed.

"You look wonderful. So full of colour." That may have been stretching it a bit. She looks weak, and it's not just because of the IV attached to her arm.

"If we count gray as a colour, that is," she says. "I'm an old, grey mare."

"You're not old. You're vintage."

Laughing, she shakes her head at me. "And you are young, lovely, and full of shit. Now, I understand you want to call off the wedding. Apparently, you're not as bright as I gave you credit for."

Well, that was a little insulting, wasn't it? "I'm afraid it's for the best. I'm not at all what Arthur will need in a queen."

"Don't worry about the queen part. It's a wife he needs."

"Yes, well, in this case I think he needs a wife who can double as an elegant queen."

"All couples have their differences. It's part of the fun. Argue, make up, argue, make up. It's a hoot if you do it right."

She waves a hand at me. "Now then, there are some things you need to know about Arthur if you're going to make this work."

"I don't think you should tell me anything, Your...Arthur and I aren't going to be able to make this work."

"Yes, I absolutely should. I know Arthur's been a bit of an arse since the engagement, but he's got good reason for it—well, what *he* would see as good reason."

She stares out the window for a moment. When she turns back to me, her eyes glisten with tears. "His mother's death affected him more than anyone realizes. Even Arthur himself."

Oh, dear. This took a turn I wasn't expecting. "I assure you I was very careful in my deliberations before making this decision. I know how hard it was for him to let anyone get so close to him."

"You don't know because he never would have told you." Her eyes bore into mine. "He just shut down completely. Wouldn't talk about her. I tried very hard to comfort him and get him to talk about his feelings, but he wouldn't. Just sat, silently. He would sit in the hall, staring at her painting by the hour. That's why Winston had all other photos of her removed from the family residences. He couldn't bear to see his little boy like that. Ill-advised, I know, but he thought it better to remove all signs of her, hoping Arthur would one day forget."

A lump forms in my throat.

She dabs at her eyes. "Do you know how his mother died?"

"I think I can guess."

"Good, because it wouldn't be polite to discuss it." She nods. "When Arthur found out the truth, he blamed himself for it. The day she...he'd been coming down with a fever. I don't know if you know much about children, Tessa, but they tend to misbehave when they're getting sick. Arabella was only two months, and little Arthur had been acting out like any five-year-old boy would do when his mother is preoccupied with a new baby. But that day, he told her she was the worst mummy ever and that he hated her face." Her face crinkles as she tries to fight her tears.

"Oh, God. That's awful. I mean, kids say things like that all the time, but for her to...right after..." My eyes fill with tears as I think about how young five years old is. I think of little Knox, and how innocent and naïve he is to the world. In my mind's eye, I can see Arthur at that age. Small and sad and scared. "Poor Arthur."

She reaches out and places her frail hand on mine. Warmth and comfort radiate from her. She says nothing, and when I look at her, the pain is obvious. We sit like this for a long while, both grieving for a little boy.

"He's carried that with him for a long time now, and it's time for him to set that burden down. Over the years, I've tried to help him realize it wasn't his fault, but he won't hear it. So, instead, he's spent his entire life trying to rescue Arabella and me, and now you. And I know what kind of trouble it's been causing you in particular. He's been keeping things from you that you had every right to know."

My head snaps back in surprise.

"Oh, yes, I know everything. Very little gets by me," she says. "I know my grandson better than anyone, and I can tell you he'd never stray. But he'll also never get rid of his ridiculous savior complex unless he forgives himself for his mother's death. You need to be the one to help him do that."

"I can't. I wish I could, but—"

"What? It's too hard? He's not worth the effort?"

Yeesh. She's tough for someone who just got out of surgery. "No, of course not. I just wouldn't know how."

"By standing up to him. By showing him you're strong and you won't be chased away by some idiots who disapprove. By taking him back."

"I can't. It's too late for us. The palace is making the announcement today."

"Then you'd better hurry," she says with a firm nod.

My entire body fills with nervous energy. She's right. I need to go get him back. I stand up and grab my purse. "Do you think he'll want to?"

"Of course. He's absolutely miserable without you. Now, don't just stand here. Go find him!"

TWENTY-SIX

The Patience Test

Arthur

"Ruben, please don't close the door!" The words spill out of my mouth as the door swings shut in my face. Blocking it with one foot, I say, "One minute. That's all I ask for."

Evi's voice comes from inside. "What's going on, Ruben?"

Ruben turns slightly. "It's that heartbreaking prince again. I told him she's not home, but he won't listen."

I take advantage of the distraction and press my shoulder to the door to pry it open. "Evi! I just want to know where she is."

"Honestly, Ruben, his grandmother has just had a heart attack. Let the poor boy in."

Ruben lets go of the door. The momentum from me pushing on it causes it to swing open and me to lose my balance, following the wooden slab as it crashes into the wall. "Thank you, Evi."

I straighten myself up and give her a small bow. "Very kind of you."

Ruben turns on his heel and walks away, muttering something that sounds like 'useless feck,' leaving me standing alone with his wife.

"I need to find Tessa."

"She's at work."

I shake my head. "I was just there. No sign of her."

"Nikki's?"

"I had Arabella call her. She hasn't seen her either."

Evi snaps her fingers. "Let me text her."

She walks down the hall to the kitchen, returning a moment later with her mobile phone and her reading glasses.

"Thank you, Evi. I know you have no reason to help me."

"Sure, I do. My daughter will never be happy again without you." She opens the bejeweled phone case and starts slowly typing with one finger.

I stand waiting impatiently, forcing myself not to tap my foot. Using my height to my advantage, I peer at the screen. So far, the only words she's managed are:

Tessa, it's your mother.

Dear God. She doesn't even have to include that bit. Of course she'll know it's from her mother.

"Oh, wait," she says, deleting everything she's written. "The kids keep teasing me about not texting properly. I guess you don't have to say who it is because she'll already have my number in her contacts."

"Right. Hadn't thought of that." Yes, I had. Everyone has. Just hand me the phone. Hand it to me so I can text her myself.

Prince Arthur is here looking for

"I suppose I don't need to say Prince, do I?" she asks as she deletes the entire message again.

"Perhaps, I could just—"

"You're so patient, Arthur. My kids are just awful. They keep grabbing the phone from me and doing it for me."

"I'd never dream of it."

"Such a well-mannered young man."

"Yes, well, I did go to Prince Charming school, so..."

Evi drops the phone to her side and laughs like a kookaburra. I laugh for a second with her, all the while gesturing with my hands for her to lift the phone again.

Tessa, Arthur is here looking for you. Where are you?

Push send. Push send.

But she doesn't. Instead, she looks up at me. "Do you want her to come here? Or should I tell her to meet you somewhere else?"

My voice takes on a high-pitched quality as I stifle the urge to rip the phone from her hand. "Umm, maybe just send it like that, and we'll wait for a few minutes for her to answer."

Using her texting finger, she wags at the air. "Yes. Smart."

When she finally pushes the send button, I let out a long puff of air.

And now we wait.

She and I stare at each other awkwardly for a second. Evi smiles. "Lovely weather we're having."

"Quite. Yes. Unusually warm for April."

"Indeed. How's your gran?"

"She's doing quite well, actually. She's in great spirits."

"Excellent."

Her phone makes a ping sound, and we both turn our attention to it. "Nope. Not her. Grace next door wants to see if I can verse her in Candy Crush."

"Oh."

"Do you play?"

I shake my head.

"No, I suppose you wouldn't have time for that." She makes a clicking sound with her tongue for about half a minute. "Would you like some tea?"

"Thank you, no." I check my watch. I still have two hours before the official announcement is made. Still time to turn this ship around.

"Oh! Have you tried calling that handsome Xavier? He'll know where she is."

"He's not answering, which is very odd because they're meant to have their mobile devices on at all times. Unless…" I clap my hands. "I know where she is."

"Where?"

"She's at the hospital!"

TWENTY-SEVEN

Where in the World is Arthur Landgon?

Tessa

I hurry down the long hall to the hospital with Xavier, who is double-timing it in his excitement for me to find Arthur.

"To the palace!"

"I know a shortcut," Xavier says, wrenching open the back door of the car for me.

Tires screeching, the car pulls out on the road and we zoom off toward my prince. I sit up, hands on the headrest of the passenger seat, watching out the window as Xavier weaves in and out of traffic. "This is rather exciting, isn't it?"

"Agreed! You know, you burn two extra calories per minute when your adrenaline is pumping like this."

"Do you?" I'm so happy, I don't even mind his fitness facts today. I'm going to find Arthur, and I know in my heart everything will be okay.

Gravel spins under the tires as the car skids to a stop in front of the palace. I get out and run up the steps as fast as my legs can carry me. One of the pages opens the door, and I run into the Grande Hall, stopping when I get there to decide if I should try his office or his apartment.

A door opens to my left, and the king walks out. He stops when he sees me. "Oh, it's you."

I hold my chin high. "Yes, it is. I came by to say that you and your nasty friends won't be able to chase me off. I have four older brothers, and they're all total shits to me, so I have loads of experience dealing with arseholes. So, you'd better get used to the fact that I'll be your daughter-in-law. I know that I may not be elegant or graceful or well-born, but I have a kind heart and I'm brave as fuck, and I'll protect your son with my very life if it's required, which should count for something." I take a deep breath. "And you know what else? I'm going to be the person who keeps your family in touch with the people of Avonia, which is something neither Brooke Beddingfield nor any of your other stuffy cronies could ever do. And you know what else? I saved your sorry arse during the referendum, so you should probably just say thank you and welcome me to the sodding family."

He stares at me, looking utterly shocked for a moment. My heart pounds in my chest as I wonder what the penalty is for swearing at the king. What if they *do* have some torture devices hidden in the basement? Shit.

He rubs his chin with one hand. "I'm going to say something to you I have never said in my life. I may have been wrong about you. You're tougher than I thought, which, frankly, is a job requirement. Also, I think there's a chance you'll be good for my son."

I blink in surprise, then nod. "You're bloody well right I will be. Now, where is he so I can tell him we're back on?"

King Winston shrugs. "If I had to guess, I'd say he's out looking for you."

"Thank you, Your Majesty." I curtsy, then turn and hurry to the door, calling back, "Sorry for all the swearing!"

When I get outside, Xavier is doing one-armed push-ups off the bottom step.

"He's not here!" I shout. "Let's go!"

"Where?"

"I'll figure it out when we get on the road."

I climb back into the car, then remember my phone has been shut off since I went to the hospital. I turn it on and wait impatiently for it to load. Finally, I see a text from my mum.

"Ha! He's at my house!"

"Let's go!" Xavier glances back at me, smiling in the rear-view mirror. "Oh, you may want to put on some lipstick. Do you have a hairbrush in your purse?"

Apparently, he's been spending too much time with my mother. His nagging has now extended from fitness to fashion. But to be fair, he's right—I'm a bit of a mess. I search through my handbag until I find a comb, some mints, and a tube of lip gloss. By the time we pull onto Abbott Lane, I'm semi-presentable.

"Hmm. The car's not here," Xavier mumbles.

"What?"

"I'll pull up at the house and try to reach Ollie. You run in and see if your mum knows where he went."

****

I take the stairs two at a time, then make a sharp right into the bathroom. Xavier and Ollie managed to speak, and it turns out Arthur went to the hospital to find me but is now on his way back here. According to Xavier, I have t-minus seven to get myself looking—and smelling—gorgeous. I hear the creaking of the stairs, and my mum appears at the entrance to the bathroom. She smiles at me. "So, do you finally believe it?"

"Believe what?" I squeeze too much toothpaste onto my brush, then go to work.

"That you're meant to be together."

"Yeah, I think so," I say, the words muffled.

"Believe it, Twinkle. You are enough. Just the way you are. Arthur sees it. And you need to *know* it deep down inside."

I spit out the toothpaste. "That wasn't the only reason we broke up, you know."

"Yes, it was." She pats me on the shoulder. "Otherwise, you wouldn't have started to believe that malarkey about Brooke being better. She may be better at being a lady and, well, school obviously, but she's not better at loving Arthur."

I smile. "Thanks, Mum. That's the nicest thing you've ever said to me."

"You're welcome, Twinkle." She looks me up and down. "You should really hurry and get ready. Arthur'll be here any minute and you look like an old school marm in that top."

She turns to leave, then calls over her shoulder, "Dad and I are going out for a couple of hours. I need to pick up some of that cheese at that shop I like."

****

By the time there's a knock at the door, I'm in my little black dress, fresh knickers, and lipstick, with my hair up in a loose bun. Arthur smiles down at me. "I remember that dress."

"Do you?"

"You wore it to dinner the first day we met. It drained all the blood from my brain the entire evening."

"I'll take that as a compliment." I grin up at him, desperately wanting to pull him into the house by his tie, but I hold back.

"I'm here to confess, then beg you to come back to me."

"Well, that all depends on what you're confessing to..."

He screws up his face, looking thoroughly embarrassed. "I'm the brains behind @WeLoveTessa."

"You?! But you're always saying to just ignore all of that."

"Which is why I didn't want to admit to it. It makes me a terrible hypocrite, not to mention you said my comebacks were that of a moronic teenage boy."

"I may have been a little harsh when I said that."

"I may have been a total fool to do any of it in the first place."

"Maybe." I nod.

"I also figured out who @IHateTessa was. Do you want to know?"

"Yes."

"Let's just say you won't be seeing Damien around the palace anymore."

My mouth drops. "Did you...have him offed?"

"No, this isn't Game of Thrones. We fired him."

"Oh, yeah, that makes more sense," I say. "While we're confessing, you should know I may have just zipped over to the palace and told your father off."

His mouth spreads into a wide grin. "Did you, now?"

"I did. I even said fuck and told him I saved his sorry arse in the referendum." I laugh a little, then remember Brooke. "What about Brooke? Have you figured out she likes you in a 'more than a friend' way?"

"I did when I found out who'd been feeding Damien the photos of us together."

Gasping, I say, "It was her all along?"

He shakes his head. "Her mother. Brooke tried to convince me she didn't know, but when I pressed her on the subject, she fell apart, apologized profusely, then promptly tried to stick her tongue down my throat in a last-ditch effort to make me hers."

"I knew it!" I snap my fingers, feeling temporary satisfaction at being right, which is swiftly followed by rage at the thought of her kissing Arthur. The look on my face must show what I'm thinking.

"Don't worry. I set her straight." He points to his mouth. "I told her these lips belong to Tessa Sharpe."

"Was she horribly disappointed?"

"She'll be in mourning for years to come."

My entire body smiles at the thought.

Arthur grins at me. "So, do you believe me now that nothing happened?"

"I do, and I'm sorry I didn't before." I nod.

"You're forgiven. I was acting suspicious. Very foolish of me, I know, given what was at stake."

"Yes, it was, which brings me to the next item on the agenda. I think we need to renegotiate the terms of our relationship."

"Agreed. But can I come in and kiss you first?"

I put on my most posh voice. "If you must."

"I really fucking must." He steps inside, shutting the door behind him with one foot, then takes me in his arms and lowers his mouth over mine. I close my eyes and disappear into the most passionate, amazingly wonderful, toe-curling, leg-rising-up-of-its-own-accord kiss I've ever had.

When it's over, he pulls back. "Should we go somewhere where we can be alone—for negotiation purposes? These things can take days."

"My parents have gone out, so we'll have the place to ourselves for two entire hours," I say, licking my lips. "If we're unable to resolve our differences by then, we'll have to reconvene in another location."

"You're so deliciously naughty."

"That's why you like me."

"Wrong." He gives me a quick kiss on the lips, leaving me wanting more. "That's why I love you."

"I say we try something new. Strip negotiation."

He raises one eyebrow. "I'm intrigued. What are the rules?"

"For every one of my terms you agree to I take off an item of clothing, and the same for your terms."

"Deal."

We shake hands, then he says, "Now lose the dress."

"What?"

"I just agreed to your first term. Dress. Off."

****

"This is Veronica Platt from the ABNC news desk. Breaking news from the palace as an official statement has been issued. Prince Arthur and Tessa Sharpe have called off their wedding, which was to have taken place three weeks from now. Giles Bigley is on location in front of the palace with more. Giles?"

"Yes, Veronica, shock reverberates through Avonia today as Prince Arthur and Tessa Sharpe call off their wedding."

"The statement was very vague, not providing any indication as to the reasons behind it. Are they ending their relationship or just postponing the nuptials?"

"Excellent question. The prince has remained silent on the matter and has yet to post on Instagram or Twitter in the past several days, but because the announcement comes on the heels of the Princess Dowager's open-heart surgery, it could very well be that they have elected to postpone until she is able to attend the ceremony."

Veronica's face falls a little. "Yes, I suppose that *could* be possible."

"I'd say it's highly likely, Veronica. Both Tessa and Prince Arthur were seen coming and going from Valcourt Memorial last night and earlier today. It's doubtful she would be attending the Princess Dowager's side were she and Prince Arthur calling it quits."

****

"Oh, bugger." Arthur sits up in bed suddenly.

We've been negotiating for the past three hours now with one brief break for me to text my mum and suggest they go visit Lars and Nina for a few hours. I got a quick reply from mum which included a winkie face emoticon and a promise that they'll be gone until after ten tonight. A little awkward if I'm to be honest, but we're all adults here. Mostly.

"What is it?" I ask, my brain completely unable to think up what could possibly be wrong.

"The announcement. I forgot to call Vincent to cancel."

I sit up. "Oh, bugger."

We both take to our mobile phones and stare in horror at the dozens of notifications that we're broken up. Arthur looks at me with wild eyes, then bursts out laughing. "Oh, sod it."

He grabs my mobile out of my hand and tosses it and his onto the pile of lace scraps that used to be a designer wedding gown. Then he takes me in his arms and snogs me senseless, only stopping for a second to ask, "What is that pile of shredded fabric?"

"Oh, that? My wedding dress," I say simply.

He tilts his head and nods as though that makes perfect sense. "Mr. Whiskers?"

"Mmmhmm."

"He knew we needed a fresh start."

"Genius, that cat," I say, smiling.

"This time around, we do the whole thing our way. No tiny, nasty wedding planners, no diets, no twenty-page guest lists. Just you and me and whatever kind of wedding you want."

TWENTY-EIGHT

My Not-So-Big, Relatively Lean Avonian Wedding

Arthur

June 15th - Didsbury Village

I stand at the front of the church, with Chaz, Kyle, and Timothy at my side. I honestly have no idea why men pretend they don't love weddings. I'm exhilarated, terrified, and madly, wildly in love at the same time as I wait for the heavy wooden doors to open and pour late-day sunlight into the ancient stone building. I also have no idea why anyone bothers with wedding planners. It took Tessa and me all of one evening to plan out the perfect wedding—in the village church, with our close friends and relatives.

Grandmum saved our foolish arses by putting out an official statement that, while we are very much in love, we decided to postpone the wedding until she was well. I smile over at her where she sits in the front pew and gratitude sweeps through me that she can be here for this moment in my life. I say a silent prayer that she'll be here to welcome our children to the world and love them up when they're getting in trouble from their parents, like she did for Arabella and me. I don't know who I would be if she hadn't been here, but I don't think I'd be half the man who awaits his bride.

Oh, you're probably wondering how I've become so sentimental. 'Arthur, this doesn't sound like you. You're

246

sarcastic and witty and debonair.' Relax, I'll get straight back to that as soon as the ceremony is over.

I glance to my right, where my father is waiting to bestow the title of Duchess of Wellingborne, Princess of Avonia on Tessa. Oddly enough, things have gotten much better between us since I threatened to make him do all his own work. Turns out he was waiting for me to finally stand up to him so he'd know I can handle being king someday. He's still not what you'd call a cuddly or involved dad, but he's been trying. He smiles at me and nods. I do the same.

Suddenly, the doors open and I see Tessa's nieces and nephews, who are serving as our flower girls and ring bearers, all but little Eugenia, who is sleeping soundly on her dad's shoulder in the second row. Poppy is first, sprinkling flowers on the aisle. Well, really, she's sort of chucking fistfuls of them on the carpet. Her brother, Knox, who has a slightly quicker pace, bumps into her back, and she turns around and smacks him on the arm. "Stop it!"

"Hurry up, you ninny!" he hisses.

The church roars with laughter, reminding them that they are, indeed, being watched.

The children make their way up the rest of the aisle without incident, and I give them each a wink and a fist bump as they turn to their pew.

Then I look up and see Arabella coming down the aisle, carrying a simple bouquet of wild flowers. She's already crying, poor thing, but she's smiling, too. Then Nikki is next, and I do a double-take. Her hair is light brown today. She looks...normal. Very presentable.

They make their way down the aisle, Arabella stopping to hug me. "I'm so happy!"

I hug her back. "Me, too."

She pulls back and narrows her eyes at me. "Don't fuck this up, Arthur. I swear to God, I'll kill you."

"You and Gran both."

Nikki comes up behind her and does a little curtsy in front of me and my father. I lean toward her and point to her hair. "Natural colour?"

She nods and shrugs.

"You look rather fetching."

Her cheeks turn pink. "Charmer."

The trumpets sound the first notes of Mendelssohn's "Wedding March", and I snap to attention. There she is, flanked on either side by her parents. At first she's only a silhouette against the pink and orange sky, but then she takes a few steps forward and I see her for the first time. My princess.

Her dress belonged to her grandmother. It's a simple long-sleeved lace gown that trails behind her, causing her to look like she's walking on air. Behind the veil, she smiles, her eyes set only on me as she makes her way down the aisle, arms hooked through those of her parents. Her eyes glisten with emotion, and mine do the same. Each step she takes brings me more to life, makes me that much fuller. A lump forms in my throat, and I'm not sure I'll be able to speak at all when it's time.

When they reach us, I vibrate with the purest joy. She turns to her mother, who lifts her veil and sobs loudly, then kisses her on the cheek. "Imagine my little girl becoming a princess."

Evi turns to me and says, "Be good to each other. None of the rest matters."

I nod, and we kiss each other on both cheeks. "Thanks, Mum."

As soon as I say it, I know it was a mistake because she bursts into tears, patting my cheek in a most undignified way. Oh, well, sod it all. We're family now. A little show of emotion never hurt anyone, I suppose.

Ruben shakes my hand, gripping my elbow firmly with his other hand. His eyes say what he's too polite to—and it's pretty much the same message as Arabella's.

Why is it everyone assumes *I'll* fuck this up? It could just as easily be Tessa. I nod and murmur to him, "Don't worry, sir. I'll take good care of her."

Ruben's eyes well up a bit, and he sniffles, then takes his wife's arm and leads her to the spots waiting for them in the front pew.

And now it's just the two of us grinning at each other like fools. "You're so beautiful, I can hardly breathe."

Tessa tears up, then says, "You wore your naval uniform. Good choice."

"I knew it would get you going," I whisper. "Should we do this?"

"Yes, let's get it over with," she says.

"No, I intend to savour every second of the best day of my life."

We turn to the minister, who stands next to my father. And the next ten minutes are a blur because I can't concentrate on anything other than how in love I am with the woman standing next to me.

She turns to me, and I snap out of it, remembering it's time for the vows. Little Knox, who has the real rings, stands between us, holding up the pillow and grinning smugly back at his brothers. Oh, they learn that early, don't they?

I take Tessa's ring off the pillow, then lift her left hand with mine. "I, Arthur Winston Phillip George Charles Edward, take thee, Tessa Adelaide, to be my wife. I promise to love, comfort, support, and keep you, forsaking all others, for all the days of my life."

I gently slide the ring onto her finger, and then our eyes meet. "Your turn," I whisper.

"I, Tessa Adelaide, take thee, Arthur Winston Phillip George Charles Edward, to be my husband. I promise to love, comfort, support, and keep you, forsaking all others, for all the days of my life."

I watch as she slides the most symbolic and meaningful piece of jewelry I'll ever wear onto my finger.

Then we turn to the minister, who says a whole bunch of things about love and marriage and commitment that I miss because I'm thinking about how damn relieved I am to have gotten this far.

My father steps down and stands in front of Tessa while Vincent hurries over to place a kneeling stool for her. She takes my hand, and I help steady her while she kneels in front of my father. His smile is genuine as he unsheathes his sword (not that kind of sword—good God, you have sick mind). He taps her left shoulder with it and says, "I, Winston Phillip George Edwin Charles, rightful Monarch of the Kingdom of Avonia, Duke of Canterboroguh, Count of Middlesbury, by right of arms dub thee Princess Tessa, Duchess of Wellingborne."

Lifting the sword over her head, he taps her right shoulder. "Rise up, madam, and join the ranks of your peers."

Tessa stands and curtseys deeply to my father, looking very much like she was born into all this silliness. When she rises, my father takes her hand and smiles, then quietly says, "Well done, Tessa. I know we got off to a rocky start, but I want to thank you for everything you've done for my family and for my son. You've turned him into the man I should have, and you're just the person to make sure he'll be the leader this nation needs someday."

Tessa tears up. "Hopefully, that will be a very long time from now, Your Majesty."

"Call me..." he gives her a thoughtful look, then says, "Winston."

****

"This is Giles Bigley on location in Didsbury, where the bells have just begun ringing, indicating that Prince Arthur, rightful heir to the throne of Avonia, has indeed married Tessa Sharpe, who will henceforth be known as Princess Tessa, Duchess of Wellingborne.

"Any second now the doors will open, and the happy couple will emerge and get into the waiting carriage for a short tour around the village and off to Didsbury Castle for an intimate reception. Even though they've broken nearly every royal protocol today, the excitement in this tiny village, and indeed around the kingdom, is unbelievable. I've never seen so many smiling faces in all my days as a reporter. People rushing around the cobblestone streets wishing each other well and laughing together, thrilled to be among the very few in attendance on this beautiful June afternoon.

"The couple will honeymoon here for two days, then head to Valcourt for the official wedding parade, followed by a luncheon with dignitaries and royals from around the globe. Once the celebrations are over, they will commence a one-month honeymoon trip including Maui, Mauritius, and the Maldives…"

TWENTY-NINE

Three Cheers for Birthing Hips

Tessa

"We did it!" I say to Arthur once we settle into the carriage for the ride to the castle.

"Yes, we certainly did!" He beams and kisses me right on the lips, not caring who happens to be watching. "Now all that's left to do is live happily ever after."

"But first, let's party."

We wave and smile at the crowd, Arthur holding my hand up in the air between us as though we've just taken gold at the Olympics—and in a way, we have. We've taken the top prize of love—a lifetime with the right person.

"Hey! I just realized that you're going to be King Arthur someday."

He gives me an amused look. "I can't decide if my mother had a bit of a sense of humour or was just a real romantic."

"Maybe it was both."

****

It's ten in the evening, and the reception is in full swing. I've just returned from the ladies' room, where I patted my hot face with a towel and reapplied my lipstick. I'm a bit tipsy, but more on the excitement of the day than Champagne. I stand near the door and laugh as the guests do the Chicken Dance—a request to the band from my mum, no doubt. Arthur is in the center of the floor, giving it all he's got along with her, Nina, Isa, Nikki, and the kids.

I think about how funny life is and how it can change on a dime. I think about the life we're starting today and what it will be like. We've decided we'll live part-time here at the castle and part-time in one of the larger empty apartments at the palace with four bedrooms, one of which will become Dexter's. Arthur came by my parents' place a couple of days ago and loaded all my things into the limo himself so everything will be set when we get home. *Home.* That has a wonderful ring to it. And even if it will be a strange sort of life in a lot of ways, the scones are to die for.

Arthur has declared that we will take every Sunday off so we can just be together and do nothing. Or something. Or somethin' somethin'.

"Well, this has been quite the hoot, my dear."

I look to my left and see the Princess Dowager at my side. "It has been wonderful, hasn't it?"

"Quite. Your people are an absolute blast. Not a stuffed shirt in the bunch. I think I'll fit in quite well with them."

"You will indeed. I've already had all four of my brothers give me what for over not inviting you to Sunday dinner yet."

She laughs. "I'd love that. Now, which ones are single again?"

"Bram and Finn. Although, from the looks of things, I think Bram and Irene over there are going to make a go of it."

"Finn, it is, then." She gives me a wry smile. "And how lovely for you that you don't have to worry about the wedding night."

I feel my face warm at her meaning, and I laugh.

"Good that you young ladies do a test drive before you make a final decision," she says with a firm nod. "Although in my case, it all worked out very nicely in that regard."

"I'm glad to hear it." I put one arm over her shoulder and pull her in for a side hug.

She bristles for a moment, then seems to relax, so I go all in and give her a kiss on the cheek. "Thank you."

"For what?"

"For giving me a chance, for getting Arthur and me back together, for lending me this gorgeous tiara for today, for welcoming me—"

"Don't get all sentimental on me. I'll lose all respect for you." She reaches up and pats me on the cheek. "Now, I'll be expecting great-grandchildren right away. With those excellent birthing hips of yours, it shouldn't be much trouble at all for you."

I laugh, covering my mouth with one hand.

The Princess Dowager breaks away from my hold and says, "Oh, there's that handsome Xavier. I'm going to make him dance with me."

"Be gentle with him!" I call as she walks away.

I look around and see my father and King Winston standing next to the bar, laughing with each other. They've been deep in conversation for the better part of an hour now, which, I have to say, warms my heart. I'm suddenly proud of my father, who has the ability to be uniquely himself no matter who he's with. I resolve to tell him as much as soon as I can pry him away from King Winston long enough for a dance.

As I scan the room and take it all in, it occurs to me that I need to be more like my dad, which is to say, happy to be me. I'll never manage to make everyone like or accept me, but I can be my best self wherever I go.

I am Tessa Langdon, Princess of Avonia, Duchess of Wellingborne, Potty-Mouth Extraordinaire, Former Blogger, Recently Retired Reporter, and Soon-to-be Board Member of the three dozen charities I have taken on.

And best of all, I am brave, I am strong, and I am loved.

AVAILABLE NOW

The Royal Delivery
(A Crown Jewels Romance, Book 3)

Don't miss the heartwarming, laugh-out-loud conclusion of The Crown Jewels Romantic Comedy Trilogy for fans of both Bridget Jones and The Shopaholic...

After one year of marriage, Crown Prince Arthur and his lovely, albeit accident-prone wife, Princess Tessa, are preparing to bring an heir to the tiny kingdom of Avonia. With all eyes on Tessa, she's determined to be one of those fabulously fit pregnant women. She could do it too if it weren't for all the freshly-baked scones. Soon dubbed the *Countess of Camembert,* Tessa wants to go into hiding until after the baby is born, but royal life won't wait, and she needs to figure out how to make the best of a desperate situation and win the people over once and for all.

Prince Author never thought he'd find himself involved in horribly awkward conversations about the first day of his wife's last period, but that's precisely what happens after that plus sign shows up on the pregnancy test. With a baby on the way, Arthur's overprotective streak comes out in spades, and he finds himself attributing ill-intentions to everyone he meets, from the vagina-fixated obstetricians to the potential pedos everywhere.

Will Arthur calm down in time to welcome the baby? Will Tessa manage to figure out how to be mother to the kingdom's next heir? And most importantly, will the happy couple still be happy when the baby arrives?

A NOTE FROM MELANIE

I hope you loved this installment of Arthur and Tessa's story! I hope it made you smile and laugh out loud and feel good. If you enjoyed it, please leave a review.

Oh, and tell everyone you know/meet they simply must read The Crown Jewels Romantic Comedy Series. Wink Wink.

Reviews are a true gift to writers. They are the best way for other readers to find our work and for us to figure out if we're on the right track, so thank you if you are one of those kind folks out there to take time out of your day to leave a review!

If you'd like to find out about my upcoming releases, sign up for my newsletter on www.mjsummersbooks.com.

All the very best to you and yours,
Melanie

ALSO AVAILABLE

The Honeymooner
(Paradise Bay, Book 1)

From bestselling author Melanie Summers comes the wickedly funny, ridiculously romantic spinoff of her highly-acclaimed Crown Jewels Series...

Twenty-nine-year-old workaholic Libby Dewitt lives by the motto 'if you fail to plan, you plan to fail.' She's finally about to start her dream life with her steady-as-a-rock fiancé, Richard Tomy. Together, they're the perfect power couple—right down to the fact that he's agreed to use their honeymoon to help further her career in mergers and acquisitions. But ten minutes before the wedding, her dreams dissolve via text message.

Devastated and humiliated, Libby escapes to Paradise Bay alone. She's got two goals for her trip: to devise a plan to get Richard back and to convince resort owner Harrison Banks to sell his property to her company. Unfortunately, when she arrives, she discovers that tall, dark, and built, Harrison is not about to make anything easy for her.

Instead, he derails her plans while at the same time, bringing out a side of Libby she's kept carefully tucked away— a carefree, adrenaline junkie. After a few days together, Harrison's got her wondering if the life she always wanted was meant for some other girl. Suddenly, Libby must decide which version of herself she wants to be.

Will she go back to her comfortable, safe life, or risk everything to be with the only man who's ever made her feel truly alive?

Made in the USA
Monee, IL
19 September 2020